# WUTHERING HEIGHTS

# WUTHERING HEIGHTS

*by*

EMILY BRONTE

ABRIDGED

A BANCROFT

CLASSIC

BANCROFT BOOKS

LONDON

BANCROFT BOOKS
*49–50 Poland Street*
*London W. 1*

*First published in the "Bancroft Classics" 1967*
*This impression 1970*

430 00083 9

# Chapter 1

1801. I have just returned from a visit to my landlord—the solitary neighbour that I shall be troubled with. This is certainly a beautiful country! In all England, I do not believe that I could have fixed on a situation so completely removed from the stir of society. A perfect misanthropist's heaven: and Mr. Heathcliff and I are such a suitable pair to divide the desolation between us. A capital fellow! He little imagined how my heart warmed towards him when I beheld his black eyes withdraw so suspiciously under their brows, as I rode up, and when his fingers sheltered themselves, with a jealous resolution, still further in his waistcoat, as I announced my name.

"Mr. Heathcliff?" I said.

A nod was the answer.

"Mr. Lockwood your new tenant, sir. I do myself the honour of calling as soon as possible after my arrival, to express the hope that I have not inconvenienced you by my perseverance in soliciting the occupation of Thrushcross Grange: I heard yesterday you had had some thoughts —"

"Thrushcross Grange is my own, sir," he interrupted, wincing. "I should not allow any one to inconvenience me, if I could hinder it—walk in!"

The "walk in" was uttered with closed teeth, and expressed the sentiment, "Go to the Deuce:" even the gate over which he leant manifested no sympathizing movement to the words; and I think that circumstances determined me to accept the invitation: I felt interested in a man who seemed more exaggeratedly reserved than myself.

When he saw my horse's breast fairly pushing the barrier, he did put out his hand to unchain it, and then sullenly preceded me up the causeway, calling, as we entered the court,—"Joseph, take Mr. Lockwood's horse; and bring up some wine."

"Here we have the whole establishment of domestics, I suppose," was the reflection suggested by this compound order. "No wonder the grass grows up between the flags, and cattle are the only hedgecutters."

Joseph was an elderly, nay, an old man: very old, perhaps, though hale and sinewy. "The Lord help us!" he soliloquized in an undertone of peevish displeasure, while relieving me of my horse: looking, meantime, in my face so sourly that I charitably conjectured he must have need of divine aid to digest his dinner, and his pious ejaculation had no reference to my unexpected advent.

Wuthering Heights is the name of Mr. Heathcliff's dwelling. "Wuthering" being a significant provincial adjective, descriptive of the atmospheric tumult to which its station is exposed in stormy weather. Pure, bracing ventilation they must have up there at all times, indeed: one may guess the power of the north wind blowing over the edge, by the excessive slant of a few stunted firs at the end of the house; and by a range of gaunt thorns all stretching their limbs one way, as if craving alms of the sun. Happily, the architect had foresight to build it strong: the narrow windows are deeply set in the wall, and the corners defended with large jutting stones.

Before passing the threshold, I paused to admire a quantity of grotesque carving lavished over the front, and especially about the principal door; above which, among a wilderness of crumbling griffins and shameless little boys, I detected the date "1500," and the name "Hareton Earnshaw." I would have made a few comments, and requested a short history of the place from the surly owner; but his attitude at the door appeared to demand my speedy entrance, or complete departure, and I had no desire to aggravate his impatience previous to inspecting the penetralium.

One step brought us into the family sitting-room, without any introductory lobby or passage: they call it here "the house" pre-eminently. It includes kitchen and parlour, generally; but I believe at Wuthering Heights the kitchen is forced to retreat altogether into another quarter: at least I distinguished a chatter of tongues, and a clatter of culinary utensils, deep within; and I observed no signs of roasting, boiling, or baking, about the huge fire-place; nor any glitter of copper saucepans and tin cullenders on the walls. One end, indeed, reflected splendidly both light and heat from ranks of immense pewter dishes, interspersed with silver jugs and tankards, towering row after row, on a vast oak dresser, to the very roof. The latter had never been underdrawn: its entire anatomy lay bare to an inquiring eye, except where a frame of wood laden with oatcakes and clusters of legs of beef, mutton, and ham, concealed it. Above the chimney were sundry villanous old guns, and a couple of horse pistols: and, by way of ornament, three gaudily painted canisters disposed along its ledge. The floor was of smooth, white stone; the chairs, high-backed, primitive structures, painted green: one or two heavy black ones lurking in the shade. In an arch under the dresser, reposed a huge, liver-coloured bitch pointer, surrounded by a swarm of squealing puppies; and other dogs haunted other recesses.

The apartment and furniture would have been nothing extraordinary as belonging to a homely, northern farmer, with a stubborn countenance, and stalwart limbs set out to advantage in kneebreeches and gaiters. Such an individual seated in his arm-chair, his mug of ale frothing on the round table before him, is to be seen in any circuit of five or six miles among these hills, if you go at the right time after dinner. But Mr. Heathcliff forms a singular contrast to his abode and style of living. He is a dark-skinned gipsy in aspect, in dress and manners a gentleman: that is, as much a gentleman as many a country squire: rather slovenly, perhaps, yet not looking amiss with his negligence, because he has an erect and handsome figure; and rather morose.

I took a seat at the end of the hearthstone opposite that towards which my landlord advanced, and filled up an interval of silence by attempting to caress the canine mother, who had left her nursery, and was sneaking wolfishly to the back of my legs, her lip curled up, and her white teeth watering for a snatch. My caress provoked a long, guttural snarl.

"You'd better let the dog alone," growled Mr. Heathcliff in unsion, checking fiercer demonstrations with a punch of his foot. "She's not accustomed to be spoiled—not kept for a pet." Then, striding to a side door, he shouted again, "Joseph!"

Joseph mumbled indistinctly in the depths of the cellar, but gave no intimation of ascending; so his master dived down to him, leaving me *vis-s-vis* the ruffianly bitch and a pair of grim shaggy sheep-dogs, who shared with her a jealous guardianship over all my movements. Not anxious to come in contact with their fangs, I sat still; but, imagining they would scarcely understand tacit insults, I unfortunately indulged in winking and making faces at the trio, and some turn of my physiognomy so irritated madam, that she suddenly broke into a fury and leapt on my knees. I flung her back, and hastened to interpose the table between us. This proceeding roused the whole hive: half a dozen four-footed fiends, of various sizes and ages, issued from hidden dens to the common centre. I felt my heels and coat-laps peculiar subjects of assault; and, parrying off the larger combatants as effectually as I could with the poker, I was constrained to demand, aloud, assistance from some of the household in re-establishing peace.

Mr. Heathcliff and his man climbed the cellar steps with vexatious phlegm: I don't think they moved one second faster than usual, though the hearth was an absolute tempest of worrying and yelping. Happily, an inhabitant of the kitchen made more despatch: a lusty dame, with tucked-up gown, bare arms, and fire-flushed cheeks, rushed into the midst of us flourishing a frying-pan; and used that weapon, and her tongue, to such purpose, that the storm subsided magically, and she only remained, heaving like a sea after a high wind, when her master entered on the scene.

"Not bitten, are you?"

"If I had been, I would have set my signet on the biter."

Heathcliff's countenance relaxed into a grin.

"Come, come," he said, "you are flurried, Mr. Lockwood. Here, take a little wine. Guests are so exceedingly rare in this house that I and my dogs, I am willing to own, hardly know how to receive them. Your health, sir!"

I bowed and returned the pledge; beginning to perceive that it would be foolish to sit sulking for the misbehaviour of a pack of curs: besides, I felt loath to yield the fellow further amusement at my expense; since his humour took that turn. He—probably swayed by prudential consideration of the folly of offending a good tenant—relaxed a little in the laconic style of chipping off his pronouns and auxiliary verbs, and introduced what he supposed would be a subject of interest to me,—a discourse on the advantages and disadvantages of my present place of retirement. I found him very intelligent on the topics we touched; and before I went home, I was encouraged so far as to volunteer another visit to-morrow. He evidently wished no repetition of my intrusion. I shall go, notwithstanding. It is astonishing how sociable I feel myself compared with him.

## Chapter 2

YESTERDAY afternoon set in misty and cold. I had half a mind to spend it by my study fire, instead of wading through heath and mud to Wuthering Heights. On coming up from dinner, however, on mounting the stairs and stepping into the room, I saw a servant girl on her knees surrounded by brushes and coal-scuttles, and raising an infernal dust as she extinguished the flames with heaps of cinders. This spectacle drove me back immediately; I took my hat, and, after a four miles' walk, arrived at Heathcliff's garden gate just in time to escape the first feathery flakes of a snow-shower.

On that bleak hill-top the earth was hard with a black frost, and the air made me shiver through every limb. Being unable to remove the chain, I jumped over, and, running up the flagged causeway, knocked vainly for admittance, till my knuckles tingled and the dogs howled.

The snow began to drive thickly. I seized the handle to essay another trial; when a young man without coat, and shouldering a pitchfork, appeared in the yard behind. He hailed me to follow him, and, after marching through a washhouse, and a paved area containing a coal-shed, pump, and pigeon-cot, we at length arrived in the huge, warm, cheerful apartment, where I was formerly received. It glowed delightfully in the radiance of an immense fire, compounded of coal, peat, and wood; and near the table, laid for a plentiful evening meal, I was pleased to observe the "missis," an individual whose existence I had never previously suspected. I bowed and waited, thinking she would bid me take a seat. She looked at me, leaning back in her chair, and remained motionless and mute.

"Rough weather!" I remarked. "I'm afraid, Mrs. Heathcliff, the door must bear the consequences of your servants' leisure attendance: I had hard work to make them hear me."

"You should not have come out," she said, rising and reaching from the chimney-piece two of the painted canisters.

Her position before was sheltered from the light; now, I had a distinct view of her whole figure and countenance. She was slender, and apparently scarcely past girlhood: an admirable form, and the most exquisite little face that I have ever had the pleasure of beholding, small features, very fair; flaxen ringlets, or rather golden, hanging loose on her delicate neck; and eyes, had they been agreeable in expression, that would have been irresistible.

"Were you asked to tea?" she demanded, tying an apron over her neat black frock, and standing with a spoonful of the leaf poised over the pot.

"I shall be glad to have a cup," I answered.

"Were you asked?" she repeated.

"No," I said, half smiling. "You are the proper person to ask me."

She flung the tea back, spoon and all, and resumed her chair in a pet; her forehead corrugated, and her red under-lip pushed out, like a child's ready to cry.

Meanwhile, the young man had slung on to his person a decidedly shabby upper garment, and, erecting himself before the blaze, looked down on me from the corner of his eyes, for all the world as if there were some mortal feud unavenged between us. I began to doubt whether he were a servant or not: his dress and speech were both rude, entirely devoid of the superiority observable in Mr. and Mrs. Heathcliff; his thick, brown curls were rough and uncultivated, his whiskers encroached bearishly over his cheeks, and his hands were enbrowned like those of a common labourer: still his bearing was free, almost haughty, and he showed none of a domestic's assiduity, in attending on the lady of the house. In the absence of clear proofs of his condition, I deemed it best to abstain from noticing his curious conduct; and, five minutes afterwards, the entrance of Heathcliff relieved me, in some measure, from my uncomfortable state.

"Are you going to make th' tea?" demanded he of the shabby coat, shifting his ferocious gaze from me to the young lady.

"Is *he* to have any?" she asked, appealing to Heathcliff.

"Get it ready, will you?" was the answer, uttered so savagely that I started. The tone in which the words were said revealed a genuine bad nature. I no longer felt inclined to call Heathcliff a capital fellow. When the preparations were finished, he invited me with—"Now, sir, bring forward your chair." And we all, including the rustic youth, drew round the table: an austere silence prevailing while we discussed our meal.

Then it flashed upon me—"The clown at my elbow, who is drinking his

9

tea out of a basin and eating his bread with unwashed hands, may be her husband: Heathcliff junior, of course."

"Mrs. Heathcliff is my daughter-in-law," said Heathcliff, corroborating my surmise. He turned, as he spoke, a peculiar look in her direction: a look of hatred; unless he has a most perverse set of facial muscles that will not, like those of other people, interpret the language of his soul.

"Ah, certainly—I see now: you are the favoured possessor of the beneficent fairy," I remarked, turning to my neighbour.

This was worse than before: the youth grew crimson, and clenched his fist, with every appearance of a meditated assault. But he seemed to recollect himself presently, and smothered the storm in a brutal curse, muttered on my behalf: which, however, I took care not to notice.

"Unhappy in your conjectures, sir," observed my host; "we neither of us have the privilege of owning your good fairy; her mate is dead. I said she was my daughter-in-law, therefore, she must have married my son."

"And this young man is——"

"My name is Hareton Earnshaw," growled the other; "and I'd counsel you to respect it!"

The business of eating being concluded, and no one uttering a word of sociable conversation, I approached a window to examine the weather. A sorrowful sight I saw: dark night coming down prematurely, and sky and hills mingled in one bitter whirl of wind and suffocating snow.

"I don't think it possible for me to get home now without a guide," I could not help exclaiming. "The roads will be buried already; and, if they were bare, I could scarcely distinguish a foot in advance."

"Hareton, drive those dozen sheep into the barn porch. They'll be covered if left in the fold all night: and put a plank before them," said Heathcliff.

"How must I do?" I continued, with rising irritation.

There was no reply to my question; and on looking round I saw only Mrs. Heathcliff leaning over the fire.

"I hope it will be a lesson to you to make no more rash journeys on these hills," cried Heathcliff's stern voice from the kitchen entrance. "As to staying here, I don't keep accommodations for visitors: you must share a bed with Hareton or Joseph, if you do."

"I can sleep on a chair in this room," I replied.

"No, no! A stranger is a stranger, be he rich or poor: it will not suit me to permit any one the range of the place while I am off guard!" said the unmannerly wretch.

With this insult, my patience was at an end. I uttered an expression of disgust, and pushed past him into the yard, running against Earnshaw in my haste. It was so dark that I could not see the means of exit.

Joseph sat within earshot, milking the cows by the light of a lantern, which I seized unceremoniously, and, calling out that I would send it back on the morrow, rushed to the nearest postern.

"Maister, maister, he's staling t'lanthern!" shouted the ancient, pursuing my retreat. "Hey, Gnasher! Hey, dog! Hey, Wolf, holld him, holld him!"

On opening the little door, two hairy monsters flew at my throat, bearing me down and extinguishing the light; while a mingled guffaw from Heathcliff and Hareton, put the copestone on my rage and humiliation. Fortunately, the beasts seemed more bent on stretching their paws and yawning, and flourishing their tails, than devouring me alive; but they would suffer no resurrection, and I was forced to lie till their malignant masters pleased to deliver me: then, hatless and trembling with wrath, I ordered the miscreants to let me out—on their peril to keep me one minute longer—with several incoherent threats of retaliation that, in their indefinite depth of virulency, smacked of King Lear.

The vehemence of my agitation brought on a copious bleeding at the nose, and still Heathcliff laughed, and still I scolded. I don't know what would have concluded the scene, had there not been one person at hand rather more rational than myself, and more benevolent than my entertainer. This was Zillah, the stout housewife; who at length issued forth to inquire into the nature of the uproar. She thought that some of them had been laying violent hands on me; and, not daring to attack her master, she turned her vocal artillery against the younger scoundrel.

"Well, Mr. Earnshaw," she cried, "I wonder what you'll have agait next! Are we going to murder folk on our very door-stones! I see this house will never do for me—look at t' poor lad, he's fair choking! Wisht, wisht! you mun'n't go on so. Come in, and I'll cure that: there now, hold ye still."

With these words she suddenly splashed a point of icy water down my neck, and pulled me into the kitchen. Mr. Heathcliff followed, his accidental merriment expiring quickly in his habitual moroseness.

I was sick exceedingly, and dizzy and faint; and thus compelled perforce to accept lodgings under his roof. He told Zillah to give me a glass of brandy, and then passed on to the inner room; while she condoled with me on my sorry predicament, and having obeyed his order, whereby I was somewhat revived, ushered me to bed.

# Chapter 3

WHILE leading the way upstairs, she recommended that I should hide the candle, and not make a noise; for her master had an odd notion about the chamber she would put me in, and never let anybody lodge there willingly. I asked the reason. She did not know, she answered: she had only lived there a year or two; and they had so many queer goings on, she could not begin to be curious.

Too stupefied to be curious myself, I fastened my door and glanced round for the bed. The whole furniture consisted of a chair, a clothes-press, and a large oak case, with squares cut out near the top, resembling coach windows. Having approached this structure, I looked inside, and perceived it to be a singular sort of old-fashioned couch, very conveniently designed to obviate the necessity for every member of the family having a room to himself. In fact, it formed a little closet, and the ledge of a window, which it enclosed, served as a table. I slid back the panelled sides, got in with my light, pulled them together again, and felt secure against the vigilance of Heathcliff, and every one else.

The ledge, where I placed my candle, had a few mildewed books piled up in one corner; and it was covered with writing scratched on the paint. This writing, however, was nothing but a name repeated in all kinds of characters, large and small—*Catherine Earnshaw,* here and there varied to *Catherine Heathcliff,* and then again to *Catherine Linton.*

In vapid listlessness I leant my head against the window, and continued spelling over Catherine Earnshaw—Heathcliff—Linton, till my eyes closed; but they had not rested five minutes when a glare of white letters started from the dark, as vivid as spectres—the air swarmed with Catherines; and rousing myself to dispel the obtrusive name, I discovered my candle-wick reclining on one of the antique volumes, and perfuming the place with an odour of roasted calf-skin. I snuffed it off, and, very ill at ease under the influence of cold and lingering nausea, sat up and spread open the injured tome on my knee. It was a Testament, in lean type, and smelling dreadfully musty: a fly-leaf bore the inscription—"Catherine Earnshaw, her book," and a date some quarter of a century back. I shut it, and took up another, and another, till I had examined all. Catherine's library was select, and its state of dilapidation proved it to have been well used; though not altogether for a legitimate purpose: scarcely one chapter had escaped a pen-and-ink commentary—at least, the appearance of one—covering every morsel of blank that the printer had left. Some were de-tached sentences; other parts took the form of a regular diary, scrawled in an unformed, childish hand. At the top of an extra page (quite a trea-sure, probably, when first lighted on) I was greatly amused to behold an excellent caricature of my friend Joseph,—rudely yet powerfully sketched. An immediate interest kindled within me for the unknown Catherine, and I began forthwith to decypher her faded hieroglyphics.

"How little did I dream that Hindley would ever make me cry so!" she wrote. "My head aches, till I cannot keep it on the pillow; and still I can't give over. Poor Heathcliff! Hindley calls him a vagabond, and won't let him sit with us, nor eat with us any more; and, he says, he and I must not play together, and threatens to turn him out of the house if we break his orders. He has been blaming our father (how dared he?) for treating H. too liberally; and swears he will reduce him to his right place——"

I began to nod drowsily over the dim page: my eye wandered from manuscript to print. I sank back in bed, and fell asleep. Alas, for the effects of bad tea and bad temper! What else could it be that made me pass such a terrible night? I don't remember another that I can at all compare with it since I was capable of suffering.

I began to dream, almost before I ceased to be sensible of my locality.

I remembered I was lying in the oak closet, and I heard distinctly a gusty wind, and the driving of the snow; I heard, also, a fir-bough touch my lattice and rattle its dry cones against the panes: but it annoyed me so much, that I resolved to silence it, if possible; and, I thought, I rose and endeavoured to unhasp the casement. The hook was soldered into the staple: a circumstance observed by me when awake, but forgotten. "I must stop it, nevertheless!" I muttered, knocking my knuckles through the glass, and stretching an arm out to seize the importunate branch; instead of which, my fingers closed on the fingers of a little, ice-cold hand! The intense horror of nightmare came over me: I tried to draw back my arm, but the hand clung to it, and a most melancholy voice sobbed, "Let me in—let me in!" "Who are you?" I asked, struggling, meanwhile, to disengage myself. "Catherine Linton," it replied, shiveringly (why did I think of Linton? I had read Earnshaw twenty times for Linton), "I'm come home: I'd lost my way on the moor!" As it spoke, I discerned, obscurely, a child's face looking through the window. Terror made me cruel; and, finding it useless to attempt shaking the creature off, I pulled its wrist on to the broken pane, and rubbed it to and fro till the blood ran down and soaked the bedclothes: still it wailed, "Let me in!" and maintained its tenacious gripe. I tried to jumb up; but could not stir a limb; and so yelled aloud, in a frenzy of fright. To my confusion, I discovered the yell was not ideal: hasty footsteps approached my chamber door; somebody pushed it open, with a vigorous hand, and a light glimmered through the squares at the top of the bed. I sat shuddering yet, and wiping the perspiration from my forehead: the intruder appeared to hesitate, and muttered to himself. At last, he said in a half-whisper, plainly not expecting an answer, "Is any one here?" I considered it best to confess my presence; for I knew Heathcliff's accents, and feared he might search further, if I kept quiet. With this intention, I turned and opened the panels. I shall not soon forget the effect my action produced.

Heathcliff stood near the entrance, in his shirt and trousers; with a candle dripping over his fingers, and his face as white as the wall behind him. The first creak of the oak startled him like an electric shock: the light leaped from his hold to a distance of some feet, and his agitation was so extreme, that he could hardly pick it up.

"It is only your guest, sir," I called out, desirous to spare him the humiliation of exposing his cowardice further. "I had the misfortune to scream in my sleep, owing to a frightful nightmare. I'm sorry I disturbed you."

"Oh, God confound you, Mr. Lockwood! I wish you were at the——" commenced my host, setting the candle on a chair, because he found it impossible to hold it steady. "And who showed you up into this room?" he continued, crushing his nails into his palms, and grinding his teeth to subdue the maxillary convulsions. "Who was it? I've a good mind to turn them out of the house this moment!"

"It was your servant, Zillah," I replied, flinging myself on to the floor, and rapidly resuming my garments. "I should not care if you did, Mr. Heathcliff; she richly deserves it. I suppose that she wanted to get another proof that the place was haunted, at my expense. Well, it is—swarming with ghosts and goblins! You have reason in shutting it up, I assure you. No one will thank you for a doze in such a den!"

"What do you mean?" asked Heathcliff, "and what are you doing? Lie down and finish out the night, since you *are* here; but, for Heaven's sake! don't repeat that horrid noise: nothing could excuse it, unless you were having your throat cut!"

"If the little fiend had got in at the window, she probably would have strangled me!" I returned. "I'm not going to endure the persecutions of your hospitable ancestors again. Was not the Reverend Jabes Branderham akin to you on the mother's side? And that minx, Catherine Linton, or Earnshaw, or however she was called—she must have been a changeling—wicked little soul! She told me she had been walking the earth these twenty years: a just punishment for her mortal transgressions, I've no doubt!"

"What *can* you mean by talking in this way to *me*?" thundered Heathcliff with savage vehemence. "How—how *dare* you, under my roof?—God! he's mad to speak so!" And he struck his forehead with rage.

I obeyed, so far as to quit the chamber; when, ignorant where the narrow lobbies led, I stood still, and was witness involuntarily, to a piece of superstition on the part of my landlord, which belied, oddly, his apparent sense. He got on to the bed, and wrenched open the lattice, bursting, as he pulled at it, into an uncontrollable passion of tears. "Come in! come in!" he sobbed. "Cathy, do come. Oh do—*once* more! Oh! my heart's darling! hear me *this* time, Catherine, at last!" The spectre showed a spectre's ordinary caprice; it gave no sign of being; but the snow and wind whirled wildly through, even reaching my station, and blowing out the light.

There was such anguish in the gush of grief that accompanied this raving, that my compassion made me overlook its folly, and I drew off, half angry to have listened at all, and vexed at having related my ridiculous nightmare, since it produced that agony; though *why*, was beyond my comprehension. I descended cautiously to the lower regions, and landed in the back-kitchen, where a gleam of fire, raked compactly together, enabled me to rekindle my candle. Nothing was stirring except a brindled, grey cat, which crept from the ashes, and saluted me with a querulous mew.

Two benches, shaped in sections of a circle, nearly enclosed the hearth; on one of these I stretched myself, and Grimalkin mounted the other. We were both of us nodding, ere any one invaded our retreat, and then it was Joseph, shuffling down a wooden ladder that vanished in the roof, through a trap: the ascent to his garret, I suppose. He cast a sinister look at the little flame which I had enticed to play between the ribs, swept the cat from its elevation, and bestowing himself in the vacancy, commenced the operation of stuffing a three-inch pipe with tobacco. My presence in his sanctum was evidently esteemed a piece of impudence too shameful for remark: he silently applied the tube to his lips, folded his arms, and puffed away. I let him enjoy the luxury unannoyed; and after sucking out his last breath, and heaving a profound sigh, he got up, and departed as solemnly as he came.

A more elastic footstep entered next; and now I opened my mouth for a "good morning," but closed it again, the salutation unachieved; for Hareton Earnshaw was performing his orisons *sotto voce,* in a series of curses directed against every object he touched, while he rummaged a corner for a spade or shovel to dig through the drifts. He glanced over the back of the bench, dilating his nostrils, and thought as little of exchanging civilities with me as with my companion the cat. I guessed, by his preparations, that egress was allowed, and, leaving my hard couch, made a movement to follow him. He noticed this, and thrust at an inner door with the end of his spade, intimating by an inarticulate sound that there was the place where I must go, if I changed my locality.

It opened into the house, where the females were already astir. Zillah urging flakes of flame up the chimney with a colossal bellows; and Mrs. Heathcliff, kneeling on the hearth, reading a book by the aid of the blaze. She held her hand interposed between the furnace heat and her eyes, and seemed absorbed in her occupation; desisting from it only to chide the servant for covering her with sparks, or to push away a dog, now and then, that snoozled its nose over-forwardly into her face. I was surprised to see Heathcliff there also. He stood by the fire, his back towards me, just finishing a stormy scene to poor Zillah; who ever and anon interrupted her labour to pluck up the corner of her apron, and heave an indignant groan.

"And you, you worthless——" he broke out as I entered, turning to his daughter-in-law, and employing an epithet as harmless as duck, or sheep, but generally represented by a dash——. Having no desire to be entertained by a cat-and-dog combat, I stepped forward briskly, as if eager to partake the warmth of the hearth, and innocent of any knowledge of the interrupted dispute. Each had enough decorum to suspend further hostilities: Heathcliff placed his fists, out of temptation, in his pockets; Mrs. Heathcliff curled her lip, and walked to a seat far off, where she kept her word by playing the part of a statue during the remainder of my stay. That was not long. I declined joining their breakfast, and, at the first gleam of dawn, took an opportunity of escaping into the free air, now clear, and still, and cold as impalpable ice.

## *Chapter 4*

WHAT vain weather-cocks we are! I, who had determined to hold myself independent of all social intercourse, and thanked my stars that, at length, I had lighted on a spot where it was next to impracticable—I, weak wretch, after maintaining till dusk a struggle with low spirits and solitude, was finally compelled to strike my colours; and, under pretence of gaining information concerning the necessities of my establishment, I desired Mrs. Dean, when she brought in supper, to sit down while I ate it; hoping sincerely she would prove a regular gossip, and either rouse me to animation or lull me to sleep by her talk.

"You have lived here a considerable time," I commenced; "did you not say sixteen years?"

"Eighteen, sir: I came, when the mistress was married, to wait on her; after she died, the master retained me for his housekepper."

"Indeed."

I asked Mrs. Dean why Heathcliff let Thrushcross Grange, and preferred living in a situation and residence so much inferior. "Is he not rich enough to keep the estate in good order?" I inquired.

"Rich, sir!" she returned. "He has, nobody knows what money, and every year it increases. Yes, yes, he's rich enough to live in a finer house than this: but he's very near—close-handed; and, if he had meant to flit to Trushcross Grange, as soon as he heard of a good tenant he could not have borne to miss the chance of getting a few hundred more. It is strange people should be so greedy, when they are alone in the world!"

"He had a son, it seems?"

"Yes, he had one—he is dead."

"And that young lady, Mrs. Heathcliff, is his widow?"

"Yes."

"Where did she come from originally?"

"Why, sir, she is my late master's daughter: Catherine Linton was her maiden name. I nursed her, poor thing! I did wish Mr. Heathcliff would remove here, and then we might have been together again."

"What! Catherine Linton?" I exclaimed, astonished. But a minute's reflection convinced me it was not my ghostly Catherine. "Then," I continued, "my predecessor's name was Linton?"

"It was."

"And who is that Earnshaw: Hareton Earnshaw, who lives with Mr. Heathcliff? are they relations?"

"No; he is the late Mrs. Linton's nephew."

"The young lady's cousin, then?"

"Yes; and her husband was her cousin also: one on the mother's, the other on the father's side: Heathcliff married Mr. Linton's sister."

"I see the house at Wuthering Heights has 'Earnshaw' carved over the front door. Are they an old family?"

"Very old, sir; and Hareton is the last of them, as our Miss Cathy is of us—I mean, of the Lintons. Have you been to Wuthering Heights? I beg pardon for asking; but I should like to hear how she is?"

"Mrs. Heathcliff? she looked very well, and very handsome; yet, I think, not very happy."

"Oh dear, I don't wonder! And how did you like the master?"

"A rough fellow, rather, Mrs. Dean. Is not that his character?"

"Rough as a saw-edge, and hard as whinstone! The less you meddle with him the better."

"He must have had some ups and downs in life to make him such a churl. Do you know anything of his history?"

"It's a cuckoo's, sir—I know all about it: except where he was born, and who were his parents, and how he got his money, at first. And Hareton has been cast out like an unfledged dunnock! The unfortunate lad is the only one in all this parish that does not guess how he has been cheated."

"Well, Mrs. Dean, it will be a charitable deed to tell me something of my neighbours: I feel I shall not rest, if I go to bed; so be good enough to sit and chat an hour."

"Oh, certainly, sir! I'll just fetch a little sewing, and then I'll sit as long as you please. But you've caught cold: I saw you shivering, and you must have some gruel to drive it out."

The worthy woman bustled off, and I crouched nearer the fire; my head felt hot, and the rest of me chill: moreover, I was excited, almost to a pitch of foolishness, through my nerves and brain. She returned presently, bringing a smoking basin and a basket of work; and, having placed the former on the hob, drew in her seat, evidently pleased to find me so companionable.

Before I came to live here, she commenced—waiting no farther invitation to her story—I was almost always at Wuthering Heights; because my mother had nursed Mr. Hindley Earnshaw, that was Hareton's father, and I got used to playing with the children: I ran errands too, and helped to make hay, and hung about the farm ready for anything that anybody would set me to. One fine summer morning—it was the beginning of harvest, I remember—Mr. Earnshaw, the old master, came downstairs, dressed for a journey; and after he had told Joseph what was to be done during the day, he turned to Hindley, and Cathy, and me—for I sat eating my porridge with them—and he said, speaking to his son, "Now my bonny man, I'm going to Liverpool to-day, what shall I bring you? You may choose what you like: only let it be little, for I shall walk there and back: sixty miles each way, that is a long spell!" Hindley named a fiddle, and then he asked Miss Cathy; she was hardly six years old, but she could ride any horse in the stable, and she chose a whip. He did not forget me; for he had a kind heart, though he was rather severe sometimes. He promised to bring me a pocketful of apples and pears, and then he kissed his children, said good-bye, and set off.

It seemed a long while to us all—the three days of his absence—and often did little Cathy ask when he would be home. Mrs. Earnshaw expected him by supper-time, on the third evening, and she put the meal off hour after hour; there were no signs of his coming, however, and at last the children got tired of running down to the gate to look. Then it grew dark; she would have had them to bed, but they begged sadly to be allowed to stay up; and, just about eleven o'clock, the door-latch was raised quietly and in stepped the master. He threw himself into a chair, laughing and groaning, and bid them all stand off, for he was nearly killed—he would not have such another walk for the three kingdoms.

"And at the end of it, to be flighted to death!" he said opening his great coat, which he held bundled up in his arms. "See here, wife! I was never so beaten with anything in my life: but you must e'en take it as a gift of God; though it's as dark almost as if it came from the devil."

We crowded round, and over Miss Cathy's head, I had a peep at a dirty, ragged, black-haired child; big enough both to walk and talk: indeed, its face looked older than Catherine's; yet, when it was set on its feet, it only stared round, and repeated over and over again some gibberish, that nobody could understand. I was frightened, and Mrs. Earnshaw was ready to fling it out of doors: she did fly up, asking how he could fashion to bring that gipsy brat into the house, when they had their own bairns to feed and fend for? What he meant to do with it, and whether he were mad? The master tried to explain the matter; but he was really half dead with fatigue, and all that I could make out, amongst her scolding, was a tale of his seeing it starving, and houseless, and as good as dumb, in the streets of Liverpool; where he picked it up and inquired for its owner. Not a soul knew to whom it belonged, he said; and his money and time being both limited, he thought it better to take it home with him at once, than run unto vain expenses there: because he was determined he would not leave it as he found it. Well, the conclusion was that my mistress grumbled herself calm; and Mr. Earnshaw told me to wash it, and give it clean things, and let it sleep with the children.

Hindley and Cathy contented themselves with looking and listening till peace was restored: then, both began searching their father's pockets for the presents he had promised them. The former was a boy of fourteen, but when he drew out what had been a fiddle, crushed to morsels in the great coat, he blubbered aloud; and Cathy, when she learned the master had lost her whip in attending on the stranger, showed her humour by grinning and spitting at the stupid little thing; earning for her pains a sound blow from her father to teach her cleaner manners. They entirely refused to have it in bed with them, or even in their room; and I had no more sense, so I put it on the landing of the stairs, hoping it might be gone on the morrow. By chance, or else attracted by hearing his voice, it crept to Mr. Earnshaw's door, and there he found it on quitting his chamber. Inquiries were made as to how it got there; I was obliged to confess, and in recompense for my cowardice and inhumanity was sent out of the house.

This was Heathcliff's first introduction to the family. On coming back a few days afterwards (for I did not consider my banishment perpetual) I found they had christened him "Heathcliff": it was the name of a son who died in childhood, and it has served him ever since, both for Christian and surname. Miss Cathy and he were now very thick; but Hindley hated him: and to say the truth I did the same; and we plagued and went on with him shamefully: for I wasn't reasonable enough to feel my injustice, and the mistress never put in a word on his behalf when she saw him wronged.

So, from the very beginning, he bred bad feeling in the house; and at Mrs. Earnshaw's death, which happened in less than two years after, the young master had learned to regard his father as an oppressor rather than a friend, and Heathcliff as a usurper of his parent's affections and his privileges; and he grew bitter with brooding over these injuries.

I couldn't dote on Heathcliff, and I wondered often what my master saw to admire so much in the sullen boy. He was not insolent to his benefactor, he was simply insensible; though knowing perfectly the hold he had on his heart, and conscious he had only to speak and all the house would be obliged to bend to his wishes.

## Chapter 5

IN THE course of time, Mr. Earnshaw began to fail. He had been active and healthy, yet his strength left him suddenly; and when he was confined to the chimney-corner he grew grievously irritable. A nothing vexed him; and suspected slights of his authority nearly threw him into fits. This was especially to be remarked if any one attempted to impose upon, or domineer over, his favourite: he was painfully jealous lest a word should be spoken amiss to him; seeming to have got into his head the notion that, because he liked Heathcliff, all hated, and longed to do him an ill-turn.

It was a disadvantage to the lad; for the kinder among us did not wish to fret the master, so we humoured his partiality; and that humouring was rich nourishment to the child's pride and black tempers. Still it became in a manner necessary; twice, or thrice, Hindley's manifestation of scorn, while his father was near, roused the old man to a fury: he seized his stick to strike him, and shook with rage that he could not do it.

At last, our curate advised that the young man should be sent to college; and Mr. Earnshaw agreed, though with a heavy spirit, for he said— "Hindley was nought, and would never thrive as where he wandered."

But the hour came, at last, that ended Mr. Earnshaw's troubles on earth. He died quietly in his chair one October evening, seated by the fireside. A high wind blustered round the house, and roared in the chimney: it sounded wild and stormy, yet it was not cold, and we were all together—I, a little removed from the hearth, busy at my knitting, and Joseph reading his Bible near the table (for the servants generally sat in the house then, after their work was done). Miss Cathy had been sick, and that made her still; she leant against her father's knee, and Heathcliff was lying on the floor with his head in her lap. I remember the master, before he fell into a doze, stroking her bonny hair—it pleased him rarely to see her gentle—and saying—"Why canst thou not always be a good lass, Cathy?" And she turned her face up to his, and laughed, and answered, "Why cannot you always be a good man, father?" But as soon as she saw him vexed again, she kissed his hand, and said she would sing him to sleep. She began singing very low, till his fingers dropped from hers, and his head sank on his breast. Then I told her to hush, and not stir, for fear she should wake him. We all kept as mute as mice a full half-hour, and should have done so longer, only Joseph, having finished his chapter, got up and said that he must rouse the master for prayers and bed. He stepped forward, and called him by name, and touched his shoulder; but he would not move, so he took the candle and looked at him. I thought there was something wrong as he set down the light; and seizing the children each by an arm, whispered them to "frame upstairs, and make little din—they might pray alone that evening—he had summut to do."

"I shall bid father good-night first," said Catherine, putting her arms round his neck, before he could hinder her. The poor thing discovered her loss directly—she screamed out—"Oh, he's dead, Heathcliff! he's dead!" And they both set up a heart-breaking cry.

I joined my wail to theirs, loud and bitter; but Joseph asked what we could be thinking of to roar in that way over a saint in heaven. He told me to put on my cloak and run to Gimmerton for the doctor and the parson. I could not guess the use that either would be of, then. However, I went through wind and rain, and brought one, the doctor, back with me; the other said he would come in the morning. Leaving Joseph to explain matters, I ran to the children's room: their door was ajar, I saw they had never laid down, though it was past midnight; but they were calmer, and did not need me to console them. The little souls were comforting each other with better thoughts than I could have hit on: no parson in the world ever pictured heaven so beautifully as they did, in their innocent talk; and, while I sobbed and listened, I could not help wishing we were all there safe together.

## Chapter 6

MR. HINDLEY came home to the funeral; and—a thing that amazed us, and set the neighbours gossiping right and left—he brought a wife with him. What she was, and where she was born, he never informed us: probably, she had neither money nor name to recommend her, or he would scarcely have kept the union from his father.

Young Earnshaw was altered considerably in the three years of his absence. He had grown sparer, and lost his colour, and spoke and dressed quite differently; and, on the very day of his return, he told Joseph and me we must thenceforth quarter ourselves in the backkitchen, and leave the house for him. Indeed, he would have carpeted and papered a small spare room for a parlour; but his wife expressed such pleasure at the white floor and huge glowing fire-place, at the pewter dishes and delf-case, and dog-kennel, and the wide space there was to move about in where they usually sat, that he thought it unnecessary to her comfort, and so dropped the intention.

She expressed pleasure, too, at finding a sister among her new acquaintance; and she prattled to Catherine, and kissed her, and ran about with her, and gave her quantities of presents, at the beginning. Her affection tired very soon, however, and when she grew peevish, Hindley became tyrannical. A few words from her, evincing a dislike to Heathcliff, were enough to rouse in him all his old hatred of the boy. He drove him from their company to the servants, deprived him of the instructions of the curate, and insisted that he should labour out of doors instead; compelling him to do so as hard as any other lad on the farm.

Heathcliff bore his degradation pretty well at first, because Cathy taught him what she learnt, and worked or played with him in the fields. They both promised fair to grow up as rude as savages; the young master being entirely negligent how they behaved, and what they did, so they kept clear of him. One Sunday evening, it chanced that they were banished from the sitting-room, for making a noise, or a light offence of the kind; and when I went to call them to supper, I could discover them nowhere. We searched the house, above and below, and the yard and stables; they were invisible: and, at last, Hindley in a passion told us to bolt the doors, and swore nobody should let them in that night. The household went to

21

bed; and I, too, anxious to lie down, opened my lattice and put my head out to hearken, though it rained: determined to admit them in spite of the prohibition, should they return. In a while, I distinguished steps coming up the road, and the light of a lantern glimmered through the gate. I threw a shawl over my head and ran to prevent them from waking Mr. Earnshaw by knocking. There was Heathcliff, by himself: it gave me a start to see him alone.

"Where is Miss Catherine?" I cried hurriedly. "No accident, I hope?" "At Thrushcross Grange," he answered; "and I would have been there too, but they had not the manners to ask me to stay." "Well, you will catch it!" I said: "you'll never be content till you're sent about your business. What in the world led you to wandering to Thrushcross Grange?" "Let me get off my wet clothes, and I'll tell you all about it, Nelly," he replied. I bid him beware of rousing the master, and while he undressed and I waited to put out the candle, he continued—"Cathy and I escaped from the wash-house to have a ramble at liberty, and getting a glimpse of the Grange lights, we thought we would just go and see whether the Lintons passed their Sunday evenings standing shivering in corners, while their father and mother sat eating and drinking, and singing and laughing, and burning their eyes out before the fire. We ran from the top of the Heights to the park, without stopping—Catherine completely beaten in the race, because she was barefoot. You'll have to seek for her shoes in the bog to-morrow. We crept through a broken hedge, groped our way up the path, and planted ourselves on a flower-plot under the drawing-room window. The light came from thence; they had not put up the shutters, and the curtains were only half closed. Both of us were able to look in by standing on the basement, and clinging to the ledge, and we saw—ah! it was beautiful—a splendid place carpeted with crimson, and crimson-covered chairs and tables, and a pure white ceiling bordered by gold, a shower of glass-drops hanging in silver chains from the centre, and shimmering with little soft tapers. Old Mr. and Mrs. Linton were not there; Edgar and his sister had it entirely to themselves. Shouldn't they have been happy? We should have thought ourselves in heaven! And now, guess what your good children were doing? Isabella—I believe she is eleven, a year younger than Cathy—lay screaming at the farther end of the room, shrieking as if witches were running red-hot needles into her. Edgar stood on the hearth weeping silently, and in the middle of the table sat a little dog, shaking its paw and yelping; which, from their mutual accusations, we understood they had nearly pulled in two between them. The idiots! That was their pleasure! to quarrel who should hold a heap of warm hair, and each begin to cry because both, after struggling to get it, refused to take it. We laughed outright at the petted things; we did despise them!

"The Lintons heard us, and with one accord, they shot like arrows to the door; there was silence, and then a cry, 'Oh, mamma, mamma! Oh, papa! Oh, mamma, come here. Oh, papa, oh!' They really did howl out something in that way. We made frightful noises to terrify them still more, and then we dropped off the ledge, because somebody was drawing the bars, and we felt we had better flee. I had Cathy by the hand, and was urging her on, when all at once she fell down. 'Run, Heathcliff, run!' she whispered. 'They have let the bull-dog loose, and he holds me!' The devil had seized her ankle, Nelly: I heard his abominable snorting. She did not yell out—no! she would have scorned to do it, if she had been spitted on the horns of a mad cow. I did, though: I vociferated curses enough to annihilate any fiend in Christendom; and I got a stone and thrust it between his jaws, and tried with all my might to cram it down his throat. A beast of a servant came up with a lantern, at last, shouting—'Keep fast, Skulker, keep fast!' He changed his note, however, when he saw Skulker's game. The dog was throttled off; his huge, purple tongue hanging half a foot out of his mouth, and his pendent lips streaming with bloody slaver. The man took Cathy up; she was sick: not from fear, I'm certain, but from pain. He carried her in; I followed, grumbling execrations and vengeance. 'What prey, Robert?' hallooed Linton from the entrance. 'Skulker has caught a little girl, sir,' he replied; 'and there's a lad here,' he added, making a clutch at me, 'who looks an out-and-outer! Come in; I'll furnish them a reception. There, John, fasten the chain. Give Skulker some water, Jenny. To beard a magistrate in his stronghold, and on the Sabbath, too! Where will their insolence stop? Oh, my dear Mary, look here! Don't be afraid, it is but a boy—yet the villain scowls so plainly in his face; would it not be a kindness to the country to hang him at once, before he shows his nature in acts as well as features?' He pulled me under the chandelier, and Mrs. Linton placed her spectacles on her nose and raised her hands in horror. The cowardly children crept nearer, also, Isabella lisping—'Frightful thing! Put him in the cellar, papa. He's exactly like the son of the fortune-teller, that stole my tame pheasant. Isn't he, Edgar?'

"While they examined me, Cathy came round; she heard the last speech, and laughed. Edgar Linton, after an inquisitive stare, collected sufficient wit to recognise her. They see us at church, you know, though we seldom met them elsewhere. 'That's Miss Earnshaw!' he whispered to his mother, 'and look how Skulker has bitten her—how her foot bleeds!'

"'Miss Earnshaw? Nonsense!' cried the dame; 'Miss Earnshaw scouring the country with a gipsy! And yet, my dear, the child is in mourning—surely it is—and she may be lamed for life!'

"Robert was ordered to take me off. I refused to go without Cathy; he dragged me into the garden, pushed the lantern into my hand, assured me that Mr. Earnshaw should be informed of my behaviour, and, bidding me march directly, secured the door again. The curtains were still looped up at one corner, and I saw they were full of stupid admiration; she is so immeasurably superior to them—to everybody on earth, is she not, Nelly?"

"There will more come of this business than you reckon on," I answered, covering him up and extinguishing the light. "You are incurable, Heathcliff; and Mr. Hindley will have to proceed to extremities, see if he won't." My words came truer than I desired. The luckless adventure made Earnshaw furious. And then Mr. Linton, to mend manners, paid us a visit himself on the morrow; and read the young master such a lecture on the road he guided his family, that he was stirred to look about him, in earnest.


# Chapter 7

CATHY stayed at Thrushcross Grange five weeks: till Christmas. By that time her ankle was thoroughly cured, and her manners much improved. The mistress visited her often in the interval, and commenced her plan of reform by trying to raise her self-respect with fine clothes and flattery, which she took readily; so that, instead of a wild, hatless little savage jumping into the house, and rushing to squeeze us all breathless, there 'lighted from a handsome black pony a very dignified person, with brown ringlets falling from the cover of a feathered beaver, and a long cloth habit, which she was obliged to hold up with both hands that she might sail in. Hindley lifted her from her horse, exclaiming delightedly, "Why Cathy, you are quite a beauty! I should scarcely have known you: you look like a lady now. Ellen, help Miss Catherine off with her things—Stay, dear, you will disarrange your curls—let me untie your hat."

I removed the habit, and there shone forth beneath, a grand plaid silk frock, white trousers, and burnished shoes; and, while her eyes sparkled joyfully when the dogs came bounding to welcome her, she dare hardly touch them lest they should fawn upon her splendid garments. She kissed me gently: I was all flour making the Christmas cake, and it would not have done to give me a hug; and, then, she looked round for Heathcliff.

Heathcliff was hard to discover, at first. If he were careless, and uncared for, before Catherine's absence, he had been ten times more so, since. Nobody but I even did him the kindness to call him a dirty boy, and bid him wash himself, once a week; and children of his age seldom have a natural pleasure in soap and water. Therefore, not to mention his clothes, which had seen three months' service in mire and dust, and his thick uncombed hair, the surface of his face and hands was dismally beclouded.

"Heathcliff, you may come forward," cried Mr. Hindley, enjoying his discomfiture, and gratified to see what a forbidding young blackguard he would be compelled to present himself. "You may come and wish Miss Catherine welcome, like the other servants."

Cathy, catching a glimpse of her friend in his concealment, flew to embrace him; she bestowed seven or eight kisses on his cheek within the second, and then stopped, and drawing back, burst into a laugh, exclaiming,

"Why, how very black and cross you look! and how—how funny and grim! But that's because I'm used to Edgar and Isabella Linton. Well, Heathcliff, have you forgotten me?"

"Shake hands, Heathcliff," said Mr. Earnshaw, condescendingly; "once in a way, that is permitted."

"I shall not," replied the boy, finding his tongue at last; "I shall not stand to be laughed at. I shall not bear it!"

With that he dashed head foremost out of the room, amid the merriment of the master and mistress, and to the serious disturbance of Catherine; who could not comprehend how her remarks should have produced such an exhibition of bad temper.

After playing lady's maid to the new comer, and putting my cakes in the oven, and making the house and kitchen cheerful with great fires, befitting Christmas eve, I prepared to sit down and amuse myself by singing carols, all alone; regardless of Joseph's affirmations that he considered the merry tunes I chose as next door to songs. He had retired to private prayer in his chamber, and Mr. and Mrs. Earnshaw were engaging Missy's attention by sundry gay trifles bought for her to present to the little Lintons, as an acknowledgment of their kindness. They had invited them to spend the morrow at Wuthering Heights, and the invitation had been accepted, on one condition: Mrs. Linton begged that her darlings might be kept carefully apart from that "naughty swearing boy."

Under these circumstances I remained solitary. I gave due inward applause to every object, and then I remembered how old Earnshaw used to come in when all was tidied, and call me a cant lass, and slip a shilling into my hand as a Christmas-box; and from that I went on to think of his fondness for Heathcliff, and his dread lest he should suffer neglect after death had removed him; and that naturally led me to consider the poor lad's situation now, and from singing I changed my mind to crying. I got up and walked into the court to seek him. He was not far; I found him smoothing the glossy coat of the new pony in the stable, and feeding the other beasts according to custom.

"Make haste, Heathcliff!" I said, "the kitchen is so comfortable; and Joseph is upstairs: make haste, and let me dress you smart before Miss Cathy comes out, and then you can sit together, with the whole hearth to yourselves, and have a long chatter till bedtime."

He proceeded with his task and never turned his head towards me.

I waited five minutes, but getting no answer left him. Catherine supped with her brother and sister-in-law: Joseph and I joined at an unsociable meal, seasoned with reproofs on one side and sauciness on the other. His cake and cheese remained on the table all night for the fairies. He managed to continue work till nine-o'clock, and then marched dumb and dour to his chamber. Cathy sat up late, having a world of things to order for the reception of her new friends: she came into the kitchen once to speak to her old one; but he was gone, and she only stayed to ask what was the matter with him, and then went back. In the morning he rose early; and as it was a holiday, carried his ill-humour on to the moors; not re-appearing till the family were departed for church. Fasting and reflection seemed to have brought him to a better spirit. He hung about me for a while, and having screwed up his courage, exclaimed abruptly—

"Nelly, make me decent, I'm going to be good."

"High time, Heathcliff," I said; "you *have* grieved Catherine: she's sorry she ever came home, I dare say! It looks as if you envied her, because she is more thought of than you."

So I chatted on; and Heathcliff gradually lost his frown and began to look quite pleasant, when all at once our conversation was interrupted by a rumbling sound moving up the road and entering the court. He ran to the window and I to the door, just in time to behold the two Lintons descend from the family carriage, smothered in cloaks and furs, and the Earnshaws dismount from their horses: they often rode to church in winter. Catherine took a hand of each of the children, and brought them into the house and set them before the fire, which quickly put colour into their white faces.

I urged my companion to hasten now and show his amiable humour, and he willingly obeyed; but ill luck would have it that, as he opened the door leading from the kitchen on one side, Hindley opened it on the other. They met, and the master irritated at seeing him clean and cheerful; or, perhaps, eager to keep his promise to Mrs. Linton, shoved him back with a sudden thrust, and angrily bade Joseph "keep the fellow out of the room—send him into the garret till dinner is over. He'll be cramming his fingers in the tarts and stealing the fruit, if left alone with them a minute."

"Nay, sir," I could not avoid answering, "he'll touch nothing, not he: and I suppose he must have his share of the dainties as well as we."

"He shall have his share of my hand, if I catch him downstairs till dark," cried Hindley. "Begone, you vagabond! What! you are attempting the coxcomb, are you? Wait till I get hold of those elegant locks—see if I won't pull them a bit longer!"

"They are long enough already," observed Master Linton, peeping from the doorway; "I wonder they don't make his head ache. It's like a colt's mane over his eyes!"

He ventured this remark without any intention to insult; but Heathcliff's violent nature was not prepared to endure the appearance of impertinence from one whom he seemed to hate, even then, as a rival. He seized a tureen of hot apple sauce (the first thing that came under his gripe) and dashed it full against the speaker's face and neck; who instantly commenced a lament that brought Isabella and Catherine hurrying to the place. Mr. Earnshaw snatched up the culprit directly and conveyed him to his chamber; where, doubtless, he administered a rough remedy to cool the fit of passion, for he appeared red and breathless. I got the dish-cloth, and rather spitefully scrubbed Edgar's nose and mouth, affirming it served him right for meddling. His sister began weeping to go home, and Cathy stood by confounded, blushing for all.

"There, there, children—to your seats!" cried Hindley, bustling in. "That brute of a lad has warmed me nicely. Next time, Master Edgar, take the law into your own fists—it will give you an appetite!"

The little party recovered its equanimity at sight of the fragrant feast. They were hungry after their ride, and easily consoled, since no real harm had befallen them. Mr. Earnshaw carved bountiful platefuls, and the mistress made them merry with lively talk. I waited behind her chair, and was pained to behold Catherine, with dry eyes and an indifferent air, commence cutting up the wing of a goose before her. "An unfeeling child," I thought to myself; "how lightly she dismisses her old playmate's troubles. I could not have imagined her to be so selfish." She lifted a mouthful to her lips; then she set it down again: her cheeks flushed, and the tears gushed over them. She slipped her fork to the floor, and hastily dived under the cloth to conceal her emotion. I did not call her unfeeling long; for I perceived she was in purgatory throughout the day a take back to end of preceding line.

## *Chapter 8*

On the morning of a fine June day, my first bonny little nursling, and the last of the ancient Earnshaw stock, was born. We were busy with the hay in a far away field, when the girl that usually brought our breakfasts, came running an hour too soon, across the meadow and up the lane, calling me as she ran.

"Oh, such a grand bairn!" she panted out. "The finest lad that ever breathed! But the doctor says missis must go: he says she's been in a consumption these many months. I heard him tell Mr. Hindley: and now she has nothing to keep her, and she'll be dead before winter. You must come home directly. You're to nurse it, Nelly: to feed it with sugar and milk, and take care of it day and night, I wish I were you, because it will be all yours when there is no missis!"

When we got to Wuthering Heights, there he stood at the front door; and, as I passed in, I asked, "how was the baby?"

"Nearly ready to run about, Nell!" he replied, putting on a cheerful smile.

"And the mistress?" I ventured to inquire; "the doctor says she's——"

"Damn the doctor!" he interrupted, reddening. "Frances is quite right; she'll be perfectly well by this time next week."

He told his wife the same story, and she seemed to believe him; but one night, while leaning on his shoulder, in the act of saying she thought she should be able to get up to-morrow, a fit of coughing took her—a very slight one—he raised her in his arms; she put her two hands about his neck, her face changed, and she was dead.

As the girl had anticipated, the child Hareton fell wholly into my hands. Mr. Earnshaw, provided he saw him healthy and never heard him cry, was contented, as far as regarded him. For himself, he grew desperate: his sorrow was of that kind that will not lament. He neither wept nor prayed; he cursed and defied: execrated God and man, and gave himself up to reckless dissipation. The servants could not bear his tyrannical and evil conduct long: Joseph and I were the only two that would stay.

The master's bad ways and bad companions formed a pretty example for Catherine and Heathcliff. His treatment of the latter was enough to make a fiend of a saint. And, truly, it appeared as if the lad *were* possessed of something diabolical at that period. He delighted to witness Hindley degrading himself past redemption; and became daily more notable for savage sullenness and ferocity. I could not half tell what an infernal house we had. The curate dropped calling, and nobody decent came near us, at last; unless Edgar Linton's visits to Miss Cathy might be an exception. At fifteen she was the queen of the country-side; she had no peer; and she did turn out a haughty, headstrong creature! I own I did not like her, after her infancy was past; and I vexed her frequently by trying to bring down her arrogance: she never took an aversion to me, though. She had a wondrous constancy to old attachments: even Heathcliff kept his hold on her affections unalterably; and young Linton, with all his superiority, found it difficult to make an equally deep impression.

Mr. Edgar seldom mustered courage to visit Wuthering Heights openly. He had a terror of Earnshaw's reputation, and shrunk from encountering him; and yet he was always received with our best attempts at civility: the master himself avoided offending him, knowing why he came; and if he could not be gracious, kept out of the way. I rather think his appearance there was distasteful to Catherine: she was not artful, never played the coquette, and had evidently an objection to her two friends meeting at all; for when Heathcliff expressed contempt of Linton in his presence, she could not half coincide, as she did in his absence; and when Linton evinced disgust and antipathy to Heathcliff, she dare not treat his sentiments with indifference, as if depreciation of her playmate were of scarcely any consequence to her.

Intelligence of Mr. Hindley's arrival drove Linton speedily to his horse, and Catherine to her chamber. I went to hide little Hareton, and to take the shot out of the master's fowling-piece, which he was fond of playing with in his insane excitement, to the hazard of the lives of any who provoked, or even attracted his notice too much; and I had hit upon the plan of removing it, that he might do less mischief if he did go the length of firing the gun.

28

## Chapter 9

HE ENTERED, vociferating oaths dreadful to hear; and caught me in the act of stowing his son away in the kitchen cupboard. Hareton was impressed with a wholesome terror of encountering either his wild beast's fondness or his madman's rage; for in one he ran a chance of being squeezed and kissed to death, and in the other of being flung into the fire, or dashed against the wall; and the poor thing remained perfectly quiet wherever I chose to put him.

"There, I've found it out at last!" cried Hindley, pulling me back by the shin of my neck, like a dog. "By heaven and hell, you've sworn between you to murder that child! I know how it is, now, that he is always out of my way. But, with the help of Satan, I shall make you swallow the carving-knife Nelly! You needn't laugh; for I've just crammed Kenneth, head-downmost, in the Blackhorse marsh; and two is the same as one—and I want to kill some of you: I shall have no rest till I do!"

Poor Hareton was squalling and kicking in his father's arms with all his might, and redoubled his yells when he carried him upstairs and lifted him over the banister. I cried out that he would frighten the child into fits, and ran to rescue him. As I reached them, Hindley leant forward on the rails to listen to a noise below; almost forgetting what he had in his hands. "Who is that?" he asked, hearing some one approaching the stair's foot. I leant forward also, for the purpose of signing to Heathcliff, whose step I recognised, not to come further; and, at the instant when my eye quitted Hareton, he gave a sudden spring, delivered himself from the careless grasp that held him, and fell.

There was scarcely time to experience a thrill of horror before we saw that the little wretch was safe. Heathcliff arrived underneath just at the critical moment; by a natural impulse, he arrested his descent, and setting him on his feet, looked up to discover the author of the accident. Hindley descended more leisurely, sobered and abashed.

I went into the kitchen, and sat down to lull my little lamb to sleep. Heathcliff, as I thought, walked through to the barn. It turned out afterwards that he only got as far as the other side the settle, when he flung himself on a bench by the wall, removed from the fire, and remained silent.

I was rocking Hareton on my knee, and humming a song when Miss Cathy, who had listened to the hubbub from her room, put her head in, and whispered,—

"Are you alone, Nelly?"

"Yes, miss," I replied.

She entered and approached the hearth. I, supposing she was going to say something, looked up. The expression of her face seemed disturbed and anxious. Her lips were half asunder, as if she meant to speak, and she drew a breath; but it escaped in a sigh instead of a sentence. I resumed my song; not having forgotten her recent behaviour.

"Nelly, will you keep a secret for me?" she pursued, kneeling down by me, and lifting her winsome eyes to my face with that sort of look which turns off bad temper, even when one has all the right in the world to indulge it.

"Is it worth keeping?" I inquired, less sulkily.

"Yes, and it worries me, and I must let it out! I want to know what I should do. To-day, Edgar Linton has asked me to marry him, and I've given him an answer. Now, before I tell you whether it was a consent or denial, you tell me which it ought to have been."

"Really, Miss Catherine, how can I know?" I replied. "To be sure, considering the exhibition you performed in his presence this afternoon, I might say it would be wise to refuse him: since he asked you after that, he must either be hopelessly stupid or a venturesome fool."

"If you talk so, I won't tell you any more," she returned, peevishly, rising to her feet. "I accepted him, Nelly. Be quick, and say whether I was wrong!"

"Perfectly right; if people be right to marry only for the present, and now, let us hear what you are unhappy about. Your brother will be pleased; the old lady and gentleman will not object, I think; you will escape from a disorderly, comfortless home into a wealthy, respectable one; and you love Edgar, and Edgar loves you. All seems smooth and easy: where is the obstacle?"

"*Here!* and *here!*" replied Catherine, striking one hand on her forehead, and the other on her breast; "in whichever place the soul lives. In my soul and in my heart, I'm convinced I'm wrong!"

"That's very strange! I cannot make it out."

"It's my secret. But if you will not mock at me, I'll explain it: I can't do it distinctly; but I'll give you a feeling of how I feel."

She seated herself by me again: her countenance grew sadder and graver, and her clasped hands trembled.

"If I were in heaven, Nelly, I should be extremely miserable."

"Because you are not fit to go there," I answered. "All sinners would be miserable in heaven."

"But it is not for that. I dreamt once that I was there."

"I won't hearken to your dreams, Miss Catherine! I'll go to bed," I interrupted again.

She laughed, and held me down; for I made a motion to leave my chair.

"This is nothing," cried she: "I was only going to say that heaven did not seem to be my home; and I broke my heart with weeping to come back to earth; and the angels were so angry that they flung me out into the middle of the heath on the top of Wuthering Heights; where I woke

30

sobbing for joy. That will do to explain my secret, as well as the other. I've no more business to marry Edgar Linton than I have to be in heaven; and if the wicked man in there had not brought Heathcliff so low, I shouldn't have thought of it. It would degrade me to marry Heathcliff now; so he shall never know how I love him: and that, not because he's handsome, Nelly, but because he's more myself than I am. Whatever our souls are made of, his and mine are the same; and Linton's is as different as a moonbeam from lightning, or frost from fire."

Ere this speech ended, I became sensible of Heathcliff's presence. Having noticed a slight movement, I turned my head, and saw him rise from the bench, and steal out noiselessly. He had listened till he heard Catherine say it would degrade her to marry him, and then he stayed to hear no further. My companion, sitting on the ground, was prevented by the back of the settle from remarking his presence or departure; but I started, and bade her hush!

"Why?" she asked, gazing nervously round.

"Joseph is here," I answered, catching opportunely the roll of his cartwheels up the road; "and Heathcliff will come in with him. I'm not sure whether he were not at the door this moment."

"Oh, he couldn't overhear me at the door!" said she. "Give me Hareton, while you get the supper, and when it is ready ask me to sup with you. I want to cheat my uncomfortable conscience, and be convinced that Heathcliff has no notion of these things. He has not, has he? He does not know what being in love is?"

"If I can make any sense of your nonsense, miss," I said, "it only goes to convince me that you are ignorant of the duties you undertake in marrying; or else that you are a wicked, unprincipled girl. But trouble me with no more secrets: I'll not promise to keep them."

"You'll keep that?" she asked, eagerly.

"No, I'll not promise," I repeated.

She was about to insist, when the entrance of Joseph finished our conversation: and Catherine removed her seat to a corner, and nursed Hareton, while I made the supper. After it was cooked, my fellow-servant and I began to quarrel who should carry some to Mr. Hindley; and we didn't settle it till all was nearly cold. Then we came to the agreement that we would let him ask, if he wanted any; for we feared particularly to go into his presence when he had been some time alone.

"And how isn't that nowt comed in fro' th' field, be this time? What is he about? girt idle seeght!" demanded the old man, looking round for Heathcliff.

"I'll call him," I replied. "He's in the barn, I've no doubt." I went and called, but got no answer. On returning, I whispered to Catherine that he had heard a good part of what she said, I was sure; and told how I saw him quit the kitchen just as she complained of her brother's conduct regarding him. She jumped up in a fine fright, flung Hareton on to the settle, and ran to seek for her friend herself; not taking leisure to consider why she was so flurried, or how her talk would have affected him. She was absent such a while that Joseph proposed we should wait no longer. He cunningly conjectured they were staying away in order to avoid hearing his protracted blessing. They were "ill eneugh for ony fahl manners," he affirmed. And on their behalf he added that night a special prayer to the usual quarter of an hour's supplication before meat, and would have tacked another to the end of the grace, had not his young mistress broken in upon him with a hurried command that he must run down the road, and, wherever Heathcliff had rambled, find and make him re-enter directly!

It was a very dark evening for summer: the clouds appeared inclined to thunder, and I said we had better all sit down; the approaching rain would be certain to bring him home without further trouble. However, Catherine would not be persuaded into tranquillity. She kept wandering to and fro, from the gate to the door, in a state of agitation which permitted no repose; and at length took up a permanent situation on one side of the wall, near the road: where, heedless of my expostulations and the growling thunder, and the great drops that began to plash around her, she remained, calling at intervals, and then listening, and then crying outright.

About midnight, while we still sat up, the storm came rattling over the Heights in full fury. There was a violent wind, as well as thunder, and a huge bough fell across the roof, and knocked down a portion of the east chimney-stack, sending a clatter of stones and soot into the kitchen fire. But the uproar passed away in twenty minutes, leaving us all unharmed; excepting Cathy, who got thoroughly drenched for her obstinacy in refusing to take shelter, and standing bonnetless and shawlless to catch as much water as she could with her hair and clothes. She came in and lay down on the settle, all soaked as she was, turning her face to the back.

"Well, miss!" I exclaimed, touching her shoulder; "you are not bent on getting your death, are you? Do you know what o'clock it is? Half-past twelve. Come, come to bed! there's no use waiting longer on that foolish boy: he'll be gone to Gimmerton, and he'll stay there now. He guesses we shouldn't wake for him till this late hour: at least, he guesses that only Mr. Hindley would be up; and he'd rather avoid having the door opened by the master."

"Nay, nay, he's noan at Gimmerton," said Joseph. "I's niver wonder but he's at t' botham of a bog-hoile. This visitation worn't for nowt, and I wod hev ye to look out, miss—yah muh be t' next. Thank Hivin for all! All warks togither for gooid to them as is chozzen, and piked out fro' th' rubbidge! Yah knaw whet t' Scripture ses." And he began quoting several texts, refering us to chapters and verses where we might find them.

I, having vainly begged the wilful girl to rise and remove her wet things, left him preaching and her shivering, and betook myself to bed with little Hareton, who slept as fast as if everyone had been sleeping round him. I heard Joseph read on a while afterwards; then I distinguished his slow step on the ladder, and then I dropped asleep.

Coming down somewhat later than usual, I saw, by the sunbeams piercing the chinks of the shutters, Miss Catherine still seated near the fireplace. The house door was ajar, too; light entered from its unclosed windows; Hindley had come out, and stood on the kitchen heath, haggard and drowsy.

"What ails you, Cathy?" he was saying when I entered: "You look as dismal as a drowned whelp. Why are you so damp and pale, child?"

"I've been wet," she answered reluctantly, "and I'm cold, that's all."

"Oh, she is naughty!" I cried, perceiving the master to be tolerably sober. "She got steeped in the shower of yesterday evening, and there she has sat the night through, and I couldn't prevail on her to stir."

"She's ill," said Hindley, taking her wrist; "I suppose that's the reason she would not go to bed. Damn it! I don't want to be troubled with more sickness here. What took you into the rain?"

"Running after t' lads, as usuald!" croaked Joseph, catching an opportunity, from our hesitation, to thrust in his evil tongue. "If I war yah, maister, I'd just slam t' boards i' their faces all on 'em, gentle and simple! Never a day ut yah're off, but yon cat o' Linton comes sneaking hither; and Miss Nelly, shoo's a fine lass! shoo sits watching for ye i' t' kitchen; and as yah're in at one door, he's out at t' other; and, then, wer grand lady goes a coorting of her side! It's bonny behaviour, lurking amang t' fields, after twelve ut' night, wi' that fahl, flaysome divil of a gipsy, Heathcliff! They think *I'm* blind; but I'm noan: no'wt ut t' soart!— I seed young Linton boath coming and going, and I seed *yah*" (directing his discourse to me), "yah guid fur nowt, slattenly witch! nip up and bolt into th' house, t' minute yah heard t' maister's horse fit clatter up t' road."

Hindley lavished on her a torrent of scornful abuse, and bade her get to her room immediately, or she shouldn't cry for nothing! I obliged her to obey; and I shall never forget what a scene she acted when we reached her chamber: it terrified me. I thought she was going mad, and I begged Joseph to run for the doctor. It proved the commencement of delirium: Mr. Kenneth, as soon as he saw her, pronounced her dangerously ill; she had a fever. He bled her, and he told me to let her live on whey and water-gruel, and take care she did not throw herself downstairs or out of the window.

Though I cannot say I made a gentle nurse, and Joseph and the master were no better; and though our patient was as wearisome and headstrong as a patient could be, she weathered it through. Old Mrs. Linton paid us several visits, to be sure, and set things to rights, and scolded and ordered us all; and when Catherine was convalescent, she insisted on conveying her to Thrushcross Grange; for which deliverance we were very grateful. But the poor dame had reason to repent of her kindness: she and her husband both took the fever, and died within a few days of each other.

Our young lady returned to us, saucier and more passionate, and haughtier than ever. Heathcliff had never been heard of since the evening of the thunderstorm; and, one day, I had the misfortune, when she had provoked me exceedingly, to lay the blame of his disappearance on her: where indeed it belonged, as she well knew. From that period, for several months, she ceased to hold any communication with me, save in the relation of a mere servant. From Mr. Earnshaw and his companions she kept aloof; her brother allowed her whatever she pleased to demand, and generally avoided aggravating her fiery temper. He was rather *too* indulgent in humouring her caprices; not from affection, but from pride; he wished earnestly to see her bring honour to the family by an alliance with the Lintons, and as long as she let him alone she might trample on us like slaves, for aught he cared! Edgar Linton, as multitudes have been before and will be after him, was infatuated; and believed himself the happiest man alive on the day he led her to Gimmerton Chapel, three years subsequent to his father's death.

Much against my inclination, I was persuaded to leave Wuthering Heights and accompany her here. Little Hareton was nearly five years old, and I had just begun to teach him his letters. We made a sad parting; but Catherine's tears were more powerful than ours. When I refused to go, and when she found her entreaties did not move me, she went lamenting to her husband and brother. The former offered me munificent wages; the latter ordered me to pack up: he wanted no women in the house, he said, now that there was no mistress; and as to Hareton, the curate should take him in hand, by-and-by. And so I had but one choice left: to do as I was ordered. I told the master he got rid of all decent people only to run to ruin a little faster; I kissed Hareton, said good-bye; and since then he has been a stranger: and it's very queer to think it, but I've no doubt he has completely forgotten all about Ellen Dean, and that he was ever more than all the world to her, and she to him!

At this point of the housekeeper's story, she chanced to glance towards the time-piece over the chimney; and was in amazement on seeing the minute-hand measure half-past one. She would not hear of staying a second longer: in truth, I felt rather disposed to defer the sequel of her narrative, myself. And now that she is vanished to her rest, and I have meditated for another hour or two, I shall summon courage to go, also, in spite of aching laziness of head and limbs.

# Chapter 10

A CHARMING introduction to a hermit's life! Four weeks' torture, tossing, and sickness! Oh, these bleak winds and bitter northern skies, and impassable roads, and dilatory country surgeons! And, oh, this dearth of the human physiognomy! and, worse than all, the terrible intimation of Kenneth that I need not expect to be out of doors till spring!

Mr. Heathcliff has just honoured me with a call. About seven days ago he sent me a brace of grouse—the last of the season. Scoundrel! He is not altogether guiltless in this illness of mine; and that I had a great mind to tell him. But, alas! how could I offend a man who was charitable enough to sit at my bedside a good hour, and talk on some other subject than pills and draughts, blisters and leeches? This is quite an easy interval. I am too weak to read; yet I feel as if could enjoy something interesting. Why not have up Mrs. Dean to finish her tale? I can recollect its chief incidents, as far as she had gone. Yes: I remember her hero had run off, and never been heard of for three years; and the heroine was married. I'll ring: she'll be delighted to find me capable of talking cheerfully. Mrs. Dean came.

"It wants twenty minutes, sir, to taking the medicine," she commenced.

"Away, away with it!" I replied; "I desire to have——"

"The doctor says you must drop the powders."

"With all my heart! Don't interrupt me. Come and take your seat here. Keep your fingers from that bitter phalanx of vials. Draw your knitting out of your pocket—that will do—now continue the history of Mr. Heathcliff, from where you left off, to the present day. Did he finish his education on the Continent, and come back a gentleman—or did he get a sizar's place at college, or escape to America, and earn honours by drawing blood from his foster-country? or make a fortune more promptly on the English highways?"

"He may have done a little in all these vocations, Mr. Lockwood; but I couldn't give my word for any. I stated before that I didn't know how he gained his money; neither am I aware of the means he took to raise his mind from the savage ignorance into which it was sunk: but, with your leave, I'll proceed in my own fashion, if you think it will amuse and not weary you. Are you feeling better this morning?"

"Much."

"That's good news. I got Miss Catherine and myself to Thrushcross Grange; and, to my agreeable disappointment, she behaved infinitely better than I dared to expect. She seemed almost over fond of Mr. Linton; and even to his sister, she showed plenty of affection. They were both very attentive to her comfort, certainly. It was not the thorn bending to the honeysuckles, but the honeysuckles embracing the thorn. There were no mutual concessions: one stood erect, and the others yielded: and who *can* be ill-natured and bad-tempered when they encounter neither opposition nor indifference? I observed that Mr. Edgar had a deep-rooted fear of ruffling her humour. He concealed it from her; but if ever he heard me answer sharply, or saw any other servant grow cloudy at some imperious order of hers, he would show his trouble by a frown of displeasure that never darkened on his own account. He many a time spoke sternly to me about my pertness; and averred that the stab of a knife could not inflict a worse pang than he suffered at seeing his lady vexed. Not to grieve a kind master, I learned to be less touchy; and, for the space of half a year, the gunpowder lay as harmless as sand, because no fire came near to explode it. Catherine had seasons of gloom and silence now and then: they were respected with sympathizing silence by her husband, who ascribed them to an alteration in her constitution, produced by her perilous illness; as she was never subject to depression of spirits before. The return of sunshine was welcomed by answering sunshine from him. I believe I may assert that they were really in possession of deep and growing happiness.

It ended. Well, we *must* be for ourselves in the long run; the mild and generous are only more justly selfish than the domineering; and it ended when circumstances caused each to feel that the one's interest was not the chief consideration in the other's thoughts. On a mellow evening in September, I was coming from the garden with a heavy basket of apples which I had been gathering. It had got dusk, and the moon looked over the high wall of the court, causing undefined shadows to lurk in the corners of the numerous projecting portions of the building. I set my burden on the house steps by the kitchen door, and lingered to rest, and drew in a few more breaths of the soft, sweet air; my eyes were on the moon, and my back to the entrance, when I heard a voice behind me say,—

"Nelly, is that you?"

It was a deep voice, and foreign in tone; yet there was something in the manner of pronouncing my name which made it sound familiar. I turned about to discover who spoke, fearfully; for the doors were shut, and I had seen nobody on approaching the steps. Something stirred in the porch; and, moving nearer, I distinguished a tall man dressed in dark clothes, with dark face and hair. He leant against the side, and held his fingers on the latch as if intending to open for himself. "Who can it be?" I thought. "Mr. Earnshaw? Oh, no! The voice has no resemblance to his."

A ray fell on his features; the cheeks were sallow, and half-covered with black whiskers; the brows lowering, the eyes deep set and singular. I remembered the eyes.

"What!" I cried, uncertain whether to regard him as a worldly visitor, and I raised my hands in amazement. "What! you come back? Is it really you? Is it?"

"Yes, Heathcliff," he replied, glancing from me up to the windows, which reflected a score of glittering moons, but showed no lights from within. "Are they at home? where is she? Nelly, you are not glad! you needn't be so disturbed. Is she here? Speak! I want to have one word with her—your mistress. Go, and say some person from Gimmerton desires to see her."

He lifted the latch, and I entered; but when I got to the parlour where Mr. and Mrs. Linton were, I could not persuade myself to proceed. At length, I resolved on making an excuse to ask if they would have the candles lighted, and I opened the door.

They sat together in a window whose lattice lay back against the wall, and displayed, beyond the garden trees and the wild green park, the valley of Gimmerton, with a long line of mist winding nearly to its top (for very soon after you pass the chapel, as you may have noticed, the sough that runs from the marshes joins a beck which follows the bend of the glen). Wuthering Heights rose above this silvery vapour; but our old house was invisible; it rather dips down on the other side. Both the room and its occupants, and the scene they gazed on, looked wondrously peaceful. I shrank reluctantly from performing my errand; and was actually going away leaving it unsaid, after having put my question about the candles, when a sense of my folly compelled me to return, and mutter:—"A person from Gimmerton wishes to see you, ma'am."

"What does he want?" asked Mrs. Linton.

"I did not question him," I answered.

"Well, close the curtains, Nelly," she said; "and bring up tea. I'll be back again directly."

She quitted the apartment; Mr. Edgar inquired, carelessly, who it was.

"Some one mistress does not expect," I replied. "That Heathcliff—you recollect him, sir,—who used to live at Mr. Earnshaw's."

Mr. Linton walked to a window on the other side of the room that overlooked the court. He unfastened it, and leant out. I suppose they were below, for he exclaimed quickly:—"Don't stand there, love! Bring the person in if it be any one particular." Ere long, I heard the click of the latch, and Catherine flew upstairs, breathless and wild; too excited to show gladness: indeed, by her face, you would rather have surmised an awful calamity.

"Oh, Edgar, Edgar!" she panted, flinging her arms round his neck. "Oh, Edgar, darling! Heathcliff's come back—he is!" And she tightened her embrace to a squeeze.

"Well, well," cried her husband, crossly, "don't strangle me for that! He never struck me as such a marvellous treasure. There is no need to be frantic!"

"I know you didn't like him," she answered, repressing a little the intensity of her delight. "Yet, for my sake, you must be friends now. Shall I tell him to come up?"

She was about to dart off again; but Edgar arrested her.

"*You* bid him step up," he said, addressing me; "and, Catherine, try to be glad, without being absurd! The whole household need not witness the sight of your welcoming a runaway servant as a brother."

I descended, and found Heathcliff waiting under the porch, evidently anticipating an invitation to enter. He followed my guidance without waste of words, and I ushered him into the presence of the master and mistress, whose flushed cheeks betrayed signs of warm talking. But the lady's glowed with another feeling when her friend appeared at the door: she sprang forward, took both his hands, and led him to Linton; and then she seized Linton's reluctant fingers and crushed them into his. Now fully revealed by the fire and candlelight, I was amazed, more than ever, to behold the transformation of Heathcliff. He had grown a tall, athletic, well-formed man; beside whom, my master seemed quite slender and youth-like. His upright carriage suggested the idea of his having been in the army. His countenance was much older in expression and decision of feature than Mr. Linton's; it looked intelligent, and retained no marks of former degradation. A half-civilized ferocity lurked yet in the depressed brows and eyes full of black fire, but it was subdued; and his manner was even dignified: quite divested of roughness, though too stern for grace. My master's surprise equalled or exceeded mine: he remained for a minute at a loss how to address the ploughboy, as he had called him. Heathcliff dropped his slight hand, and stood looking at him coolly till he chose to speak.

"Sit down, sir," he said, at length, "Mrs. Linton, recalling old times, would have me give you a cordial reception; and, of course, I am gratified when anything occurs to please her."

She took her post before the urn; and Miss Isabella came, summoned by the bell; then, having handed their chairs forward, I left the room. The meal hardly endured ten minutes. Catherine's cup was never filled: she could neither eat nor drink. Edgar had made a slop in his saucer, and scarcely swallowed a mouthful. Their guest did not protract his stay that evening above an hour longer. I asked, as he departed, if he went to Gimmerton?

"No, to Wuthering Heights," he answered: "Mr. Earnshaw invited me, when I called this morning."

Mr. Earnshaw invited *him!* and *he* called on Mr. Earnshaw! I pondered this sentence painfully, after he was gone. Is he turning out a bit of a hypocrite, and coming into the country to work mischief under a cloak? I mused: I had a presentiment in the bottom of my heart that he had better have remained away.

About the middle of the night, I was wakened from my first nap by Mrs. Linton gliding into my chamber, taking a seat on my bedside, and pulling me by the hair to rouse me.

"I cannot rest, Ellen," she said, by way of apology. "And I want some living creature to keep me company in my happiness! Edgar is sulky, be-

38

cause I'm glad of a thing that does not interest him: he refuses to open his mouth, except to utter pettish, silly speeches; and he affirmed I was cruel and selfish for wishing to talk when he was so sick and sleepy. He always contrives to be sick at the least cross! I gave a few sentences of commendation to Heathcliff, and he, either for a headache or a pang of envy, began to cry: so I got up and left him."

"What do you think of his going to Wuthering Heights?" I inquired. "He is reformed in every respect, apparently: quite a Christian: offering the right hand of fellowship to his enemies all around!"

"He explained it," she replied. "I wonder as much as you. He said he called to gather information concering me from you, supposing you resided there still; and Joseph told Hindley, who came out and fell to questioning him of what he had been doing, and how he had been living; and finally, desired him to walk in. There were some persons sitting at cards; Heathcliff joined them; my brother lost some money to him, and, finding him plentifully supplied, he requested that he would come again in the evening: to which he consented. Hindley is too reckless to select his acquaintance prudently: he doesn't trouble himself to reflect on the causes he might have for mistrusting one whom he has basely injured. But Heathcliff affirms his principal reason for resuming a connection with his ancient persecutor is a wish to install himself in quarters at walking distance from the Grange, and an attachment to the house where we lived together; and likewise a hope that I shall have more opportunities of seeing him there than I could have if he settled in Gimmerton. He means to offer liberal payment for permission to lodge at the Heights; and doubtless my brother's covetousness will prompt him to accept the terms: he was always greedy; though what he grasps with one hand he flings away with the other."

Heathcliff—Mr. Heathcliff I should say in future—used the liberty of visiting at Thrushcross Grange cautiously, at first: he seemed estimating how far its owner would bear his intrusion. Catherine, also, deemed it judicious to moderate her expressions of pleasure in receiving him; and he gradually established his right to be expected. He retained a great deal of the reserve for which his boyhood was remarkable; and that served to repress all startling demonstrations of feeling. My master's uneasiness experienced a lull, and further circumstances diverted it into another channel for a space.

We had all remarked, during some time, that Miss Linton fretted and pined over something. She grew cross and wearisome; snapping at and teasing Catherine continually, at the imminent risk of exhausting her limited patience. We excused her, to a certain extent, on the plea of ill-health: she was dwindling and fading before our eyes. But one day, when she had been peculiarly wayward, rejecting her breakfast, complaining that the servants did not do what she told them; that the mistress would allow her to be nothing in the house, and Edgar neglected her; that she had caught a cold with the doors being left open, and we let the parlour fire go out on purpose to vex her, with a hundred yet more frivolous accusations, Mrs. Linton peremptorily insisted that she should get to bed; and, having scolded her heartily, threatened to send for the doctor. Mention of Kenneth caused her to exclaim, instantly, that her health was perfect, and it was only Catherine's harshness which made her unhappy.

"How can you say I am harsh, you naughty fondling?" cried the mistress, amazed at the unreasonable assertion. "You are surely losing your reason. When have I been harsh, tell me?"

"Yesterday," sobbed Isabella, "and now!"

"Yesterday!" said her sister-in-law. "On what occasion?"

"In our walk along the moor: you told me to ramble where I pleased, while you sauntered on with Mr. Heathcliff."

"And that's your notion of harshness?" said Catherine, laughing. "It was no hint that your company was superfluous: we didn't care whether you kept with us or not; I merely thought Heathcliff's talk would have nothing entertaining for your ears."

"Oh no," wept the young lady; "you wished me away, because you knew I liked to be there!"

"Is she sane?" asked Mrs. Linton, appealing to me. "I'll repeat our conversation, word for word, Isabella; and you point out any charm it could have had for you."

"I don't mind the conversation," she answered. "I wanted to be with——"

"Well!" said Catherine, perceiving her hesitate to complete the sentence.

"With him: and I won't always be sent off!" she continued, kindling up. "You are a dog in the manger, Cathy, and desire no one to be loved but yourself!"

"You are an impertinent little monkey!" exclaimed Mrs. Linton, in surprise. "But I'll not believe this idiocy! It is impossible that you can covet the admiration of Heathcliff—that you consider him an agreeable person! I hope I have misunderstood you, Isabella?"

"No you have not," said the infatuated girl. "I love him more than ever you loved Edgar; and he might love me, if you would let him!"

"I wouldn't be you for a kingdom, then!" Catherine declared, emphatically: and she seemed to speak sincerely. "Nelly, help me to convince her of her madness. Tell her what Heathcliff is: an unreclaimed creature, without refinement, without cultivation: an arid wilderness of furze and whinstone. I'd as soon put that little canary into the park on a winter's day, as recommend you to bestow your heart on him! It is deplorable ignorance of his character, child, and nothing else, which makes that dream enter your head. Pray, don't imagine that he conceals depths of benevolence and affection beneath a stern exterior! He's not a rough diamond—a pearl-containing oyster of a rustic: he's a fierce, pitiless, wolfish man. I never say to him 'Let this or that enemy alone, because it would be ungenerous or cruel to harm them:' I say 'Let them alone, because *I* should hate them to be wronged:' and he'd crush you like a sparrow's egg, Isabella, if he found you a troublesome charge. I know he couldn't love a Linton; and yet he'd be quite capable of marrying your fortune and expectations: avarice is growing with him a besetting sin. That's my picture: and I'm his friend—so much so, that had he thought seriously to catch you, I should, perhaps, have held my tongue, and let you fall into his trap."

Miss Linton regarded her sister-in-law with indignation.

"For shame! for shame!" she repeated, angrily. "You are worse than twenty foes, you poisonous friend!"

"Ah! you won't believe me, then?" said Catherine. "You think I speak from wicked selfishness?"

"I'm certain you do," retorted Isabella; "and I shudder at you!"

"Good!" cried the other. "Try for yourself, if that be your spirit: I have done, and yield the argument to your saucy insolence."

"And I must suffer for her egotism!" she sobbed, as Mrs. Linton left the room. "All, all is against me: she has blighted my single consolation. But she uttered falsehoods, didn't she? Mr. Heathcliff is not a fiend: he has an honourable soul, and a true one, or how could he remember her?"

"Banish him from your thoughts, miss," I said. "He's a bird of bad omen: no mate for you. Mrs. Linton spoke strongly, and yet I can't contradict her. She is better acquainted with his heart than I, or any one besides; and she never would represent him as worse than he is. Honest people don't hide their deeds. How has he been living? how has he got rich? why is he staying at Wuthering Heights, the house of a man whom he abhors? They say Mr. Earnshaw is worse and worse since he came. They sit up all night together continually, and Hindley has been borrowing money on his land, and does nothing but play and drink: I heard only a week ago—it was Joseph who told me—I met him at Gimmerton."

"You are leagued with the rest, Ellen!" she replied. "I'll not listen to your slanders. What malevolence you must have to wish to convince me that there is no happiness in the world!"

Whether she would have got over this fancy left to herself, or persevered in nursing it perpetually, I cannot say: she had little time to reflect. The day after, there was a justice-meeting at the next town; my master was obliged to attend; and Mr. Heathcliff, aware of his absence, called rather earlier than usual. Catherine and Isabella were sitting in the library, on hostile terms, but silent. The latter alarmed at her recent indiscretion, and the disclosure she had made of her secret feelings in a transient fit of passion; the former, on mature consideration, really offended with her companion; and, if she laughed again at her pertness, inclined to make it no laughing matter to *her*. She did laugh as she saw Heathcliff pass the window. I was sweeping the hearth, and I noticed a mischievous smile on her lips. Isabella, absorbed in her meditations, or a book, remained till the door opened; and it was too late to attempt an escape, which she would gladly have done had it been practicable.

"Come in, that's right!" exclaimed the mistress, gaily, pulling a chair to the fire. "Here are two people sadly in need of a third to thaw the ice between them; and you are the very one we should both of us choose. Heathcliff, I'm proud to show you, at last, somebody that dotes on you more than myself. I expect you to feel flattered. Nay, it's not Nelly: don't look at her! My poor little sister-in-law is breaking her heart by mere contemplation of your physical and moral beauty. It lies in your own power to be Edgar's brother! No, no, Isabella, you shan't run off," she continued, arresting, with feigned playfulness, the confounded girl, who had risen indignantly. "We were quarrelling like cats about you, Heathcliff; and I was fairly beaten in protestations of devotion and admiration: and, moreover, I was informed that if I would but have the manners to stand aside, my rival, as she will have herself to be, would shoot a shaft into your soul that would fix you for ever, and send my image into eternal oblivion!"

"I think you belie her," said Heathcliff, twisting his chair to face them. "She wishes to be out of my society now, at any rate!"

And he stared hard at the object of discourse, as one might do at a strange repulsive animal: a centipede from the Indies. for instance, which curiosity leads one to examine in spite of the aversion it raises. The poor thing couldn't bear that: she grew white and red in rapid succession, and, while tears beaded her lashes, bent the strength of her small fingers to loosen the firm clutch of Catherine; and perceiving that as fast as she raised one finger off her arm another closed down, and she could not remove the whole together, she began to make use of her nails; and their sharpness presently ornamented the detainer's with crescents of red.

"There's a tigress!" exclaimed Mrs. Linton, setting her free, and shaking her hand with pain. "Begone, for God's sake, and hide your vixen face! How foolish to reveal those talons to *him*. Can't you fancy the conclusions he'll draw? Look, Heathcliff! they are instruments that will do execution—you must beware of your eyes."

"I'd wrench them off her fingers, if they ever menaced me," he answered, brutally, when the door had closed after her. "But what did you mean by teasing the creature in that manner, Cathy? You were not speaking the truth, were you?"

"I assure you I was," she returned. "She has been dying for your sake several weeks; and raving about you this morning, and pouring forth a deluge of abuse, because I represented your failings in a plain light, for the purpose of mitigating her adoration. But don't notice it further: I wished to punish her sauciness, that's all. I like her too well, my dear Heathcliff, to let you absolutely seize and devour her up."

42

# Chapter 11

SOMETIMES, while meditating on these things in solitude, I've got up in a sudden terror, and put on my bonnet to go see how all was at the farm. I've persuaded my conscience that it was a duty to warn him how people talked regarding his ways; and then I've recollected his confirmed bad habits, and, hopeless of benefiting him, have flinched from re-entering the dismal house, doubting if I could bear to be taken at my word.

The next time Heathcliff came, my young lady chanced to be feeding some pigeons in the court. She had never spoken a word to her sister-in-law for three days; but she had likewise dropped her fretful complaining, and we found it a great comfort. Heathcliff had not the habit of bestowing a single unnecessary civility on Miss Linton, I knew. Now, as soon as he beheld her, his first precaution was to take a sweeping survey of the house-front. I was standing by the kitchen window, but I drew out of sight. He then stepped across the pavement to her, and said something: she seemed embarrassed, and desirous of getting away; to prevent it, he laid his hand on her arm. She averted her face: he apparently put some question which she had no mind to answer. There was another rapid glance at the house, and supposing himself unseen, the scoundrel had the impudence to embrace her.

"Judas! Traitor!" I ejaculated. "You are a hyprocrite, too, are you? A deliberate deceiver."

"Who is, Nelly?" said Catherine's voice at my elbow: I had been over intent on watching the pair outside to mark her entrance.

"Your worthless friend!" I answered, warmly; "the sneaking rascal yonder. Ah, he has caught a glimpse of us—he is coming in! I wonder will he have the heart to find a plausible excuse for making love to Miss, when he told you he hated her?"

Mrs. Linton saw Isabella tear herself free, and run into the garden; and a minute after, Heathcliff opened the door. I couldn't withhold giving some loose to my indignation; but Catherine angrily insisted on silence, and threatened to order me out of the kitchen, if I dared to be so presumptuous as to put in my insolent tongue.

"To hear you, people might think you were the mistress!" she cried. "You want setting down in your right place! Heathcliff, what are you about, raising this stir? I said you must let Isabella alone!—I beg you will, unless you are tired of being received here, and wish Linton to draw the bolts against you!"

"He might spare himself the trouble," said Heathcliff: "I could do as well without his approbation. And as to you, Catherine, I have a mind to speak a few words now, while we are at it. I want you to be aware that I _know_ you have treated me infernally—infernally! Do you hear? And if you flatter yourself that I don't perceive it, you are a fool; and if you think I can be consoled by sweet words, you are an idiot; and if you fancy I'll suffer unrevenged, I'll convince you of the contrary, in a very little while! Meantime, thank you for telling me your sister-in-law's secret: I swear I'll make the most of it. And stand you aside!"

The conversation ceased. Mrs. Linton sat down by the fire, flushed and gloomy. The spirit which served her was growing intractable: she could neither lay nor control it. He stood on the hearth with folded arms, brooding on his evil thoughts; and in this position I left them to seek the master, who was wondering what kept Catherine below so long.

"Ellen," said he, when I entered, "have you seen your mistress?"

"Yes; she's in the kitchen, sir," I answered. "She's sadly put out by Mr. Heathcliff's behaviour; and, indeed, I do think it's time to arrange his visits on another footing. There's harm in being too soft, and now it's come to this——" And I related the scene in the court, and, as near as I dared, the whole subsequent dispute. I fancied it could not be very prejudicial to Mrs. Linton; unless she made it so afterwards, by assuming the defensive for her guest. Edgar Linton had difficulty in hearing me to the close. His first words revealed that he did not clear his wife of blame.

"This is insufferable!" he exclaimed. "It is disgraceful that she should own him for a friend, and force his company on me! Call me two men out of the hall, Ellen. Catherine shall linger no longer to argue with the low ruffian—I have humoured her enough."

He descended, and bidding the servants wait in the passage, went, followed by me, to the kitchen. Its occupants had recommenced their angry discussion: Mrs. Linton, at least, was scolding with renewed vigour; Heathcliff had moved to the window, and hung his head, somewhat cowed by her violent rating, apparently. He saw the master first, and made a hasty motion that she should be silent; which she obeyed, abruptly, on discovering the reason of his intimation.

My master glanced towards the passage, and signed me to fetch the men: he had no intention of hazarding a personal encounter. I obeyed the hint; but Mrs. Linton, suspecting something, followed; and when I attempted to call them, she pulled me back, slammed the door to, and locked it.

"Fair means!" she said, in answer to her husband's look of angry surprise. "If you have not courage to attack him, make an apology, or allow yourself to be beaten. It will correct you of feigning more valour than you possess. No, I'll swallow the key before you shall get it! I'm delightfully rewarded for my kindness to each! After constant indulgence, of one's weak nature, and the other's bad one, I earn for thanks two samples of blind ingratitude, stupid to absurdity! Edgar, I was defending you and yours; and I wish Heathcliff may flog you sick, for daring to think an evil thought of me!"

It did not need the medium of a flogging to produce that effect on the master. He tried to wrest the key from Catherine's grasp, and for safety she flung it into the hottest part of the fire, whereupon Mr. Edgar was taken with a nervous trembling, and his countenance grew deadly pale. For his life he could not avert that excess of emotion: mingled anguish and humiliation overcame him completely. He leant on the back of a chair, and covered his face.

"I wish you joy of the milk-blooded coward, Cathy!" said her friend. "I compliment you on your taste. And that is the slavering, shivering thing you preferred to me! I would not strike him with my fist, but I'd kick him with my foot, and experience considerable satisfaction. Is he weeping, or is he going to faint for fear?"

The fellow approached and gave the chair on which Linton rested a push. He'd better have kept his distance; my master quickly sprang erect, and struck him full on the throat a blow that would have levelled a slighter man. It took his breath for a minute; and while he choked, Mr. Linton walked out by the back door into the yard.

"There! you've done with coming here," cried Catherine. "Get away, now; he'll return with a brace of pistols, and half a dozen assistants. If he did overhear us, of course he'd never forgive you. You've played me an ill turn, Heathcliff! But go! I'd rather see Edgar at bay than you."

"Do you suppose I'm going with that blow burning in my gullet?" he thundered. "By hell, no! I'll crush his ribs in like a rotten hazelnut before I cross the threshold! If I don't floor him now, I shall murder him some time; so, as you value his existence, let me get at him!"

"He is not coming," I interposed, framing a bit of a lie. "There's the coachman and the two gardeners; you'll surely not wait to be thrust into the road by them! Each has a bludgeon; and master will, very likely, be watching from the parlour windows, to see that they fulfil his orders."

The gardeners and the coachman *were* there; but Linton was with them. They had already entered the court. Heathcliff, on the second thoughts, resolved to avoid a struggle against three underlings; he seized the poker, smashed the lock from the inner door, and made his escape as they tramped in.

Mrs. Linton, who was very much excited, bade me accompany her upstairs. She did not know my share in contributing to the disturbance, and I was anxious to keep her in ignorance.

As she never offered to descend to breakfast next morning, I went to ask whether she would have some carried up. "No!" she replied, peremptorily. The same question was repeated at dinner and tea; and again on the morrow after, and received the same answer. Mr. Linton, on his part, spent his time in the library, and did not inquire concerning his wife's occupations. Isabella and he had had an hour's interview, during which he tried to elicit from her some sentiment of proper horror for Heathcliff's advances; but he could make nothing of her evasive replies, and was obliged to close the examination unsatisfactorily; adding, however, a solemn warning, that if she were so insane as to encourage that worthless suitor, it would dissolve all bonds of relationship between her and him.

## Chapter 12

WHILE Miss Linton moped about the park and garden, always silent, and almost always in tears; and her brother shut himself up among books that he never opened—wearying, I guessed, with a continual vague expectation that Catherine, repenting her conduct, would come of her own accord to ask pardon, and seek a reconciliation—and *she* fasted pertinaciously, under the idea, probably, that at every meal, Edgar was ready to choke for her absence, and pride alone held him from running to cast himself at her feet; I went about my household duties, convinced that the Grange had but one sensible soul in its walls, and that lodged in my body. I wasted no condolences on Miss, nor any expostulations on my mistress; nor did I pay much attention to the sighs of my master, who yearned to hear his lady's name, since he might not hear her voice. I determined they should come about as they pleased for me; and though it was a tiresomely slow process, I began to rejoice at length in a faint dawn of its progress: as I thought at first.

Mrs. Linton, on the third day, unbarred her door, and having finished the water in her pitcher and decanter, desired a renewed supply, and a basin of gruel, for she believed she was dying. That I set down as a speech meant for Edgar's ears; I believed no such thing, so I kept it to myself and brought her some tea and dry toast. She ate and drank eagerly; and sank back on her pillow again clenching her hands and groaning. "Oh, I will die," she exclaimed, "since no one cares anything about me. I wish I had not taken that." Then a good while after I heard her murmur, "No, I'll not die—he'd be glad—he does not love me at all—be would never miss me!"

"Did you want anything, ma'am?" I inquired, still preserving my external composure, in spite of her ghastly countenance and strange exaggerated manner.

"What is that apathetic being doing?" she demanded, pushing the thick entangled locks from her wasted face. "Has he fallen into a lethargy, or is he dead?"

"Neither," replied I; "if you mean Mr. Linton. He's tolerably well, I think, though his studies occupy him rather more than they ought: he is continually among his books, since he has no other society."

She could not bear the notion which I had put into her head of Mr. Linton's philosophical resignation. Tossing about, she increased her feverish bewilderment to madness, and tore the pillow with her teeth; then raising herself up all burning, desired that I would open the window. We were in the middle of winter, the wind blew strong from the north-east, and I objected. Both the expressions flitting over her face, and the changes of her moods, began to alarm me terribly; and brought to my recollection her former illness, and the doctor's injunction that she should not be crossed. A minute previously she was violent; now, supported on one arm, and not noticing my refusal to obey her, she seemed to find childish diversion in pulling the feathers from the rents she had just made, and ranging them on the sheet according to their different species: her mind had strayed to other associations.

"I see in you, Nelly," she continued, dreamily, "an aged woman; you have grey hair and bent shoulders. This bed is the fairy cave under Peniston Crag, and you are gathering elf-bolts to hurt our heifers; pretending, while I am near, that they are only locks of wool. That's what you'll come to fifty years hence: I know you are not so now. I'm not wandering: you're mistaken, or else I should believe you really *were* that withered hag, and I should think I *was* under Peniston Crag; and I'm conscious it's night, and there are two candles on the table making the black press shine like jet."

"The black press? where is that?" I asked. "You are talking in your sleep!"

"It's against the wall, as it always is," she replied. "It *does* appear odd— I see a face in it!"

"There's no press in the room, and never was," said I, resuming my seat, and looping up the curtain that I might watch her.

"Don't *you* see that face?" she enquired, gazing earnestly at the mirror.

And say what I could, I was incapable of making her comprehend it to be her own; so I rose and covered it with a shawl.

"It's behind there still!" she pursued, anxiously. "And it stirred. Who is it? I hope it will not come out when you are gone! Oh! Nelly, the room is haunted! I'm afraid of being alone!"

I took her hand in mine, and bid her be composed; for a succession of shudders convulsed her frame, and she *would* keep straining her gaze towards the glass.

"There's nobody here!" I insisted. "It was *yourself*, Mrs. Linton: you knew it a while since."

"Myself!" she gasped, "and the clock is striking twelve! It's true, then! that's dreadful!"

Her fingers clutched the clothes, and gathered them over her eyes. I attempted to steal to the door with an intention of calling her husband; but I was summoned back by a piercing shriek—the shawl had dropped from the frame.

"Why, what *is* the matter?" cried I. "Who is coward now? Wake up!

47

That is the glass—the mirror, Mrs. Linton; and you see yourself in it, and there am I too, by your side."

Trembling and bewildered, she held me fast, but the horror gradually passed from her countenance; its paleness gave place to a glow of shame.

"Oh, dear! I thought I was at home," she sighed. "I thought I was lying in my chamber at Wuthering Heights. Because I'm weak, my brain got confused, and I screamed unconsciously. Don't say anything; but stay with me. I dread sleeping: my dreams appal me."

"A sound sleep would do you good, ma'am," I answered; "and I hope this suffering will prevent your trying starving again."

"Oh, if I were but in my own bed in the old house!" she went on bitterly, wringing her hands. "And that wind sounding in the firs by the lattice. Do let me feel it—it comes straight down the moor—do let me have one breath!"

To pacify her, I held the casement ajar a few seconds. A cold blast rushed through.

Perceiving it vain to argue against her insanity, I was planning how I could reach something to wrap about her, without quitting my hold of herself (for I could not trust her alone by the gaping lattice), when, to my consternation, I heard the rattle of the door handle, and Mr. Linton entered. He had only then come from the library; and, in passing through the lobby, had noticed our talking and been attracted by curiosity, or fear, to examine what it signified, at that late hour.

"Oh, sir!" I cried, checking the exclamation risen to his lips at the sight which met him, and the bleak atmosphere of the chamber. "My poor mistress is ill, and she quite masters me: I cannot manage her at all; pray, come and persuade her to go to bed. Forget your anger, for she's hard to guide any way but her own."

At first she gave him no glance of recognition: he was invisible to her abstracted gaze. The delirium was not fixed, however; having weaned her eyes from contemplating the outer darkness, by degrees she centred her attention on him, and discovered who it was that held her.

"Ah! you are come, are you, Edgar Linton?" she said, with angry animation. "You are one of those things that are ever found when least wanted, and when you are wanted, never! I suppose we shall have plenty of lamentations now—I see we shall—but they can't keep me from my narrow home out yonder: my resting-place, where I'm bound before spring is over! There it is: not among the Lintons, mind, under the chapel-roof, but in the open air, with a head-stone; and you may please yourself, whether you go to them or come to me!"

"Catherine, what have you done?" commenced the master. "Am I nothing to you any more? Do you love that wretch Heath——"

"Hush!" cried Mrs. Linton. "Hush, this moment! You mention that name and I end the matter instantly, by a spring from the window! What you touch at present you may have; but my soul will be on that hill-top before you lay hands on me again. I don't want you, Edgar: I'm past wanting you. Return to your books. I'm glad you possess a consolation, for all you had in me is gone."

"Her mind wanders, sir," I interposed. "She has been talking nonsense the whole evening; but let her have quiet, and proper attendance, and she'll rally. Hereafter, we must be cautious how we vex her."

"The next time you bring a tale to me, you shall quit my service, Ellen Dean," he replied.

"You'd rather hear nothing about it, I suppose, then, Mr. Linton?" said I. "Heathcliff has your permission to come a courting to Miss, and to drop in at every opportunity your absence offers, on purpose to poison the mistress against you?"

Confused as Catherine was, her wits were alert at applying our conversation.

"Ah! Nelly has played traitor," she exclaimed, passionately. "Nelly is my hidden enemy. You witch! So you do seek elf-bolts to hurt us! Let me go, and I'll make her rue! I'll make her howl a recantation!"

A maniac's fury kindled under her brows; she struggled desperately to disengage herself from Linton's arms. I felt no inclination to tarry the event; and, resolving to seek medical aid on my own responsibility, I quitted the chamber.

In passing the garden to reach the road, at a place where a bridle hook is driven into the wall, I saw something white moved irregularly, evidently by another agent than the wind. Notwithstanding my hurry, I stayed to examine it, lest ever after I should have the conviction impressed on my imagination that it was a creature of the other world. My surprise and perplexity were great on discovering, by touch more than vision, Miss Isabella's springer, Fanny, suspended by a handkerchief, and nearly at its last gasp. I quickly released the animal, and lifted it into the garden. I had seen it follow its mistress upstairs when she went to bed; and wondered much how it could have got out there, and what mischievous person had treated it so. While untying the knot round the hook, it seemed to me that I repeatedly caught the beat of horses' feet galloping at some distance; but there were such a number of things to occupy my reflections that I hardly gave the circumstance a thought: though it was a strange sound, in that place, at two o'clock in the morning.

Mr. Kenneth was fortunately just issuing from his house to see a patient in the village as I came up the street; and my account of Catherine Linton's malady induced him to accompany me back immediately. He was a plain rough man; and he made no scruple to speak his doubts of her surviving this second attack; unless she were more submissive to his directions than she had shown herself before.

"Mr. Linton will be sorry?" observed Kenneth, interrogatively.

"Sorry? he'll break his heart should anything happen!" I replied. "Don't alarm him more than necessary."

"Well, I told him to beware," said my companion; "and he must bide the consequences of neglecting my warning! Hasn't he been intimate with Mr. Heathcliff lately?"

"Heathcliff frequently visits the Grange," answered I, "though more on the strength of the mistress having known him when a boy, than because the master likes his company. At present, he's discharged from the trouble of calling; owing to some presumptuous aspirations after Miss Linton which he manifested. I hardly think he'll be taken in again."

"And does Miss Linton turn a cold shoulder on him?" was the doctor's next question.

"I'm not in her confidence," returned I, reluctant to continue the subject.

"No, she's a sly one," he remarked, shaking his head.

"She keeps her own counsel! But she's a real little fool. I have it from good authority, that, last night (and a pretty night it was!) she and Heathcliff were walking in the plantation at the back of your house, above two hours; and he pressed her not to go in again, but just mount his horse and away with him! My informant said she could only put him off by pledging her word of honour to be prepared on their first meeting after that: when it was to be he didn't hear, but you urge Mr. Linton to look sharp!"

This news filled me with fresh fears; I outstripped Kenneth, and ran most of the way back. The little dog was yelping in the garden yet. I spared a minute to open the gate for it, but instead of going to the house door, it coursed up and down snuffing the grass, and would have escaped to the road, had I not seized and conveyed it in with me. On ascending to Isabella's room, my suspicions were confirmed: it was empty. Had I been a few hours sooner, Mrs. Linton's illness might have arrested her rash step. But what could be done now? There was a bare possibility of overtaking them if pursued instantly. *I* could not pursue them, however; and I dare not rouse the family, and fill the place with confusion; still less unfold the business to my master, absorbed as he was in his present calamity, and having no heart to spare for a second grief! I saw nothing for it but to hold my tongue, and suffer matters to take their course; and Kenneth being arrived, I went with a badly composed countenance to announce him. Catherine lay in a troubled sleep: her husband had succeeded in soothing the excess of frenzy; he now hung over her pillow, watching every shade, and every change of her painfully expressive features.

I did not close my eyes that night, nor did Mr. Linton: indeed, we never went to bed: and the servants were all up long before the usual hour, moving through the house with stealthy tread, and exchanging whispers as they encountered each other in their vocations. Every one was active, but Miss Isabella; and they began to remark how sound she slept: her brother, too, asked if she had risen, and seemed impatient for her presence, and hurt that she showed so little anxiety for her sister-in-law. I trembled lest he should send me to call her; but I was spared the pain of being the first proclaimant of her flight. One of the maids, a thoughtless girl, who had been on an early errand to Gimmerton, came panting upstairs, open mouthed, and dashed into the chamber, crying:

"Oh, dear, dear! What mun we have next? Master, master, our young lady—"

"Hold your noise!" cried I hastily, enraged at her clamorous manner.

"Speak lower, Mary— What is the matter?" said Mr. Linton. "What ails your young lady?"

"She's gone, she's gone! Yon' Heathcliff's run off wi' her!" gasped the girl.

"That is not true!" exclaimed Mr. Linton, rising in agitation. "It cannot be: how has the idea entered your head? Ellen Dean, go and seek her. It is incredible: it cannot be."

I ran and peeped, for form's sake, into Isabella's room; confirming, when I returned, the servant's statement. Mr. Linton had resumed his seat by the bed; on my re-entrance, he raised his eyes, read the meaning of my blank aspect, and dropped them without giving an order, or uttering a word.

## Chapter 13

FOR two months the fugitives remained absent; in those two months, Mrs. Linton encountered and conquered the worst shock of what was denominated a brain fever. No mother could have nursed an only child more devotedly than Edgar tended her. Day and night he was watching, and patiently enduring all the annoyances that irritable nerves and a shaken reason could inflict; and, though Kenneth remarked that what he saved from the grave would only recompense his care by forming the source of constant future anxiety—in fact, that his health and strength were being sacrificed to preserve a mere ruin of humanity—he knew no limits in gratitude and joy when Catherine's life was declared out of danger; and hour after hour he would sit beside her, tracing the gradual return to bodily health, and flattering his too sanguine hopes with the illusion that her mind would settle back to its right balance also, and she would soon be entirely her former self.

The first time she left her chamber was at the commencement of the following March. Mr. Linton had put on her pillow, in the morning, a handful of golden crocuses; her eye, long stranger to any gleam of pleasure, caught them in waking, and shone delighted as she gathered them eagerly together.

"These are the earliest flowers at the Heights," she exclaimed. "They remind me of soft thaw winds, and warm sunshine, and nearly melted snow. Edgar, is there not a south wind, and is not the snow almost gone?"

"The snow is quite gone down here, darling," replied her husband; "and I only see two white spots on the whole range of moors: the sky is blue, and the larks are singing, and the becks and brooks are all brim full. Catherine, last spring at this time, I was longing to have you under this roof; now, I wish you were a mile or two up those hills: the air blows so sweetly, I feel that it would cure you."

"I shall never be there but once more," said the invalid; "and then you'll leave me, and I shall remain for ever. Next spring you'll long again to have me under this roof, and you'll look back and think you were happy to-day."

Linton lavished on her the kindest caresses, and tried to cheer her by the fondest words; but, vaguely regarding the flowers, she let the tears collect on her lashes and stream down her cheeks unheeding. We knew she was really better, and, therefore, decided that long confinement to a single place produced much of this despondency, and it might be partially removed by a change of scene. The master told me to light a fire in the many-weeks deserted parlour, and to set an easy-chair in the sunshine by the window; and then he brought her down, and she sat a long while enjoying the genial heat, and, as we expected, revived by the objects round her: which, though familiar, were free from the dreary associations investing her hated sick chamber. By evening, she seemed greatly exhausted; yet no arguments could persuade her to return to that apartment, and I had to arrange the parlour sofa for her bed, till another room could be prepared. To obviate the fatigue of mounting and descending the stairs, we fitted up this, where you lie at present: on the same floor with the parlour; and she was soon strong enough to move from one to the other, leaning on Edgar's arm. Ah, I thought myself, she might recover, so waited on as she was. And there was double cause to desire it, for on her existence depended that of another: we cherished the hope that in a little while, Mr. Linton's heart would be gladdened, and his lands secured from a stranger's gripe, by the birth of an heir.

I should mention that Isabella sent to her brother, some six weeks from her departure, a short note, announcing her marriage with Heathcliff. It appeared dry and cold; but at the bottom was dotted in with pencil an obscure apology, and an entreaty for kind remembrance and reconciliation, if her proceeding had offended him: asserting that she could not help it then, and being done, she had now no power to repeal it. Linton did not reply to this, I believe; and, in a fortnight more, I got a long letter which I considered odd, coming from the pen of a bride just out of the honeymoon. I'll read it: for I keep it yet. Any relic of the dead is precious, if they were valued living.

DEAR ELLEN, it begins.

I came last night to Wuthering Heights, and heard, for the first time, that Catherine has been, and is yet, very ill. I must not write to her, I suppose, and my brother is either too angry or too distressed to answer what I sent him. Still, I must write to somebody, and the only choice left me is you.

Inform Edgar that I'd give the world to see his face again—that my heart returned to Thrushcross Grange in twenty-four hours after I left it, and is there at this moment, full of warm feelings for him, and Catherine! *I can't follow it, though*—(those words are underlined) they need not expect me, and they may draw what conclusions they please; taking care, however, to lay nothing at the door of my weak will or deficient affection.

The remainder of the letter is for yourself alone. I want to ask you two questions: the first is,—How did you contrive to preserve the common sympathies of human nature when you resided here? I cannot recognise any sentiment which those around share with me.

The second question, I have great interest in; it is this—Is Mr. Heathcliff a man? If so, is he mad? And if not, is he a devil? I shan't tell my reasons for making this enquiry; but, I beseech you to explain, if you can, what I have married; that is, when you call to see me; and you must call, Ellen, very soon. Don't write, but come and bring me something from Edgar.

Now, you shall hear how I have been received in my new home, as I am led to imagine the Heights will be. It is to amuse myself that I dwell on such subjects as the lack of external comforts: they never occupy my thoughts, except at the moment when I miss them. I should laugh and dance for joy, if I found their absence was the the total of my miseries, and the rest was an unnatural dream!

The sun set behind the Grange, as we turned on to the moors; by that, I judged it to be six o'clock; and my companion halted half an hour, to inspect the park, and the gardens, and, probably, the place itself, as well as he could; so it was dark when we dismounted in the paved yard of the farm-house, and your old fellow-servant, Joseph, issued out to receive us by the light of a dip candle. He did it with a courtesy that redounded to his credit. His first act was to elevate his torch to a level with my face, squint malignantly, project his under lip, and turn away. Then he took the two horses, and led them into the stables, reappearing for the purpose of locking the outer gate, as if we lived in an ancient castle.

Heathcliff stayed to speak to him, and I entered the kitchen—a dingy, untidy hole; I dare say you would not know it, it is so changed since it was in your charge. By the fire stood a ruffianly child, strong in limb and dirty in garb, with a look of Catherine in his eyes and about his mouth.

"This is Edgar's legal nephew," I reffected—"mine in a manner; I must shake hands, and—yes—I must kiss him. It is right to establish a good understanding at the beginning."

I approached, and, attempting to take his chubby fist, said:

"How do you do, my dear?"

He replied in a jargon I did not comprehend.

"Shall you and I be friends, Hareton?" was my next essay at conversation.

An oath, and a threat to set Throttler on me if I did not "frame off" rewarded my perseverance.

"Hey, Throttler, lad!" whispered the little wretch, rousing a half breed bull-dog from its lair in the corner. "Now, wilt thou be ganging?" he asked authoritatively.

I walked round the yard, and through a wicket, to another door, at which I took the liberty of knocking, in hopes some more civil servant might show himself. After a short suspense, it was opened by a tall, gaunt man, without neckerchief, and otherwise extremely slovenly; his features were lost in masses of shaggy hair that hung on his shoulders; and *his* eyes, too, were like a ghostly Catherine's with all their beauty annihilated.

"What's your business here?" he demanded, grimly. "Who are you?"

"My name *was* Isabella Linton," I replied. "You've seen me before, sir. I'm lately married to Mr. Heathcliff, and he has brought me here—I suppose by your permission."

"Is he come back, then?" asked the hermit, glaring like a hungry wolf.

"Yes—we came just now," I said; "but he left me by the kitchen door; and when I would have gone in, your little boy played sentinel over the place, and frightened me off by the help of a bull-dog."

"It's well the hellish villain has kept his word!" growled my future host, searching the darkness beyond me in expectation of discovering Heathcliff; and then he indulged in a soliloquy of execrations, and threats of what he would have done had the "fiend" deceived him.

I repented having tried this second entrance, and was almost inclined to slip away before he finished cursing, but ere I could execute that intention, he ordered me in, and shut and re-fastened the door. There was a great fire, and that was all the light in the huge apartment, whose floor had grown a uniform grey; and the once brilliant pewter dishes, which used to attract my gaze when I was a girl, partook of a similar obscurity, created by tarnish and dust. I inquired whether I might call the maid, and be conducted to a bedroom? Mr. Earnshaw vouchsafed no answer. He walked up and down, with his hands in his pockets, apparently quite forgetting my presence; and his abstraction was evidently so deep, and his whole aspect so misanthropical, that I shrank from disturbing him again.

I sat and thought a doleful time: the clock struck eight, and nine, and still my companion paced to and fro, his head bent on his breast, and perfectly silent, unless a groan or a bitter ejaculation forced itself out at intervals. I listened to detect a woman's voice in the house, and filled the interim with wild regrets and dismal anticipations, which, at last, spoke audibly in irrepressible sighing and weeping. I was not aware how openly I grieved, till Earnshaw halted opposite, in his measured walk, and gave me a stare of newly-awakened surprise. Taking advantage of his recovered attention, I exclaimed:

"I'm tired with my journey, and I want to go to bed! Where is the maid-servant? Direct me to her, as she won't come to me!"

"We have none," he answered; "you must wait on yourself!"

"Where must I sleep, then?" I sobbed; I was beyond regarding self-respect, weighed down by fatigue and wretchedness.

"Joseph will show you Heathcliff's chamber," said he; "open that door—he's in there."

I was going to obey, but he suddenly arrested me, and added in the strangest tone:

"Be so good as to turn your lock, and draw your bolt—don't omit it!"

"Well!" I said. "But why, Mr. Earnshaw?" I did not relish the notion of deliberately fastening myself in with Heathcliff.

"Look here!" he replied, pulling from his waistcoat a curiously constructed pistol, having a double-edged spring knife attached to the barrel. "That's a great tempter to a desperate man, is it not? I cannot resist going up with this every night, and trying his door. If once I find it open he's done for! I do it invariably, even though the minute before I have been recalling a hundred reasons that should make me refrain: it is some devil that urges me to thwart my own schemes by killing him. You fight against that devil for love as long as you may; when the time comes, not all the angels in heaven shall save him!"

I surveyed the weapon inquisitively. A hideous notion struck me: how powerful I should be possessing such an instrument! I took it from his hand, and touched the blade. He looked astonished at the expression my face assumed during a brief second: it was not horror, it was covetousness. He snatched the pistol back, jealously; shut the knife, and returned it to its concealment.

"I don't care if you tell him," said he. "Put him on his guard, and watch for him. You know the terms we are on, I see: his danger does not shock you."

"What has Heathcliff done to you?" I asked. "In what has he wronged you, to warrant this appalling hatred? Wouldn't it be wiser to bid him quit the house?"

"No!" thundered Earnshaw, "should he offer to leave me, he's a dead man: persuade him to attempt it, and you are a murderess! Am I to lose *all*, without a chance of retrieval? Is Hareton to be a beggar? Oh, damnation! I *will* have it back: and I'll have *his* gold too; and then his

55

blood; and hell shall have his soul! It will be ten times blacker with that guest than it ever was before!"

"You've acquainted me, Ellen, with your old master's habits. He is clearly on the verge of madness: he was so last night at least. I shuddered to be near him, and thought on the servant's ill-bred moroseness as comparatively agreeable. He now recommenced his moody walk, and I raised the latch, and escaped into the kitchen. Joseph was bending over the fire, peering into a large pan that swung above it; and a wooden bowl of oatmeal stood on the settle close by. The contents of the pan began to boil, and he turned to plunge his hand into the bowl; I conjectured that this preparation was probably for our supper, and, being hungry, I resolved it should be eatable; so, crying out sharply, "*I'll* make the porridge!" I removed the vessel out of his reach, and proceeded to take off my hat and riding habit. "Mr. Earnshaw," I continued, "directs me to wait on myself: I will. I'm not going to act the lady among you, for fear I should starve."

"Gooid Lord!" he muttered, sitting down, and stroking his ribbed stockings from the knee to the ankle. "If there's to be fresh ortherings— just when I getten used to two maisters, if I mun hev a *mistress* set o'er my heead, it's like time to be flitting. I niver *did* think to see t' day that I mud lave th' owld place—but I doubt it's nigh at hand!"

This lamentation drew no notice from me: I went briskly to work, sighing to remember a period when it would have been all merry fun; but compelled speedily to drive off the remembrance. It racked me to recall past happiness and the greater peril there was of conjuring up its apparition, the quicker the thible ran round, and the faster the handfuls of meal fell into the water. Joseph beheld my style of cookery with growing indignation.

"It *was* rather a rough mess, I own, when poured into the basins; four had been provided, and a gallon pitcher of new milk was brought from the dairy, which Hareton seized and commenced drinking and spilling from the expansive lip. I expostulated, and desired that he should have his in a mug; affirming that I could not taste the liquid treated so dirtily.

I put my basin on a tray, and went myself to fetch some more milk. With great grumblings, the fellow rose, and preceded me in my ascent: we mounted to the garrets; he opened a door, now and then, to look into the apartments we passed.

"Here's a rahm," he said, at last, flinging back a cranky board on hinges. "It's weel eneugh to ate a few porridge in. There's a pack o' corn i' t' corner, thear, meeterly clane; if ye're feared o' mucking yer grand silk cloes, spread yer handkerchir o' t' top on 't."

The "rahm" was a kind of lumber-hole smelling strong of malt and grain; various sacks of which articles were piled around, leaving a wide, bare space in the middle.

"Why, man!" I exclaimed, facing him angrily, "this is not a place to sleep in. I wish to see my bedroom."

"*Bedrume!*" he repeated, in a tone of mockery. "Yah's see all t' *bedrumes* thear is—yon's mine."

He pointed to the second garret, only differing from the first in being more naked about the walls, and having a large, low, curtainless bed, with an indigo-coloured quilt, at one end.

"What do I want with yours?" I retorted. "I suppose Mr. Heathcliff does not lodge at the top of the house, does he?"

"Oh! it's Maister *Heathcliff's* ye're wanting?" cried he, as if making a new discovery. "Couldn't ye ha' said soa, at onst? un then, I mud ha' telled ye, baht all this wark, that that's just one ye cannot see—he allas keeps it locked, un' nob'dy iver mells on't but hisseln."

"You've a nice house, Joseph," I could not refrain from observing, "and pleasant inmates; and I think the concentrated essence of all the madness in the world took up its abode in my brain the day I linked my fate with theirs! However, that is not to the present purpose—there are other rooms. For Heaven's sake be quick, and let me settle somewhere!"

He made no reply to this adjuration; only plodding doggedly down the wooden steps, and halting before an apartment which, from that halt and the superior quality of its furniture, I conjectured to be the best one. There was a carpet: a good one, but the pattern was obliterated by dust; a fireplace hung with cut paper, dropping to pieces; a handsome oak-bedstead with ample crimson curtains of rather expensive material and modern make; but they had evidently experienced rough usage: the valances hung in festoons, wrenched from their rings, and the iron rod supporting them was bent in an arc on one side, causing the drapery to trail upon the floor. The chairs were also damaged, many of them severely; and deep indentations deformed the panels of the walls. I was endeavouring to gather resolution for entering and taking possession, when my fool of a guide announced. "This here is t' maister's." My supper by this time was cold, my appetite gone, and my patience exhausted. I insisted on being provided instantly with a place of refuge, and means of repose.

"Whear the divil?" began the religious elder. "The Lord bless us! The Lord forgie us! Whear the *hell* wold ye gang? ye marred, wearisome nowt! Ye've seen all but Hareton's bit of a cham'er. There's not another hoile to lig down in i' th' hahse!"

I was so vexed, I flung my tray and its contents on the ground; and then seated myself at the stairs-head, hid my face in my hands, and cried.

"Ech! ech!" exclaimed Joseph. "Weel done, Miss Cathy! weel done, Miss Cathy! Howsiver, t' maister sall just tum'le o'er them brocken pots; un' then we's hear summat; we's hear how it's to be. Gooid-for-naught madling! ye desarve pining fro' this to Churstmas, flinging t' precious gifts o' God under fooit i' yer flaysome rages! But, I'm mista'en

57

if ye shew yer sperrit lang. Will Heathcliff bide such bonny way's think ye? I nobbut wish he may catch ye i' that plisky. I nobbut wish he may."

And so he went on scolding to his den beneath, taking the candle with him; and I remained in the dark. The period of reflection succeeding this silly action, compelled me to admit the necessity of smothering my pride and choking my wrath, and bestirring myself to remove its effects. An unexpected aid presently appeared in the shape of Throttler, whom I now recognised as a son of our old Skulker: it had spent its whelphood at the Grange, and was given by my father to Mr. Hindley. I fancy it knew me: it pushed its nose against mine by way of salute, and then hastened to devour the porridge; while I groped from step to step, collecting the shattered earthenware, and drying the spatters of milk from the banister with my pocket-handkerchief. Our labours were scarcely over when I heard Earnshaw's tread in the passage; my assistant tucked in his tail, and pressed to the wall; I stole into the nearest doorway. The dog's endeavour to avoid him was unsuccessful; as I guessed by a scutter downstairs, and a prolonged, piteous yelping. I had better luck: he passed on, entered his chamber, and shut the door. Directly after Joseph came up with Hareton to put him to bed. I had found shelter in Hareton's room, and the old man on seeing me, said:

"They's rahm for boath ye un yer pride, now, I sud think i' the hahse. It's empty; ye may hev it all to yerseln, un Him as allas maks a third, i' sich ill company!"

Gladly did I take advantage of this intimation; and the minute I flung myself into a chair, by the fire, I nodded, and slept. My slumber was deep and sweet, though over far too soon. Mr. Heathcliff awoke me; he had just come in, and demanded, in his loving manner, what I was doing there? I told him the cause of my staying up so late—that he had the key of our room in his pocket. The adjective *our* gave mortal offence. He swore it was not, nor ever should be, mine: and he'd—But I'll not repeat his language, nor describe his habitual conduct: he is ingenious and unresting in seeking to gain my abhorrence! I sometimes wonder at him with an intensity that deadens my fear: yet, I assure you, a tiger or a venomous serpent could not rouse terror in me equal to that which he wakens. He told me of Catherine's illness, and accused my brother of causing it; promising that I should be Edgar's proxy in suffering, till he could get hold of him.

I do hate him—I am wretched—I have been a fool! Beware of uttering one breath of this to anyone at the Grange. I shall expect you every day—don't disappoint me! ISABELLA.

# Chapter 14

As soon as I had perused this epistle, I went to the master, and informed him that his sister had arrived at the Heights, and sent me a letter expressing her sorrow for Mr. Linton's situation, and her ardent desire to see him; with a wish that he would transmit to her, as early as possible, some token of forgiveness by me.

"Forgiveness!" said Linton. "I have nothing to forgive her, Ellen. You may call at Wuthering Heights, this afternoon, if you like, and say that I am not *angry*, but I'm *sorry* to have lost her; especially as I can never think she'll be happy. It is out of the question my going to see her, however: we are eternally divided; and should she really wish to oblige me, let her persuade the villain she has married to leave the country."

Mr. Edgar's coldness depressed me exceedingly; and all the way from the Grange, I puzzled my brains how to put more heart into what he said, when I repeated it; and how to soften his refusal of even a few lines to console Isabella. I dare say she had been on the watch for me since morning. I saw her looking through the lattice, as I came up the garden causeway, and I nodded to her; but she drew back, as if afraid of being observed. I entered without knocking. There never was such a dreary, dismal scene as the formerly cheerful house presented! I must confess, that if I had been in the young lady's place, I would, at least, have swept the hearth, and wiped the tables with a duster. But she already partook of the pervading spirit of neglect which encompassed her. Her pretty face was wan and listless; her hair uncurled: some locks hanging lankly down, and some carelessly twisted round her head. Probably she had not touched her dress since yester evening. Hindley was not there. Mr. Heathcliff sat at a table, turning over some papers in his pocket-book; but he rose when I appeared, asked me how I did, quite friendly, and offered me a chair. He was the only thing there that seemed decent; and I thought he never looked better. So much had circumstances altered their positions, that he would certainly have struck a stranger as a born and bred gentleman; and his wife as a thorough little slattern! She came forward eagerly to greet me; and held out her hand to take the expected letter. I shook my head.

Mrs. Heathcliff's lip quivered slightly. Her husband took his stand on the hearthstone, near me, and began to pour questions concerning Catherine. I told him as much as I thought proper of her illness, and he extorted from me, by cross-examination, most of the facts connected with its origin. I blamed her, as she deserved, for bringing it all on herself; and ended by hoping that he would follow Mr. Linton's example and avoid future interference with his family, for good or evil.

"With your aid, that may be avoided," he continued; "and should there be danger of such an event—should he be the cause of adding a single trouble to her existence more—why, I think I shall be justified in going to extremes! I wish you had sincerity enough to tell me whether Catherine would suffer greatly from his loss: the fear that she would restrains me. And there you see the distinction between our feelings: had he been in my place and I in his, though I hated him with a hatred that turned my life to gall, I never would have raised a hand against him. You may look incredulous, if you please! I never would have banished him from her society as long as she desired his. The moment her regard ceased, I would have torn his heart out, and drunk his blood! But, till then—if you don't believe me, you don't know me—till then, I would have died by inches before I touched a single hair of his head!"

"And yet," I interrupted, "you have no scruples in completely ruining all hopes of her perfect restoration, by thrusting yourself into her remembrance now, when she has nearly forgotten you, and involving her in a new tumult of discord and distress."

"You suppose she has nearly forgotten me?" he said. "Oh, Nelly! you know she has not! You know as well as I do, that for every thought she spends on Linton, she spends a thousand on me! Come here now, Nelly: I must either persuade or compel you to aid me in fulfilling my determination to see Catherine, and that without delay. I swear that I meditate no harm: I don't desire to cause any disturbance, or to exasperate or insult Mr. Linton; I only wish to hear from herself how she is, and why she has been ill; and to ask if anything I could do would be of use to her. Last night, I was in the Grange garden six hours, and I'll return there to-night; and every night I'll haunt the place, and every day, till I find an opportunity of entering. If Edgar Linton meets me, I shall not hesitate to knock him down, and give him enough to insure his quiescence while I stay. If his servants oppose me, I shall threaten them off with these pistols. But wouldn't it be better to prevent any coming in contact with them, or their master? And you could do it so easily. I'd warn you when I came, and then you might let me in unobserved, as soon as she was alone, and watch till I departed, your conscience quite calm: you would be hindering mischief."

Well, Mr. Lockwood, I argued and complained, and flatly refused him fifty times; but in the long run he forced me to an agreement. I engaged to carry a letter from him to my mistress; and should she consent, I promised to let him have intelligence of Linton's next absence from home, when he might come, and get in as he was able: I wouldn't be there, and my fellow-servants should be equally out of the way. Was it right or wrong? I fear it was wrong, though expedient. I thought I prevented another explosion by my compliance; and I thought, too, it might create a favourable crisis in Catherine's mental illness. My journey homeward was sadder than my journey thither; and many misgivings I had, ere I could prevail on myself to put the missive into Mrs. Linton's hand.

# Chapter 15

ANOTHER week over—and I am so many days nearer health, and spring! I have now heard all my neighbour's history, at different sittings, as the housekeeper could spare time from her more important occupations. I'll continue it in her own words, only a little condensed. She is, on the whole, a very fair narrator, and I don't think I could improve her style.

In the evening, she said, the evening of my visit to the Heights, I knew, as well as if I saw him, that Heathcliff was about the place; and I shunned going out, because I still carried his letter in my pocket, and didn't want to be threatened or teased any more. I had made up my mind not to give it till my master went somewhere, as I could not guess how its receipt would affect Catherine. The consequence was, that it did not reach her before the lapse of three days. The fourth was Sunday, and I brought it into her room after the family were gone to church.

"There's a letter for you, Mrs. Linton," I said, gently inserting it in one hand that rested on her knee. "You must read it immediately, because it wants an answer. Shall I break the seal?" "Yes," she answered, without altering the direction of her eyes. I opened it—it was very short. "Now," I continued, "read it." She drew away her hand, and let it fall. I replaced it in her lap, and stood waiting till it should please her to glance down; but that movement was so long delayed that at last I resumed:

"Must I read it, ma'am? It is from Mr. Heathcliff."

There was a start and a troubled gleam of recollection, and a struggle to arrange her ideas. She lifted the letter, and seemed to peruse it; and when she came to the signature she sighed; yet still I found she had not gathered its import, for, upon my desiring to hear her reply, she merely pointed to the name, and gazed at me with mournful and questioning eagerness.

"Well, he wishes to see you," said I, guessing her need of an interpreter. "He's in the garden by this time, and impatient to know what answer I shall bring."

As I spoke, I observed a large dog lying on the sunny grass beneath raise its ears as if about to bark, and then smoothing them back, announce, by wag of the tail, that some one approached whom it did not consider a stranger. Mrs. Linton bent forward, and listened breathlessly. The minute after a step traversed the hall. With straining eagerness Catherine gazed towards the entrance of her chamber. He did not hit the right room directly, she motioned me to admit him, but he found it out ere I could reach the door, and in a stride or two was at her side, and had her grasped in his arms.

He neither spoke nor loosed his hold for some five minutes, during which period he bestowed more kisses than he ever gave in his life before, I dare say: but then my mistress had kissed him first, and I plainly saw that he could hardly bear, for downright agony, to look into her face! The same conviction had stricken him as me, from the instant he beheld her, that there was no prospect of ultimate recovery there—she was fated, sure to die.

"Oh, Cathy! Oh, my life! how can I bear it?" was the first sentence he uttered, in a tone that did not seek to disguise his despair. And now he stared at her so earnestly that I thought the very intensity of his gaze would bring tears into his eyes; but they burned with anguish: they did not melt.

"What now?" said Catherine, leaning back, and returning his look with a suddenly clouded brow: her humour was a mere vane for constantly varying caprices. "You and Edgar have broken my heart, Heathcliff! And you both come to bewail the deed to me, as if *you* were the people to be pitied! I shall not pity you, not I. You have killed me—and thriven on it, I think. How strong you are! How many years do you mean to live after I am gone?"

"Are you possessed with a devil," he pursued savagely, "to talk in that manner to me when you are dying? Do you reflect that all those words will be branded in my memory, and eating deeper eternally after you have left me? You know you lie to say I have killed you: and, Catherine, you know that I could as soon forget you as my existence! Is it not sufficient for your infernal selfishness, that while you are at peace I shall writhe in the torments of hell?"

"I'm not wishing you greater torment than I have, Heathcliff. I only wish us never to be parted: and should a word of mine distress you hereafter, think I feel the same distress underground, and for my own sake, forgive me! Come here and kneel down again! You never harmed me in your life. Nay, if you nurse anger, that will be worse to remember than my harsh words! Won't you come here again? Do!"

Heathcliff went to the back of her chair, and leant over, but not so far as to let her see his face, which was livid with emotion. She bent round to look at him; he would not permit it: turning abruptly, he walked to the fireplace, where he stood, silent, with his back towards us. Mrs. Linton's glance followed him suspiciously: every movement woke a new sentiment in her. After a pause and a prolonged gaze she resumed; addressing me in accents of indignant disappointment:

"Oh, you see, Nelly, he would not relent a moment to keep me out of the grave. *That* is how I'm loved! Well, never mind. That is not *my* Heathcliff. I shall love mine yet: and take him with me; he's in my soul. And," added she musingly, "the thing that irks me most is this shattered prison, after all. I'm tired of being enclosed here. I'm wearying to escape into that glorious world, and to be always there: not seeing it dimly through tears, and yearning for it through the walls of an aching heart; but really with it, and in it. Nelly, you think you are better and more fortunate than I; in full health and strength: you are sorry for me—very soon that will be altered. I shall be sorry for *you*. I shall be incomparably beyond and above you all. I *wonder* he won't be near me!" She went on to herself. "I thought he wished it. Heathcliff, dear! you should not be sullen now. Do come to me, Heathcliff."

In her eagerness she rose and supported herself on the arm of the chair. At that earnest appeal he turned to her, looking absolutely desperate. His eyes, wide and wet, at last flashed fiercely on her: his breast heaved convulsively. An instant they held asunder, and then how they met I hardly saw, but Catherine made a spring, and he caught her, and they were locked in an embrace from which I thought my mistress would never be released alive: in fact, to my eyes, she seemed directly insensible. He flung himself into the nearest seat, and on my approaching hurriedly to ascertain if she had fainted, he gnashed at me, and foamed like a mad dog, and gathered her to him with greedy jealousy. I did not feel as if I were in the company of a creature of my own species: it appeared that he would not understand, though I spoke to him; so I stood off, and held my tongue, in great perplexity.

A movement of Catherine's relieved me a little presently: she put up her hand to clasp his neck, and bring her cheek to his as he held her; while he, in return, covering her with frantic caresses, said wildly:

"You teach me now how cruel you've been—cruel and false. *Why* did you despise me? *Why* did you betray your own heart, Cathy? I have not one word of comfort. You deserve this. You have killed yourself. Yes, you may kiss me, and cry; and ring out my kisses and tears: they'll blight you—they'll damn you. You loved me—then what *right* had you to leave me? What right—answer me—for the poor fancy you felt for Linton?"

"Let me alone. Let me alone," sobbed Catherine. "If I've done wrong, I'm dying for it. It is enough! You left me too: but I won't upbraid you! I forgive you. Forgive me!"

"It is hard to forgive, and to look at those eyes, and feel those wasted hands," he answered. "Kiss me again; and don't let me see your eyes! I forgive what you have done to me. I love *my* murderer—but *yours!* How can I?"

They were silent—their faces hid against each other, and washed by each other's tears. At least, I suppose the weeping was on both sides; as it seemed Heathcliff *could* weep on a great occasion like this.

I grew very uncomfortable, meanwhile; for the afternoon wore fast away, and I could distinguish by the shine of the western sun up the valley, a concourse thickening outside Gimmerton chapel porch.

"Service is over," I announced. "My master will be here in half an hour."

Heathcliff groaned a curse, and strained Catherine closer: she never moved.

Ere long I perceived a group of the servants passing up the road towards the kitchen wing. Mr. Linton was not far behind; he opened the gate himself and sauntered slowly up, probably enjoying the lovely afternoon that breathed as soft as summer.

"Now he is here," I exclaimed. "For Heaven's sake, hurry down! You'll not meet any one on the front stairs. Do be quick; and stay among the tress till he is fairly in."

"I must go, Cathy," said Heathcliff, seeking to extricate himself from his companion's arms. "But if I live, I'll see you again before you are asleep. I won't stray five yards from your window."

"You must not go!" she answered, holding him as firmly as her strength allowed. "You *shall* not, I tell you."

"For one hour," he pleaded earnestly.

"Not for one minute," she replied.

"I *must*—Linton will be up immediately," persisted the alarmed intruder.

He would have risen, and unfixed her fingers by the act—she clung fast, gasping: there was mad resolution in her face.

"No!" she shrieked. "Oh, don't don't go. It is the last time! Edgar will not hurt us. Heathcliff, I shall die! I shall die!"

"Damn the fool! There he is," cried Heathcliff, sinking, back into his seat. "Hush, my darling! Hush, hush, Catherine! I'll stay. If he shot me so, I'd expire with a blessing on my lips."

And there they were fast again. I heard my master mounting the stairs— the cold sweat ran from my forehead: I was horrified.

I wrung my hands, and cried out; and Mr. Linton hastened his step at the noise. In the midst of my agitation, I was sincerely glad to observe that Catherine's arms had fallen relaxed, and her head hung down.

"She's fainted, or dead," I thought: "so much the better. Far better that she should be dead, than lingering a burden and a misery maker to all about her."

Edgar sprang to his unbidden guest, blanched with astonishment and rage. What he meant to do, I cannot tell; however, the other stopped all demonstrations, at once, by placing the lifeless-looking form in his arms.

"Look there!" he said. "Unless you be a fiend, help her first—then you shall speak to me!"

He walked into the parlour, and sat down. Mr. Linton summoned me, and with great difficulty, and after resorting to many means, we managed to restore her to sensation; but she was all bewildered; she sighed, and moaned, and knew nobody. Edgar, in his anxiety for her, forgot her hated friend. I did not. I went, at the earliest opportunity, and besought him to depart; affirming that Catherine was better, and he should hear from me in the morning how she passed the night.

"I shall not refuse to go out of doors," he answered; "but I shall stay in the garden: and, Nelly, mind you keep your word to-morrow. I shall be under those larch trees. Mind! or I pay another visit, whether Linton be in or not."

He sent a rapid glance through the half-open door of the chamber, and, ascertaining that what I stated was apparently true, delivered the house of his luckless presence.

# Chapter 16

ABOUT twelve o'clock that night, was born the Catherine you saw at Wuthering Heights: a puny, seven months' child; and two hours after the mother died, having never recovered sufficient consciousness to miss Heathcliff, or know Edgar. The latter's distraction at his bereavement is a subject too painful to be dwelt on; its after effects showed how deep the sorrow sunk. A great addition, in my eyes, was his being left without an heir. I bemoaned that, as I gazed on the feeble orphan; and I mentally abused old Linton for (what was only natural partiality) the securing his estate to his own daughter, instead of his son's. An unwelcomed infant it was, poor thing! It might have wailed out of life, and nobody cared a morsel, during those first hours of its existence. We redeemed the neglect afterwards; but its beginning was as friendless as its end is likely to be.

Next morning—bright and cheerful out of doors—stole softened in through the blinds of the silent room, and suffused the couch and its occupant with a tender, mellow glow. Edgar Linton had his head laid on the pillow, and his eyes shut. His young and fair features were almost as deathlike as those of the form beside him, and almost as fixed: but *his* was the hush of exhausted anguish, and *hers* of perfect peace. Her brow smooth, her lids closed, her lips wearing the expression of a smile; no angel in heaven could be more beautiful than she appeared. And I partook of the infinite calm in which she lay: my mind was never in a holier frame than while I gazed on that untroubled image of Divine rest. I instinctively echoed the words she had uttered a few hours before: "Incomparably beyond and above us all! Whether still on earth or now in heaven, her spirit is at home with God!"

The master looked asleep, and I ventured soon after sunrise to quit the room and steal out to the pure refreshing air. The servants thought me gone to shake off the drowsiness of my protracted watch; in reality, my chief motive was seeing Mr. Heathcliff.

I was weeping as much for him as her: we do sometimes pity creatures that have none of the feeling either for themselves or others. When I first looked into his face, I perceived that he had got intelligence of the catastrophe; and a foolish notion struck me that his heart was quelled and he prayed, because his lips moved and his gaze was bent on the ground.

"Yes, she's dead!" I answered, checking my sobs and drying my cheeks. "Gone to heaven, I hope; where we may, every one, join her, if we take due warning and leave our evil ways to follow good!"

"And—did she ever mention me?" he asked, hesitating, as if he dreaded the answer to his question would introduce details that he could not bear to hear.

"Her senses never returned: she recognised nobody from the time you left her," I said. "She lies with a sweet smile on her face; and her latest ideas wandered back to pleasant early days. Her life closed in a gentle dream—may she wake as kindly in the other world!"

"May she wake in torment!" he cried, with frightful vehemence, stamping his foot, and groaning in a sudden paroxysm of ungovernable passion. "Why, she's a liar to the end! Where is she? Not *there*—not in heaven—not perished—where? Oh! you said you cared nothing for my sufferings! And I pray one prayer—I repeat it till my tongue stiffens—Catherine Earnshaw, may you not rest as long as I am living! You said I killed you—haunt me, then! The murdered *do* haunt their murderers, I believe. I know that ghosts *have* wandered on earth. Be with me always—take any form—drive me mad; only *do* not leave me in this abyss, where I cannot find you! Oh, God! it is unutterable! I *cannot* live without my life! I *cannot* live without my soul!"

He dashed his head against the knotted trunk; and, lifting up his eyes, howled, not like a man, but like a savage beast being goaded to death with knives and spears. I observed several splashes of blood about the bark of the tree, and his hand and forehead were both stained; probably the scene I witnessed was a repetition of others acted during the night. It hardly moved my compassion—it appalled me: still, I felt reluctant to quit him so. But the moment he recollected himself enough to notice me watching, he thundered a command for me to go, and I obeyed. He was beyond my skill to quiet or console!

Mrs. Linton's funeral was appointed to take place on the Friday following her decease; and till then her coffin remained uncovered, and strewn with flowers and scented leaves, in the great drawing-room. Linton spent his days and nights there, a sleepless guardian; and—a circumstance concealed from all but me—Heathcliff spent his nights, at least, outside, equally a stranger to repose. I held no communication with him: still, I was conscious of his design to enter, if he could; and on the Tuesday, a little after dark, when my master, from sheer fatigue, had been compelled to retire a couple of hours, I went and opened one of the windows; moved by his perseverance, to give him a chance of bestowing on the faded image of his idol one final adieu. He did not omit to avail himself of the opportunity, cautiously and briefly: too cautiously to betray his presence by the slightest noise. Indeed, I shouldn't have discovered that he had been there, except for the disarrangement of the drapery about the corpse's face, and for observing on the floor a curl of light hair, fastened with a silver thread; which, on examination, I ascertained to have been taken from a locket hung round Catherine's neck. Heathcliff had opened the trinket and cast out its contents, replacing them by a black lock of his own. I twisted the two, and enclosed them together.

Mr. Earnshaw was, of course, invited to attend the remains of his sister to the grave; he sent no excuse, but he never came; so that, besides her husband, the mourners were wholly composed of tenants and servants. Isabella was not asked.

The place of Catherine's interment, to the surprise of the villagers, was neither in the chapel under the carved monument of the Lintons, nor yet by the tombs of her own relations, outside. It was dug on a green slope in a corner of the kirkyard, where the wall is so low that heath and bilberry plants have climbed over it from the moor; and peat mould almost buries it. Her husband lies in the same spot now; and they have each a simple headstone above, and a plain grey block at their feet, to mark the graves.

## Chapter 17

THAT Friday made the last of our fine days for a month. In the evening, the weather broke: the wind shifted from south to north-east, and brought rain first, and then sleet and snow. On the morrow one could hardly imagine that there had been three weeks of summer: the primroses and crocuses were hidden under wintry drifts; the larks were silent, and young leaves of the early trees smitten and blackened. And dreary, and chill, and dismal, that morrow did creep over! My master kept his room; I took possession of the lonely parlour, converting it into a nursery: and there I was, sitting with the moaning doll of a child laid on my knee; rocking it to and fro, and watching, meanwhile, the still driving flakes build up the uncurtained window, when the door opened, and some person entered, out of breath and laughing! My anger was greater than my astonishment for a minute! I supposed it one of the maids, and I cried—

"Have done! How dare you show your giddiness here? What would Mr. Linton say if he heard you?"

"Excuse me!" answered a familiar voice; "but I know Edgar is in bed, and I cannot stop myself."

With that the speaker came forward to the fire, panting and holding her hand to her side.

"I have run the whole way from Wuthering Heights!" she continued, after a pause; "except where I've flown. I couldn't count the number of falls I've had. Oh, I'm aching all over! Don't be alarmed! There shall be an explanation as soon as I can give it; only just have the goodness to step out and order the carriage to take me on to Gimmerton, and tell a servant to seek up a few clothes in my wardrobe."

The intruder was Mrs. Heathcliff. She certainly seemed in no laughing predicament: her hair streamed on her shoulders, dripping with snow and water; she was dressed in the girlish dress she commonly wore, befitting her age more than her position: a low frock with short sleeves, and nothing on either head or neck. The frock was of light silk, and clung to her with wet, and her feet were protected merely by thin slippers; add to this a deep cut under one ear, which only the cold prevented from bleeding profusely, a white face scratched and bruised, and a frame hardly able to support itself, through fatigue; and you may fancy my first fright was not much allayed when I had had leisure to examine her.

"My dear young lady," I exclaimed, "I'll stir nowhere, and hear nothing, till you have removed every article of your clothes, and put on dry things; and certainly you shall not go to Gimmerton to-night, so it is needless to order the carriage."

"Certainly, I shall," she said; "walking or riding: yet I've no objection to dress myself decently. Ah—and, see how it flows down my neck now! The fire does make it smart."

She insisted on my fulfilling her directions, before she would let me touch her; and not till after the coachman had been instructed to get ready, and a maid set to pack up some necessary attire, did I obtain her consent for binding the wound and helping her to change her garments.

"Now, Ellen," she said, when my task was finished and she was seated in an easy chair on the hearth, with a cup of tea before her, "you sit down opposite me, and put poor Catherine's baby away: I don't like to see it! You mustn't think I care little for Catherine, because I behaved so foolishly on entering: I've cried, too, bitterly—yes, more than any one else has reason to cry. We parted unreconciled, you remember, and I shan't forgive myself. But, for all that, I was not going to sympathize with him—the brute beast! O, give me the poker! This is the last thing of his I have about me:" she slipped the gold ring from her third finger, and threw it on the floor. "I'll smash it!" she continued, striking it with childish spite, "and then I'll burn it!" and she took and dropped the misused article among the coals. "There! he shall buy another, if he gets me back again. He'd be capable of coming to seek me, to tease Edgar. I dare not stay, lest that notion should possess his wicked head! And besides, Edgar has not been kind, has he? And I won't come suing for his assistance; nor will I bring him into more trouble. Necessity compelled me to seek shelter here; though, if I had not learned he was out of the way, I'd have halted at the kitchen, washed my face, warmed myself, got you to bring what I wanted, and departed again to anywhere out of the reach of my accursed—of that incarnate goblin! Ah, he was in such a fury! If he had caught me! It's a pity Earnshaw is not his match in strength: I wouldn't have run till I seen him all but demolished, had Hindley been able to do it!

"Yester-evening I sat in my nook reading some old books till late on towards twelve. It seemed so dismal to go upstairs, with the wild snow blowing outside, and my thoughts continually reverting to the kirkyard and the new-made grave! I dared hardly lift my eyes from the page before me, that melancholy scene so instantly usurped its place. Hindley sat opposite, his head leant on his hand; perhaps meditating on the same subject. He had ceased drinking at a point below irrationality, and had neither stirred nor spoken during two or three hours. There was no sound through the house but the moaning wind, which shook the windows every now and then, the faint crackling of the coals, and the click of my snuffers as I removed at intervals the long wick of the candle. Hareton and Joseph were probably fast asleep in bed. It was very, very sad: and while I read I sighed, for it seemed as if all joy had vanished from the world, never to be restored.

"The doleful silence was broken at length by the sound of the kitchen latch: Heathcliff had returned earlier than usual; owing, I suppose, to the sudden storm. That entrance was fastened, and we heard him coming round to get in by the other. I rose with an irrepressible expression of what I felt on my lips, which induced my companion, who had been staring towards the door, to turn and look at me.

"'I'll keep him out five minutes,' he exclaimed. 'You won't object?'

"'No, you may keep him out the whole night for me,' I answered. 'Do! put the key in the lock, and draw the bolts.'

"Earnshaw accomplished this ere his guest reached the front; he then came and brought his chair to the other side of my table, leaning over it, and searching in my eyes for a sympathy with the burning hate that gleamed from his: as he both looked and felt like an assassin, he couldn't exactly find that; but he discovered enough to encourage him to speak.

"'You, and I,' he said, 'have each a great debt to settle with the man out yonder! If we were neither of us cowards, we might combine to discharge it. Are you as soft as your brother? Are you willing to endure to the last, and not once attempt a repayment?'

"'I'm weary of enduring now,' I replied; 'and I'd be glad of a retaliation that wouldn't recoil on myself; but treachery and violence are spears pointed at both ends: they wound those who resort to them worse than their enemies.'

"'Treachery and violence are a just return for treachery and violence!' cried Hindley. 'Mrs. Heathcliff, I'll ask you to do nothing; but sit still and be dumb. Tell me now, can you? I'm sure you would have as much pleasure as I in witnessing the conclusion of the fiend's existence; he'll be *your* death unless you overreach him; and he'll be *my* ruin. Damn the hellish villain! He knocks at the door as if he were master here already! Promise to hold your tongue, and before that clock strikes—it wants three minutes of one—you're a free woman!'

"He took implements from his breast, and would have turned down the candle. I snatched it away, however, and seized his arm.

"'I'll not hold my tongue!' I said; 'you mustn't touch him. Let the door remain shut, and be quiet!'

"'No! I've formed my resolution, and by God I'll execute it!' cried the desperate being. 'I'll do you a kindness in spite of yourself, and Hareton justice! And you needn't trouble your head to screen me; Catherine is gone. Nobody alive would regret me, or be ashamed, though I cut my throat this minute—and it's time to make an end!'

"I might as well have struggled with a bear, or reasoned with a lunatic. The only resource left me was to run to a lattice and warn his intended victim of the fate which awaited him.

"'You'd better seek shelter somewhere else to-night!' I exclaimed in rather a triumphant tone. 'Mr. Earnshaw has a mind to shoot you, if you persist in endeavouring to enter.'

"'You'd better open the door, you——' he answered, addressing me by some elegant term that I don't care to repeat.

"'I shall not meddle in the matter,' I retorted again. 'Come in and get shot, if you please! I've done my duty.'

"With that I shut the window and returned to my place by the fire; having too small a stock of hypocrisy at my command to pretend any anxiety for the danger that menaced him. Earnshaw swore passionately at me: affirming that I loved the villain yet; and calling me all sorts of names for the base spirit I evinced. And I, in my secret heart (and conscience never reproached me), thought what a blessing it would be for *him* should Heathcliff put him out of misery; and what a blessing for *me* should he send Heathcliff to his right abode! As I sat nursing these reflections, the casement behind me was banged on the floor by a blow from the latter individual, and his black countenance looked blightingly through. The stanchions stood too close to suffer his shoulders to follow, and I smiled, exulting in my fancied security. His hair and clothes were whitened with snow, and his sharp cannibal teeth, revealed by cold and wrath, gleamed through the dark.

"'Isabella, let me in, or I'll make you repent!' he 'girned,' as Joseph calls it.

"'I cannot commit murder,' I replied. 'Mr. Hindley stands sentinel with a knife and loaded pistol.'

"'Let me in by the kitchen door,' he said.

"'Hindley will be there before me,' I answered: 'and that's a poor love of yours that cannot bear a shower of snow! Heathcliff, if I were you, I'd go stretch myself over her grave and die like a faithful dog. The world is surely not worth living in now, is it? You had distinctly impressed on me the idea that Catherine was the whole joy of your life: I can't imagine how you think of surviving her loss.'

"'He's there, is he?' exclaimed my companion, rushing to the gap. 'If I can get my arm out I can hit him!'

"'I'm afraid, Ellen, you'll set me down as really wicked; but you don't know all, so don't judge. I wouldn't have aided or abetted an attempt on *his* life even for anything. Wish that he were dead, I must; and therefore I was fearfully disappointed, and unnerved by terror for the consequences of my taunting speech, when he flung himself on Earnshaw's weapon and wrenched it from his grasp.

"The charge exploded, and the knife, in springing back, closed into its owner's wrist. Heathcliff pulled it away by main force, slitting up the flesh as it passed on, and thrust it dripping into his pocket. He then took a stone, struck down the division between two windows, and sprang in. His adversary had fallen senseless with excessive pain and the flow of blood, that gushed from an artery or a large vein. The ruffian kicked and trampled on him, and dashed his head repeatedly against the flags, holding me with one hand, meantime, to prevent me summoning Joseph. He exerted preter-human self-denial in abstaining from finishing him completely; but getting out of breath he finally desisted, and dragged the apparently inanimate body on to the settle. There he tore off the sleeve of Earnshaw's coat, and bound up the wound with brutal roughness; spitting and cursing during the operation as energetically as he had kicked before. Being at liberty, I lost no time in seeking the old servant; who, having gathered by degrees the purport of my hasty tale, hurried below, gasping, as he descended the steps two at once.

"'What is ther to do, now? what is ther to do, now?'

"'There's this to do,' thundered Heathcliff, 'that your master's mad; and should he last another month, I'll have him out to an asylum. And how the devil did you come to fasten me out, you toothless hound? Don't stand muttering and mumbling there. Come, I'm not going to nurse him. Wash that stuff away; and mind the sparks of your candle—it is more than half brandy!'

"'And so, ye've been murthering on him?' exclaimed Joseph, lifting his hands and eyes in horror. 'If iver I seed a seeght loike this! May the Lord—'

"'Heathcliff gave him a push on to his knees in the middle of the blood, and flung a towel to him; but instead of proceeding to dry it up, he joined his hands and began a prayer, which excited my laughter from its odd phraseology. I was in the condition of mind to be shocked at nothing: in fact, I was as reckless as some malefactors show themselves at the foot of the gallows.

"He shook me till my teeth rattled, and pitched me beside Joseph, who steadily concluded his supplications and then rose, vowing he would set off for the Grange directly. Mr. Linton was a magistrate, and though he had fifty wives dead, he should inquire into this. He was so obstinate in his resolution, that Heathcliff deemed it expedient to compel from my lips a recapitulation of what had taken place; standing over me, heaving with malevolence, as I reluctantly delivered the account in answer to his questions. It required a great deal of labour to satisfy the old man that Heathcliff was not the aggressor; especially with my hardly-wrung replies. However, Mr. Earnshaw soon convinced him that he was alive still; Joseph hastened to administer a dose of spirits, and by their succour his master presently regained motion and consciousness. Heathcliff, aware that his opponent was ignorant of the treatment received while insensible, called him deliriously intoxicated; and said he should not notice his atrocious conduct further, but advised him to get to bed. To my joy, he left us, after

71

giving this judicious counsel, and Hindley stretched himself on the hearth-stone. I departed to my own room, marvelling that I had escaped so easily.

"This morning, when I came down, about half an hour before noon, Mr. Earnshaw was sitting by the fire, deadly sick; his evil genius, almost as gaunt and ghastly, leant against the chimney. Neither appeared inclined to dine, and, having waited till all was cold on the table, I commenced alone. Nothing hindered me from eating heartily, and I experienced a certain sense of satisfaction and superiority, as, at intervals, I cast a look towards my silent companions, and felt the comfort of a quiet conscience within me. After I had done, I ventured on the unusual liberty of drawing near the fire, going round Earnshaw's seat, and kneeling in the corner beside him.

"Mr. Earnshaw looked up, like me, to the countenance of our mutual foe; who, absorbed in his anguish, seemed insensible to anything around him: the longer he stood, the plainer his reflections revealed their blackness through his features.

"'Oh, if God would but give me strength to strangle him in my last agony, I'd go to hell with joy,' groaned the impatient man, writhing to rise, and sinking back in despair, convinced of his inadequacy for the struggle.

"'Nay, it's enough that he has murdered one of you,' I observed aloud. 'At the Grange, every one knows your sister would have been living now, had it not been for Mr. Heathcliff. After all, it is preferable to be hated than loved by him. When I recollect how happy we were—how happy Catherine was before he came—I'm fit to curse the day.'

"Most likely, Heathcliff noticed more the truth of what was said, than the spirit of the person who said it. His attention was roused. I saw, for his eyes rained down tears among the ashes, and he drew his breath in suffocating sighs. I stared full at him, and he laughed scornfully. The clouded windows of hell flashed a moment towards me; the fiend which usually looked out, however, was so dimmed and drowned that I did not fear to hazard another sound of derision.

"'Get up, and begone out of my sight' said the mourner.

"I guessed he uttered those words, at least, though his voice was hardly intelligible.

"'I beg your pardon,' I replied. 'But I loved Catherine too; and her brother requires attendance, which, for her sake, I shall supply. Now that she's dead, I see her in Hindley: Hindley has exactly her eyes, if you had not tried to gouge them out, and made them black and red; and her——'

"'Get up, wretched idiot, before I stamp you to death!' he cried, making a movement that caused me to make one also.

"'But then,' I continued, holding myself ready to flee; 'if poor Catherine had trusted you, and assumed the ridiculous, contemptible, degrading title

72

of Mrs. Heathcliff, she would soon have presented a similar picture! *She* wouldn't have borne your abominable behaviour quietly: her detestation and disgust must have found voice.'

"The back of the settle and Earnshaw's person interposed between me and him; so instead of endeavouring to reach me, he snatched a dinner knife from the table and flung it at my head. It struck beneath my ear, and stopped the sentence I was uttering; but, pulling it out, I sprang to the door and delivered another; which I hope went a little deeper than his missile. The last glimpse I caught of him was a furious rush on his part, checked by the embrace of his host; and both fell locked together on the hearth. In my flight through the kitchen I bid Joseph speed to his master; I knocked over Hareton, who was hanging a litter of puppies from a chair-back in the doorway; and, blest as a soul escaped from purgatory, I bounded, leaped, and flew down the steep road; then, quitting its windings, shot direct across the moor, rolling over banks, and wading through marshes: precipating myself, in fact, towards the beacon light of the Grange. And far rather would I be condemned to a perpetual dwelling in the infernal regions, than, even for one night, abide beneath the roof of Wuthering Heights again."

Isabella ceased speaking, and took a drink of tea; then she rose, and bidding me put on her bonnet, and a great shawl I had brought, and turning a deaf ear to my entreaties for her to remain another hour, she stepped on to a chair, kissed Edgar's and Catherine's portraits, bestowed a similar salute on me, and descended to the carriage, accompanied by Fanny, who yelped wild with joy at recovering her mistress. She was driven away, never to revisit this neighbourhood: but a regular correspondence was established between her and my master when things were more settled. I believe her new abode was in the south, near London; there she had a son born, a few months subsequent to her escape. He was christened Linton, and, from the first, she reported him to be an ailing, peevish creature.

Mr. Heathcliff, meeting me one day in the village, inquired where she lived. I refused to tell. He remarked that it was not of any moment, only she must be aware of coming to her brother: she should not be with him, if he had to keep her himself. Though I would give no information, he discovered, through some of the other servants, both her place of residence and the existence of the child. Still he didn't molest her: for which forbearance she might thank his aversion, I suppose. He often asked about the infant, when he saw me; and on hearing its name, smiled grimly, and observed:

"They wish me to hate it too, do they?"

"I don't think they wish you to know anything about it," I answered.

"But I'll have it," he said, "when I want it. They may reckon on that!"

Fortunately, its mother died before the time arrived; some thirteen years after the decease of Catherine, when Linton was twelve, or a little more.

73

On the day succeeding Isabella's unexpected visit, I had no opportunity of speaking to my master: she shunned conversation, and was fit for discussing nothing. When I could get him to listen, I saw it pleased him that his sister had left her husband; whom he abhorred with an intensity which the mildness of his nature would scarcely seem to allow. So deep and sensitive was his aversion, that he refrained from going anywhere where he was likely to see or hear of Heathcliff. Grief, and that together, transformed him into a complete hermit: he threw up his office of magistrate, ceased even to attend church, avoided the village on all occasions, and spent a life of entire seclusion within the limits of his park and grounds; only varied by solitary rambles on the moors, and visits to the grave of his wife, mostly at evening, or early morning before other wanderers were abroad. But he was too good to be thoroughly unhappy long. *He* didn't pray for Catherine's soul to haunt him. Time brought resignation, and a melancholy sweeter than common joy. He recalled her memory with ardent, tender love, and hopeful aspiring to the better world; where he doubted not she was gone.

And he had earthly consolations and affections also. For a few days, I said, he seemed regardless of the puny successor to the departed: that coldness melted as fast as snow in April, and ere the tiny thing could stammer a word or totter a step, it wielded a despot's sceptre in his heart. It was named Catherine; but he never called it the name in full, as he had never called the first Catherine short: probably because Heathcliff had a habit of doing so. The little one was always Cathy: it formed to him a distinction from the mother, and yet a connection with her; and his attachment sprang from his relation to her, far more than from its being his own.

I used to draw a comparison between him and Hindley Earnshaw, and perplex myself to explain satisfactorily why their conduct was so opposite in similar circumstances. They had both been fond husbands, and were both attached to their children; and I could not see how they shouldn't both have taken the same road, for good or evil. But, I thought in my mind, Hindley, with apparently the stronger head, has shown himself sadly the worse and the weaker man. The end of Earnshaw was what might have been expected; it followed fast on his sister's: there were scarcely six months between them.

I confess this blow was greater to me than the shock of Mrs. Linton's death: ancient associations lingered round my heart; I sat down in the porch and wept as for a blood relation. I could not hinder myself from pondering on the question—"Had he had fair play?" Whatever I did, that idea would bother me: it was so tiresomely pertinacious that I resolved on requesting leave to go to Wuthering Heights, and assist in the last duties to the dead. Mr. Linton was extremely reluctant to consent, but I pleaded eloquently for the friendless condition in which he lay; and I said my old master and foster-brother had a claim on my services as strong as his own.

Besides, I reminded him that the child Hareton was his wife's nephew, and, in the absence of nearer kin, he ought to act as its guardian; and he ought to and must inquire how the property was left, and look over the concerns of his brother-in-law. He was unfit for attending to such matters then, but he did bid me speak to his lawyer; and at length permitted me to go. His lawyer had been Earnshaw's also: I called at the village, and asked him to accompany me. He shook his head, and advised that Heathcliff should be left alone: affirming, if the truth were known, Hareton would be found little else than a beggar.

When I reached the Heights, I explained that I had come to see everything carried on decently; and Joseph, who appeared in sufficient distress, expressed satisfaction at my presence. Mr. Heathcliff said he did not perceive that I was wanted; but I might stay and order the arrangements for the funeral, if I chose.

I insisted on the funeral being respectable. Mr. Heathcliff said I might have my own way there too: only, he desired me to remember that the money for the whole affair came out of his pocket. He maintained a hard, careless deportment, indicative of neither joy nor sorrow; if anything, it expressed a flinty gratification at a piece of difficult work successfully executed. I observed once, indeed, something like exultation in his aspect: it was just when the people were bearing the coffin from the house. He had the hypocrisy to represent a mourner: and previous to following with Hareton, he lifted the unfortunate child on to the table and muttered, with peculiar gusto, "Now, my bonny lad you are *mine*! And we'll see if one tree won't grow as crooked as another, with the same wind to twist it!" The unsuspecting thing was pleased at this speech: he played with Heathcliff's whiskers, and stroked his cheek; but I divined its meaning, and observed tartly, "That boy must go back with me to Thrushcross Grange, sir. There is nothing in the world less yours than he is!"

"Well," said the scoundrel, "we'll not argue the subject now: but I have a fancy to try my hand at rearing a young one; so intimate to your master that I must supply the place of this with my own, if he attempt to remove it. I don't engage to let Hareton go undisputed; but I'll be pretty sure to make the other come! Remember me to him."

This hint was enough to bind our hands. I repeated its substance on my return; and Edgar Linton, little interested at the commencement, spoke no more of interfering. I'm not aware that he could have done it to any purpose, had he been ever so willing.

The guest was now the master of Wuthering Heights: he held firm possession, and proved to the attorney—who, in his turn, proved it to Mr. Linton—that Earnshaw had mortgaged every yard of land he owned, for cash to supply his mania for gaming; and he, Heathcliff, was the mortgagee. In that manner Hareton, who should now be the first gentleman in the neighbourhood, was reduced to a state of complete dependence on his father's inveterate enemy; and lives in his own house as a servant, deprived of the advantage of wages: quite unable to right himself, because of his friendlessness, and his ignorance that he has been wronged.

## *Chapter 18*

THE twelve years, continued Mrs. Dean, following that dismal period, were the happiest of my life: my greatest troubles in their passage rose from our little lady's trifling illnesses, which she had to experience in common with all children, rich and poor. For the rest, after the first six months, she grew like a larch, and could walk and talk too, in her own way, before the heath blossomed a second time over Mrs. Linton's dust. She was the most winning thing that ever brought sunshine into a desolate house: a real beauty in face, with the Earnshaw's handsome dark eyes, but the Linton's fair skin and small features, and yellow curling hair. Her spirit was high, though not rough, and qualified by a heart sensitive and lively to excess in its affections. That capacity for intense attachments reminded me of her mother: still she did not resemble her; for she could be soft and mild as a dove, and she had a gentle voice and pensive expression: her anger was never furious; her love never fierce; it was deep and tender.

Till she reached the age of thirteen, she had not once been beyond the range of the park by herself. Mr. Linton would take him with her a mile or so outside, on rare occasions; but he trusted her to no one else. Gimmerton was an unsubstantial name in her ears; the chapel the only building she had approached or entered, except her own home. Wuthering Heights and Mr. Heathcliff did not exist for her: she was a perfect recluse; and, apparently, perfectly contented. Sometimes, indeed, while surveying the country from her nursery window, she would observe—

"Ellen, how long will it be before I can walk to the top of those hills? I wonder what lies on the other side—is it the sea?"

One of the maids mentioning the Fairy Cave, quite turned her head with a desire to fulfil this project: she teased Mr. Linton about it; and he promised she should have the journey when she got older. But Miss Catherine measured her age by months, and, "Now, am I old enough to go to Penistone Crags?" was the constant question in her mouth. The road thither wound close by Wuthering Heights. Edgar had not the heart to pass it; so she received as constantly the answer, "Not yet, love: not yet."

I said Mrs. Heathcliff lived above a dozen years after quitting her husband. Her family were of a delicate constitution: she and Edgar both lacked the ruddy health that you will generally meet in these parts. What her last illness was, I am not certain: I conjecture, they died of the same thing, a kind of fever, slow at its commencement, but incurable, and rapidly consuming life towards the close. She wrote to inform her brother of the probable conclusion of a four month's indisposition under which she had suffered, and entreated him to come to her, if possible; for she had much to settle, and she wished to bid him adieu, and deliver Linton safely into his hands. Her hope was, that Linton might be left with him, as he had been with her: his father, she would fain convince herself, had no desire to assume the burden of his maintenance or education. My master hesitated not a moment in complying with her request: reluctant as he was to leave home at ordinary calls, he flew to answer this; commending Catherine to my peculiar vigilance, in his absence, with reiterated orders that she must not wander out of the park, even under my escort: he did not calculate on her going unaccompanied.

He was away three weeks. The first day or two, my charge sat in a corner of the library, too sad for either reading or playing: in that quiet state she caused me little trouble; but it was succeeded by an interval of impatient, fretful weariness; and being too busy, and too old then, to run up and down amusing her, I hit on a method by which she might entertain herself. I used to send her on her travels round the grounds—now on foot, and now on a pony; indulging her with a patient audience of all her real and imaginary adventures, when she returned.

The summer shone in full prime; and she took such a taste for this solitary rambling that she often contrived to remain out from breakfast till tea; and then the evenings were spent in recounting her fanciful tales. I did not fear her breaking bounds; because the gates were generally locked, and I thought she would scarcely venture forth alone, if they had stood wide open. Unluckily, my confidence proved misplaced. Catherine came to me, one morning, at eight o'clock, and said she was that day an Arabian merchant, going to cross the Desert with his caravan; and I must give her plenty of provision for herself and beasts: a horse, and three camels, personated by a large hound and a couple of pointers. I got together good store of dainties, and slung them in a basket on one side of the saddle; and she sprang up as gay as a fairy, sheltered by her wide-brimmed hat and gauze veil from the July sun, and trotted off with a merry laugh, mocking my cautious counsel to avoid galloping, and come back early. The naughty thing never made her appearance at tea. One traveller, the hound, being an old dog and fond of its ease, returned; but neither Cathy, nor the pony, nor the two pointers were visible in any direction: I despatched emissaries down this path, and that path, and at last went wandering in search of her myself. There was a labourer working at a fence round a plantation, on the borders of the grounds. I inquired of him if he had seen our young lady.

"I saw her at morn," he replied; "she would have me to cut her a hazel switch, and then she leapt her Galloway over the hedge yonder, where it is lowest, and galloped out of sight."

You may guess how I felt at hearing this news. It struck me directly she must have started for Penistone Crags. "What will become of her?" I ejaculated, pushing through a gap which the man was repairing, and making straight to the high road. I walked as if for a wager, mile after mile, till a turn brought me in view of the Heights; but no Catherine could I detect, far or near. The Crags lie about a mile and a half beyond Mr. Heathcliff's place, and that is four from the Grange, so I began to fear night would fall ere I could reach them. "And what if she should have slipped in clambering among them," I reflected, "and been killed, or broken some of her bones?" My suspense was truly painful; and, at first, it gave me delightful relief to observe, in hurrying by the farm-house, Charlie, the fiercest of the pointers, lying under a window, with swelled head and bleeding ear. I opened the wicket and ran to the door, knocking vehemently for admittance. A woman whom I knew, and who formerly lived at Gimmerton, answered: she had been servant there since the death of Mr. Earnshaw.

I entered, and beheld my stray lamb seated on the hearth, rocking herself in a little chair that had been her mother's when a child. Her hat was hung against the wall, and she seemed perfectly at home, laughing and chattering, in the best spirits imaginable, to Hareton—now a great, strong lad of eighteen—who stared at her with considerable curiosity and astonishment; comprehending precious little of the fluent succession of remarks and questions which her tongue never ceased pouring forth.

"Put that hat on, and home at once," said I. "I'm dreadfully grieved at you, Miss Cathy: you've done extremely wrong! It's no use pouting and crying: that won't repay the trouble I've had, scouring the country after you. To think how Mr. Linton charged me to keep you in; and you stealing off so! it shows you are a cunning little fox, and nobody will put faith in you any more."

"What have I done?" sobbed she, instantly checked. "Papa charged me nothing: he'll not scold me, Ellen—he's never cross, like you!"

"Come, come!" I repeated. "I'll tie the riband. Now, let us have no petulance. Oh, for shame! You thirteen years old, and such a baby!"

This exclamation was caused by her pushing the hat from her head, and retreating to the chimney out of my reach.

"Nay," said the servant, "don't be hard on the bonny lass, Mrs. Dean. We made her stop: she'd fain have ridden forwards, afeard you should be uneasy. Hareton offered to go with her, and I thought he should: it's a wild road over the hills."

Hareton, during the discussion, stood with his hands in his pockets, too awkward to speak; though he looked as if he did not relish my intrusion.

"Now, get my horse," she said, addressing her unknown kinsman as she would one of the stable-boys at the Grange. "And you may come with me.

I want to see where the goblin-hunter rises in the marsh, and to hear about the *fairishes*, as you call them: but make haste! What's the matter? Get my horse, I say."

"I'll see thee damned before I be *thy* servant!" growled the lad.

"You'll see me *what*?" asked Catherine in surprise.

"Damned—thou saucy witch!" he replied.

"There, Miss Cathy! you see you have got into pretty company," I interposed. "Nice words to be used to a young lady! Pray don't begin to dispute with him. Come, let us seek for Minny ourselves, and begone."

"But Ellen," cried she, staring, fixed in astonishment, "how dare he speak so to me? Mustn't he be made to do as I ask him? You wicked creature, I shall tell papa what you said.—Now, then!"

Hareton did not appear to feel this threat; so the tears sprang into her eyes with indignation. "You bring the pony," she exclaimed, turning to the woman, "and let my dog free this moment!"

"Softly, miss," answered she addressed: "you'll lose nothing by being civil. Though Mr. Hareton, there, be not the master's son, he's your cousin; and I was never hired to serve you."

"*He* my cousin!" cried Cathy, with a scornful laugh.

"Yes, indeed," responded her reprover.

"Oh, Ellen! don't let them say such things," she pursued in great trouble. "Papa is gone to fetch my cousin from London: my cousin is a gentleman's son. That my——" she stopped, and wept outright; upset at the bare notion of relationship with such a clown.

I was much vexed at her and the servant for their mutual revelations; having no doubt of Linton's approaching arrival, communicated by the former, being reported to Mr. Heathcliff; and feeling as confident that Catherine's first thought on her father's return, would be to seek an explanation of the latter's assertion concerning her rude-bred kindred. Hareton, recovering from his disgust at being taken for a servant, seemed moved by her distress; and, having fetched the pony round to the door, he took, to propitiate her, a fine crooked-legged terrier whelp from the kennel, and putting it into her hand bid her whist! for he meant nought. Pausing in her lamentations, she surveyed him with a glance of awe and horror, then burst forth anew.

I could scarcely refrain from smiling at this antipathy to the poor fellow; who was a well-made, athletic youth, good looking in features, stout and healthy, but attired in garments befitting his daily occupations of working on the farm, and lounging among the moors after rabbits and game. Still, I thought I could detect in his physiognomy a mind owning better qualities than his father ever possessed. But Miss Cathy rejected the peace-offering of the terrier, and demanded her own dogs, Charlie and Phœnix. They came limping, and hanging their heads; and we set out for home, sadly out of sorts, every one of us. I could not wring from my little lady how she had spent the day; except that, as I supposed, the goal of her pilgrimage was Penistone Crags; and she arrived without adventure at the gate of the farmhouse, when Hareton happened to issue forth, attended by some canine followers, who attacked her train. They had a smart battle, before their owners could separate them: that formed an introduction. Catherine told Hareton who she was, and where she was going; and asked him to show her the way: finally, beguiling him to accompany her. He opened the mysteries of the Fairy Cave, and twenty other queer places. But, being in disgrace, I was not favoured with a description of the interesting objects she saw. I could gather, however, that her guide had been a favourite till she hurt his feelings by addressing him as a servant; and Heathcliff's housekeeper hurt hers by calling him her cousin. Then the language he had held to her rankled in her heart; she who was always "love," and "darling," and "queen," and "angel," with everybody at the Grange, to be insulted so shockingly by a stranger! She did not comprehend it; and hard work I had to obtain a promise that she would not lay the grievance before her father. I explained how he objected to the whole household at the Heights, and how sorry he would be to find she had been there; but I insisted most on the fact, that if she revealed my negligence of his orders, he would perhaps be so angry, that I should have to leave; and Cathy couldn't bear that prospect: she pledged her word, and kept it, for my sake. After all, she was a sweet little girl.

## Chapter 19

A LETTER, edged with black, announced the day of my master's return. Isabella was dead; and he wrote to bid me get mourning for his daughter, and arrange a room, and other accommodations, for his youthful nephew. Catherine ran wild with joy at the idea of welcoming her father back; and indulged most sanguine anticipations of the innumerable excellences of her "real" cousin. The evening of their expected arrival came. Since early morning, she had been busy ordering her own small affairs; and now, attired in her new black frock—poor thing! her aunt's death impressed her with no definite sorrow—she obliged me, by constant worrying, to walk with her down through the grounds to meet them.

"How long they are!" she exclaimed. "Ah, I see some dust on the road—they are coming! No! when will they be here? May we not go a little way—half a mile, Ellen: only just half a mile? Do say Yes: to that clump of birches at the turn!"

I refused staunchly. At length her suspense was ended: the travelling carriage rolled in sight. Miss Cathy shrieked and stretched out her arms, as soon as she caught her father's face looking from the window. He descended, nearly as eager as herself; and a considerable interval elapsed ere they had a thought to spare for any but themselves. While they exchanged caresses, I took a peep in to see after Linton. He was asleep in a corner, wrapped in a warm, fur-lined cloak, as if it had been winter. A pale, delicate, effeminate boy, who might have been taken for my master's younger brother, so strong was the resemblance: but there was a sickly peevishness in his aspect, that Edgar Linton never had. The latter saw me looking; and having shaken hands, advised me to close the door, and leave him undisturbed; for the journey had fatigued him. Cathy would fain have taken one glance, but her father told her to come, and they walked together up the park, while I hastened before to prepare the servants.

"Now, darling," said Mr. Linton, addressing his daughter, as they halted at the bottom of the front steps: "your cousin is not so strong or so merry as you are, and he has lost his mother, remember, a very short time since; therefore, don't expect him to play and run about with you directly. And don't harass him much by talking: let him be quiet this evening, at least, will you?"

"Yes, yes, papa," answered Catherine: "but I do want to see him; and he hasn't once looked out."

The carriage stopped; and the sleeper being roused, was lifted to the ground by his uncle.

"This is your cousin Cathy, Linton," he said, putting their little hands together. "She's fond of you already; and mind you don't grieve her by crying to-night. Try to be cheerful now; the travelling is at an end, and you have nothing to do but rest and amuse yourself as you please."

"Let me go to bed, then," answered the boy, shrinking from Catherine's salute; and he put his fingers to remove incipient tears.

"Oh, he'll do very well," said the master to me, after watching them a minute. "Very well, if we can keep him, Ellen. The company of a child of his own age will instil new spirit into him soon, and by wishing for strength he'll gain it."

"Ay, if we can keep him!" I mused to myself; and sore misgivings came over me that there was slight hope of that. And then, I thought, however will that weakling live at Wuthering Heights? Between his father and Hareton, what playmates and instructors they'll be. Our doubts were presently decided—even earlier than I expected. I had just taken the children upstairs, after tea was finished, and seen Linton asleep—he would not suffer me to leave him till that was the case—I had come down, and was standing by the table in the hall, lighting a bedroom candle for Mr. Edgar, when a maid stepped out of the kitchen and informed me that Mr. Heathcliff's servant Joseph was at the door, and wished to speak with the master.

"I shall ask him what he wants first," I said, in considerable trepidation. "A very unlikely hour to be troubling people, and the instant they have returned from a long journey. I don't think the master can see him."

Joseph had advanced through the kitchen as I uttered these words, and now presented himself in the hall. He was donned in his Sunday garments, with his most sanctimonious and sourest face, and, holding his hat in one hand and his stick in the other, he proceeded to clean his shoes on the mat.

"Good evening, Joseph," I said, coldly. "What business brings you here to-night?"

"It's Maister Linton I mun spake to," he answered, waving me disdainfully aside.

"Mr. Linton is going to bed; unless you have something particular to say, I'm sure he won't hear it now," I continued. "You had better sit down in there, and entrust your message to me."

"Which is his rahm?" pursued the fellow, surveying the range of closed doors.

I perceived he was bent on refusing my mediation, so very reluctantly I went up to the library, and announced the unseasonable visitor, advising that he should be dismissed till next day. Mr. Linton had no time to empower me to do so, for Joseph mounted close at my heels, and, pushing into the apartment, planted himself at the far side of the table, with his two fists clapped on the head of his stick, and began in an elevated tone, as if anticipating opposition—

"Heathcliff has sent me for his lad, and I munn't goa back 'bout him."

Edgar Linton was silent a minute; an expression of exceeding sorrow overcast his features: he would have pitied the child on his own account; but, recalling Isabella's hopes and fears, and anxious wishes for her son, and her commendations of him to his care, he grieved bitterly at the prospect of yielding him up, and searched in his heart how it might be avoided. No plan offered itself: the very exhibition of any desire to keep him would have rendered the claimant more peremptory: there was nothing left but to resign him. However, he was not going to rouse him from his sleep.

"Tell Mr. Heathcliff," he answered clamly, "that his son shall come to Wuthering Heights to-morrow. He is in bed, and too tired to go the distance now. You may also tell him that the mother of Linton desired him to remain under my guardianship; and, at present, his health is very precarious."

"Noa!" said Joseph, giving a thud with his prop on the floor, and assuming an authoritative air: "Noa! that means naught. Heathcliff maks noa 'count o' t' mother, nor ye norther; but he'll hev his lad; und I mun tak him—soa now ye knaw!"

"You shall not to-night!" answered Linton decisively. "Walk downstairs at once, and repeat to your master what I have said. Ellen, show him down. Go——"

And, aiding the indignant elder with a lift by the arm, he rid the room of him, and closed the door.

"Varrah weell!" shouted Joseph, as he slowly drew off. "To morn, he's come hisseln, and thrust *him* out, if ye darr!"

## Chapter 20

To OBVIATE the danger of this threat being fulfilled, Mr. Linton commissioned me to take the boy home early, on Catherine's pony; and, said he:

"As we shall now have no influence over his destiny, good or bad, you must say nothing of where he is gone, to my daughter: she cannot associate with him hereafter, and it is better for her to remain in ignorance of his proximity; lest she should be restless, and anxious to visit the Heights. Merely tell her his father sent for him suddenly, and he has been obliged to leave us."

Linton was very reluctant to be roused from his bed at five o'clock, and astonished to be informed that he must prepare for further travelling; but I softened off the matter by stating that he was going to spend some time with his father, Mr. Heathcliff, who wished to see him so much, but did not like to defer the pleasure till he should recover from his late journey.

"My father!" he cried, in strange perplexity. "Mamma never told me I had a father. Where does he live? I'd rather stay with uncle."

I attempted to persuade him of the naughtiness of showing reluctance to meet his father; still he obstinately resisted any progress towards dressing, and I had to call for my master's assistance in coaxing him out of bed. The poor thing was finally got off, with several delusive assurances that his absence should be short; that Mr. Edgar and Cathy would visit him, and other promises, equally ill-founded, which I invented and reiterated at intervals throughout the way. The pure heather-scented air, the bright sunshine, and the gentle canter of Minny, relieved his despondency after a while. He began to put questions concerning his new home, and its inhabitants, with greater interest and liveliness.

"And what is my father like?" he asked. "Is he as young and handsome as uncle?"

"He's as young," said I; "but he has black hair and eyes, and looks sterner; and he is taller and bigger altogether. He'll not seem to you so gentle and kind at first, perhaps, because it is not his way: still, mind you, be frank and cordial with him; and naturally he'll be fonder of you than any uncle, for you are his own."

"Black hair and eyes!" mused Linton. "I can't fancy him. Then I am not like him, am I?"

"Not much," I answered: not a morsel, I thought, surveying with regret the white complexion and slim frame of my companion, and his large, languid eyes—his mother's eyes, save that, unless a morbid touchiness kindled them a moment, they had not a vestige of her sparkling spirit.

The boy was fully occupied with his own cogitations for the remainder of the ride, till we halted before the farmhouse garden gate. I watched to catch his impressions in his countenance. He surveyed the carved front and low-browed lattices, the straggling gooseberry bushes and crooked firs, with solemn intentness, and then shook his head: his private feelings entirely disapproved of the exterior of his new abode. But he had sense to postpone complaining: there might be compensation within. Before he dismounted, I went and opened the door. It was half-past six; the family had just finished breakfast; the servant was clearing and wiping down the table. Joseph stood by his master's chair telling some tale concerning a lame horse; and Hareton was preparing for the hay-field.

"Hallo, Nelly!" said Mr. Heathcliff, when he saw me. "I feared I should have to come down and fetch my property myself. You've brought it, have you? Let us see what we can make of it."

He got up and strode to the door: Hareton and Joseph followed in gaping curiosity. Poor Linton ran a frightened eye over the faces of the three.

"Do you know me?" asked Heathcliff.

"No," said Linton, with a gaze of vacant fear.

"You've heard of me, I dare say?"

"No," he replied again.

"No! What a shame of your mother, never to waken your filial regard for me! You are my son, then, I'll tell you; and your mother was a wicked slut to leave you in ignorance of the sort of father you possessed. Now, don't wince, and colour up! Though it *is* something to see you have not white blood. Be a good lad; and I'll do for you. Nelly, if you be tired you may sit down; if not, get home again. I guess you'll report what you hear and see to the cipher at the Grange; and this thing won't be settled while you linger about it."

"Well," replied I, "I hope you'll be kind to the boy, Mr. Heathcliff, or you'll not keep him long; and he's all you have akin in the wide world, that you will ever know—remember."

"I'll be *very* kind to him, you needn't fear," he said, laughing. "Only nobody else must be kind to him: I'm jealous of monopolizing his affection. And, to begin my kindness, Joseph, bring the lad some breakfast. Hareton, you infernal calf, begone to your work. Yes, Nell," he added, when they had departed, "my son is prospective owner of your place, and I should not wish him to die till I was certain of being his successor. Besides, he's *mine*, and I want the triumph of seeing *my* descendant fairly lord of their estates: my child hiring their children to till their father's lands for wages. That is the sole consideration which can make me endure the whelp: I despise him for himself, and hate him for the memories he revives! But that consideration is sufficient: he's as safe with me, and shall be tended as carefully as your master tends his own. I have a room up-stairs, furnished for him in handsome style; I've engaged a tutor, also, to come three times a week, from twenty miles distance, to teach him what he pleases to learn. I've ordered Hareton to obey him: and in fact I've arranged everything with a view to preserve the superior and the gentleman in him, above his associates. I do regret, however, that he so little deserves the trouble: if I wished any blessing in the world, it was to find him a worthy object of pride; and I'm bitterly disappointed with the whey-faced whining wretch!"

## Chapter 21

WE HAD sad work with little Cathy that day: she rose in high glee, eager to join her cousin, and such passionate tears and lamentations followed the news of his departure, that Edgar himself was obliged to soothe her, by affirming he should come back soon: he added, however, "if I can get him;" and there were no hopes of that. This promise poorly pacified her: but time was more potent; and though still at intervals she inquired of her father when Linton would return, before she did see him again his features had waxed so dim in her memory that she did not recognise him.

When I chanced to encounter the housekeeper of Wuthering Heights, in paying business-visits to Gimmerton, I used to ask how the young master got on; for he lived almost as secluded as Catherine herself, and was never to be seen. I could gather from her that he continued in weak health, and was a tiresome inmate. She said Mr. Heathcliff seemed to dislike him ever longer and worse, though he took some trouble to conceal it: he had an antipathy to the sound of his voice, and could not do at all with his sitting in the same room with him many minutes together. There seldom passed much talk between them: Linton learnt his lessons and spent his evenings in a small apartment they called the parlour: or else lay in bed all day: for he was constantly getting coughs, and colds, and aches, and pains of some sort.

"And I never knew such a faint-hearted creature," added the woman; "nor one so careful of hisseln. He *will* go on, if I leave the window open a bit late in the evening. Oh! it's killing, a breath of night air! And he must have a fire in the middle of summer; and Joseph's bacca pipe is poison; and he must always have sweets and dainties, and always milk, milk for ever—heeding naught how the rest of us are pinched in winter;

and there he'll sit, wrapped in his furred cloak in his chair by the fire, with some toast and water or other slop on the hob to sip at; and if Hareton, for pity, comes to amuse him—Hareton is not bad-natured, though he's rough—they're sure to part, one swearing and the other crying. I believe the master would relish Earnshaw's thrashing him to a mummy, if he were not his son; and I'm certain he would be fit to turn him out of doors, if he knew half the nursing he gives hisseln. But then, he won't go into danger of temptation: he never enters the parlour, and should Linton show those ways in the house where he is, he sends him upstairs directly."

Time wore on at the Grange in its former pleasant way, till Miss Cathy reached sixteen. On the anniversary of her birth we never manifested any signs of rejoicing, because it was also the anniversary of my late mistress's death. Her father invariably spent that day alone in the library; and walked, at dusk, as far as Gimmerton kirkyard, where he would frequently prolong his stay beyond midnight. Therefore Catherine was thrown on her own resources for amusement. This twentieth of March was a beautiful spring day, and when her father had returned, my young lady came down dressed for going out, and said she asked to have a ramble on the edge of the moor with me: Mr. Linton had given her leave, if we went only a short distance, and were back within the hour.

"So make haste, Ellen!" she cried. "I know where I wish to go; where a colony of moor-game are settled: I want to see whether they have made their nests yet."

"That must be a good distance up," I answered; "they don't breed on the edge of the moor."

"No, it's not," she said. "I've gone very near with papa."

But there were so many hillocks and banks to climb and pass, that, at length, I began to be weary, and told her we must halt, and retrace our steps. I shouted to her, as she had outstripped me a long way; she either did not hear or did not regard, for she still sprang on, and I was compelled to follow. Finally, she dived into a hollow; and before I came in sight of her again, she was two miles nearer Wuthering Heights than her own home; and I beheld a couple of persons arrest her, one of whom I felt convinced was Mr. Heathcliff himself.

Cathy had been caught in the fact of plundering or, at least, hunting out the nests of the grouse. The Heights were Heathcliff's land, and he was reproving the poacher.

"I've neither taken any nor found any," she said, as I toiled to them, expanding her hands in corroboration of the statement. "I didn't mean to take them; but papa told me there were quantities up here, and I wished to see the eggs."

Heathcliff glanced at me with an ill-meaning smile, expressing his acquaintance with the party, and consequently, his malevolence towards it, and demanded who "papa" was?

"Mr. Linton of Thrushcross Grange," she replied. "I thought you did not know me, or you wouldn't have spoken in that way."

"You suppose papa is highly esteemed and respected then?" he said, sarcastically.

"And what are you?" inquired Catherine, gazing curiously on the speaker. "That man I've seen before. Is he your son?"

"Miss Cathy," I interrupted, "it will be three hours instead of one that we are out presently. We really must go back."

"No, that man is not my son," answered Heathcliff, pushing me aside. "But I have one, and you have seen him before too; and, though your nurse is in a hurry, I think both you and she would be the better for a little rest. Will you just turn this nab of heath, and walk into my house? You'll get home earlier for the ease; and you shall receive a kind welcome."

"Mr. Heathcliff, it's very wrong," I continued; "you know you mean no good. And there she'll see Linton, and all will be told as soon as ever we return; and I shall have the blame."

"I want her to see Linton," he answered; "he's looking better these few days: it's not often he's fit to be seen. And we'll soon persuade her to keep the visit secret: where is the harm of it?"

"The harm of it is, that her father would hate me if he found I suffered her to enter your house; and I am convinced you have a bad design in encouraging her to do so," I replied.

"My design is as honest as possible. I'll inform you of its whole scope," he said. "That the two cousins may fall in love, and get married. I'm acting generously to your master: his young chit has no expectations, and should she second my wishes, she'll be provided for at once as joint successor with Linton."

"If Linton died," I answered, "and his life is quite uncertain, Catherine would be the heir."

"No, she would not," he said. "There is no clause in the will to secure it so: his property would go to me; but, to prevent disputes, I desire their union, and am resolved to bring it about."

"And I'm resolved she shall never approach your house with me again," I returned, as we reached the gate, where Miss Cathy waited our coming.

Heathcliff bade me be quiet; and, preceding us up the path, hastened to open the door. My young lady gave him several looks, as if she could not exactly make up her mind what to think of him; but now he smiled when he met her eye, and softened his voice in addressing her; and I was foolish enough to imagine the memory of her mother might disarm him from desiring her injury. Linton stood on the hearth. He had been out walking in the fields, for his cap was on, and he was calling to Joseph to bring him dry shoes. He had grown tall of his age, still wanting some months of sixteen. His features were pretty yet, and his eye and complexion brighter than I remembered them, though with merely temporary lustre borrowed from the salubrious air and genial sun.

"Now, who is that?" asked Mr. Heathcliff, turning to Cathy. "Can you tell?"

"Your son?" she said, having doubtfully surveyed, first one and then the other.

"Yes, yes," answered he: "but is this the only time you have beheld him? Think! Ah! you have a short memory. Linton, don't you recall your cousin, that you used to tease us so with wishing to see?"

"What, Linton!" cried Cathy, kindling into joyful surprise at the name. "Is that little Linton? He's taller than I am! Are you Linton?"

The youth stepped forward, and acknowledged himself: she kissed him fervently, and they gazed with wonder at the change time had wrought in the appearance of each. Catherine had reached her full height; her figure was both plump and slender, elastic as steel, and her whole aspect sparkling with health and spirits. Linton's looks and movements were very languid, and his form extremely slight; but there was a grace in his manner that mitigated these defects, and rendered him not unpleasing. After exchanging numerous marks of fondness with him, his cousin went to Mr. Heathcliff, who lingered by the door, dividing his attention between the objects inside and those that lay without: pretending, that is, to observe the latter, and really noting the former alone.

"And you are my uncle, then!" she cried, reaching up to salute him. "I thought I liked you, though you were cross at first. Why don't you visit the Grange with Linton? To live all these years such close neighbours, and never see us, is odd: what have you done so for?"

"I visited it once or twice too often before you were born," he answered. "There—damn it! If you have any kisses to spare, give them to Linton: they are thrown away on me."

"Wouldn't you rather sit here?" asked Linton, addressing Cathy in a tone which expressed reluctance to move again.

"I don't know," she replied, casting a longing look to the door, and evidently eager to be active.

He kept his seat, and shrank closer to the fire. Heathcliff rose, and went into the kitchen, and from thence to the yard, calling out for Hareton. Hareton responded, and presently the two re-entered. The young man had been washing himself, as was visible by the glow on his cheeks and his wetted hair.

"Oh, I'll ask *you*, uncle," cried Miss Cathy, recollecting the housekeeper's assertion. "That is not my cousin, is he?"

"Yes," he replied, "your mother's nephew. Don't you like him?"

Catherine looked queer.

"Is he not a handsome lad?" he continued.

The uncivil little thing stood on tiptoe, and whispered a sentence in Heathcliff's ear. He laughed; Hareton darkened: I perceived he was very sensitive to suspected slights, and had obviously a dim notion of his inferiority. But his master or guardian chased the frown by exclaiming—

"You'll be the favourite among us, Hareton! She says you are a—What was it? Well, something very flattering. Here! you go with her round the farm. And behave like a gentleman, mind! Don't use any bad words; and don't stare when the young lady is not looking at you and be ready to hide your face when she is; and, when you speak, say your words slowly, and keep your hands out of your pockets. Be off, and entertain her as nicely as you can."

Heathcliff chuckled a fiendish laugh at the idea. I made no reply, because I saw that he expected none. Meantime, our young companion, who sat too removed from us to hear what was said, began to evince symptoms of uneasiness, probably repenting that he had denied himself the treat of Catherine's society for fear of a little fatigue. His father remarked the restless glances wandering to the window, and the hand irresolutely extended towards his cap.

"Get up, you idle boy!" he exclaimed, with assumed heartiness. "Away after them! they are just at the corner, by the stand of hives."

Linton gathered his energies, and left the hearth. The lattice was open, and, as he stepped out, I heard Cathy inquiring of her unsociable attendant, what was that inscription over the door? Hareton stared up, and scratched his head like a true clown.

"It's some damnable writing," he answered. "I cannot read it."

"Can't read it?" cried Catherine; "I can read it: it's English. But I want to know why it is there."

Linton giggled: the first appearance of mirth he had exhibited.

"He does not know his letters," he said to his cousin. "Could you believe in the existence of such a colossal dunce?"

"Is he all as he should be?" asked Miss Cathy, seriously; "or is he simple: not right? I've questioned him twice now, and each time he looked so stupid I think he does not understand me. I can hardly understand *him*, I'm sure!"

Linton repeated his laugh, and glanced at Hareton tauntingly; who certainly did not seem quite clear of comprehension at that moment.

"There's nothing the matter but laziness; is there, Earnshaw?" he said. "My cousin fancies you are an idiot. There you experience the consequence of scorning 'book-larning,' as you would say. Have you noticed, Catherine, his frightful Yorkshire pronounciation?"

"Why, where the devil is the use on't?" growled Hareton, more ready in answering his daily companion. He was about to enlarge further, but the two youngsters broke into a noisy fit of merriment; my giddy miss being delighted to discover that she might turn his strange talk to matter of amusement.

"Where is the use of the devil in that sentence?" tittered Linton. "Papa told you not to say any bad words, and you can't open your mouth without one. Do try to behave like a gentleman, now do!"

"If thou weren't more a lass than a lad, I'd fell thee this minute, I would; pitiful lath of a crater!" retorted the angry boor, retreating, while his face burnt with mingled rage and mortification; for he was conscious of being insulted, and embarrassed how to resent it.

We staid till afternoon: I could not tear Miss Cathy away sooner; but happily my master had not yet quitted his apartment, and remained ignorant of our prolonged absence. As we walked home, I would fain have enlightened my charge on the characters of the people we had quitted; but she got it into her head that I was prejudiced against them.

"Aha!" she cried, "you take papa's side, Ellen: you are partial I know; or else you wouldn't have cheated me so many years into the notion that Linton lived a long way from here. I'm really extremely angry; only I'm so pleased I can't show it! But you must hold your tongue about my uncle: he's *my* uncle, remember: and I'll scold papa for quarrelling with him."

And so she ran on, till I relinquished the endeavour to convince her of her mistake. She did not mention the visit that night, because she did not see Mr. Linton. Next day it all came out, sadly to my chagrin; and still I was not altogether sorry: I thought the burden of directing and warning would be more efficiently borne by him than me. But he was too timid in giving satisfactory reasons for his wish that she should shun connection with the household of the Heights, and Catherine liked good reasons for every restraint that harassed her petted will.

"Papa!" she exclaimed, after the morning's salutations, "guess whom I saw yesterday, in my walk on the moors. Ah, papa, you started! you've not done right, have you, now? I saw—But listen, and you shall hear how I found you out; and Ellen, who is in league with you, and yet pretended to pity me so, when I kept hoping, and was always disappointed about Linton's coming back!"

She gave a faithful account of her excursion and its consequences; and my master, though he cast more than one reproachful look at me, said nothing till she had concluded. Then he drew her to him, and asked if she knew why he had concealed Linton's near neighbourhood from her? Could she think it was to deny her a pleasure that she might harmlessly enjoy?

"Then you believe I care more for my own feelings than yours, Cathy?" he said. "No, it was not because I disliked Mr. Heathcliff, but because Mr. Heathcliff dislikes me; and is a most diabolical man, delighting to wrong and ruin those he hates, if they give him the slightest opportunity. I knew that you could not keep up an acquaintance with your cousin, without being brought into contact with him; and I knew he would detest you on my account; so for your own good, and nothing else, I took precautions that you should not see Linton again. I meant to explain this some time as you grew older, and I'm sorry I delayed it."

"But Mr. Heathcliff was quite cordial, papa," observed Catherine, not at all convinced; "and *he* didn't object to our seeing each other: he said I might come to his house when I pleased; only I must not tell you, because you had quarrelled with him, and would not forgive him for marrying aunt Isabella. And you won't. *You* are the one to be blamed: he is willing to let *us* be friends, at least; Linton and I; and you are not."

My master, perceiving that she would not take his word for her uncle-in-law's evil disposition, gave a hasty sketch of his conduct to Isabella, and the manner in which Wuthering Heights became his property. He could not bear to discourse long upon the topic; for though he spoke little of it, he still felt the same horror and detestation of his ancient enemy that had occupied his heart ever since Mrs. Linton's death. "She might have been living yet, if it had not been for him!" was his constant bitter reflection; and, in his eyes, Heathcliff seemed a murderer. Miss Cathy—conversant with no bad deeds except her own slight acts of disobedience, injustice, and passion, arising from hot temper, thoughtlessness, and re-pented of on the day they were committed—was amazed at the blackness of spirit that could brood on and cover revenge for years, and deliberately prosecute its plans without a visitation of remorse. She appeared so deeply impressed and shocked at this new view of human nature—excluded from all her studies and all her ideas till now—that Mr. Edgar deemed it un-necessary to pursue the subject. He merely added,—

"You will know hereafter, darling, why I wish you to avoid his house and family; now return to your old employments and amusements, and think no more about them."

Catherine kissed her father, and sat down quietly to her lessons for a couple of hours, according to custon; then she accompanied him into the grounds, and the whole day passed as usual: but in the evening, when she had retired to her room, and I went to help her to undress, I found her crying, on her knees, by the bedside.

"Oh, fie, silly child!" I exclaimed. "If you had any real griefs, you'd be ashamed to waste a tear on this little contrariety. You never had one shadow of substantial sorrow, Miss Catherine. Suppose, for a minute, that master and I were dead, and you were by yourself in the world: how would you feel, then? Compare the present occasion with such an affliction as that, and be thankful for the friends you have, instead of coveting more."

"I'm not crying for myself, Ellen," she answered, "it's for him. He ex-pected to see me again to-morrow, and there he'll be so disappointed: and he'll wait for me, and I shan't come!"

"Nonsense!" said I, "do you imagine he has thought as much of you as you have of him? Hasn't he Hareton for a companion? Not one in a hun-dred would weep at losing a relation they had just seen twice, for two after-noons. Linton will conjecture how it is, and trouble himself no further about you."

"But may I not write a note to tell him why I cannot come?" she asked, rising to her feet. "And just send those books, I promised to lend him? His books are not as nice as mine, and he wanted to have them extremely, when I told him how interesting they were. May I not, Ellen?"

"No, indeed! no, indeed!" replied I with decision. "Then he would write to you, and there'd never be an end of it. No, Miss Catherine, the acquaintance must be dropped entirely: so papa expects, and I shall see that it is done."

"But how can  one little note——" she recommenced, putting on an imploring countenance.

"Silence!" I interrupted. "We'll not begin with your little notes. Get into bed."

She threw at me a very naughty look, so naughty that I would not kiss her good-night at first: I covered her up, and shut her door, in great displeasure; but, repenting half-way, I returned softly, and lo! there was miss standing at the table with a bit of blank paper before her and a pencil in her hand, which she guiltily slipped out of sight, on my entrance.

"You'll get nobody to take that, Catherine," I said, "if you write it; and at present I shall put out your candle."

I set the extinguisher on the flame, receiving as I did so a slap on my hand, and a petulant "cross thing!" I then quitted her again, and she drew the bolt in one of her worst, most peevish humours. The letter was finished and forwarded to its destination by a milk-fetcher who came from the village: but that I didn't learn till some time afterwards. Weeks passed on, and Cathy recovered her temper; though she grew wondrous fond of stealing off to corners by herself; and often, if I came near her suddenly while reading, she would start and bend over the book, evidently desirous to hide it; and I detected edges of loose paper sticking out beyond the leaves. She also got a trick of coming down early in the morning and lingering about the kitchen, as if she were expecting the arrival of something: and she had a small drawer in a cabinet in the library, which she would trifle over for hours, and whose key she took special care to remove when she left it.

One day, as she inspected this drawer, I observed that the playthings, and trinkets which recently formed its contents, were transmuted into bits of folded paper. My curiosity and suspicions were roused; I determined to take a peep at her mysterious treasures; so, at night, as soon as she and my master were safe upstairs, I searched and readily found among my house keys one that would fit the lock. Having opened, I emptied the whole contents into my apron, and took them with me to examine at leisure in my own chamber. Though I could not but suspect, I was still surprised to discover that they were a mass of correspondence—daily almost, it must have been—from Linton Heathcliff: answers to documents forwarded by her. The earlier dated were embarrassed and short; gradually, however, they expanded into copious love letters, foolish, as the age of the writer rendered natural, yet with touches here and there which I thought were borrowed from a more experienced source. Some of them struck me as singularly odd compounds of ardour and flatness; commencing in strong feeling, and concluding in the affected, wordy style that a schoolboy might use to a fancied, incorporeal sweetheart. Whether they satisfied Cathy, I don't know; but they appeared very worthless trash to me. After turning over as many as I thought proper, I tied them in a handkerchief and set them aside, re-locking the vacant drawer.

Following her habit, my young lady descended early, and visited the kitchen: I watched her go to the door, on the arrival of a certain little boy; and, while the dairy-maid filled his can, she tucked something into his jacket pocket, and plucked something out. I went round by the garden, and laid wait for the messenger; who fought valorously to defend his trust, and we spilt the milk between us; but I succeeded in abstracting the epistle; and, threatening serious consequences if he did not look sharp home, I remained under the wall and perused Miss Cathy's affectionate composition. It was more simple and more eloquent than her cousin's;: very pretty and very silly. I shook my head, and went meditating into the house. The day being wet, she could not divert herself with rambling about the park; so at the conclusion of her morning studies, she resorted to the solace of the drawer. Her father sat reading at the table; and I, on purpose, had sought a bit of work in some unripped fringes of the window curtain, keeping my eye steadily fixed on her proceedings. Never did any bird flying back to the plundered nest which it had left brimful of chirping young ones, express more complete despair in its anguished cries and flutterings, than she by her single "Oh!" and the change that transfigured her late happy countenance. Mr. Linton looked up.

"What is the matter, love? Have you hurt yourself?" he said.

His tone and look assured her *he* had not been the discoverer of the hoard.

"No, papa!" she gasped. "Ellen! Ellen! come upstairs—I'm sick!"

I obeyed her summons, and accompanied her out.

"Oh, Ellen! you have got them," she commenced immediately, dropping on her knees, when we were enclosed alone. "Oh, give them to me, and I'll never, never do so again! Don't tell papa. You have not told papa, Ellen? say you have not? I've been exceedingly naughty, but I won't do it any more!"

With a grave severity in my manner, I bade her stand up.

"So," I exclaimed, "Miss Catherine, you are tolerably far on, it seems: you may well be ashamed of them! A fine bundle of trash you study in your leisure hours, to be sure: why it's good enough to be printed! And what do you suppose the master will think, when I display it before him? I haven't shown it yet, but you needn't imagine I shall keep your ridiculous secrets. For shame! and you must have led the way in writing such absurdities: he would not have thought of beginning, I'm certain."

"I didn't! I didn't!" sobbed Cathy, fit to break her heart. "I didn't once think of loving him till——"

"*Loving!*" cried I, as scornfully as I could utter the word. "*Loving!* Did anybody ever hear the like! I might just as well talk of loving the miller who comes once a year to buy our corn. Pretty loving, indeed! and both times together you have seen Linton hardly four hours in your life! Now here is the babyish trash. I'm going with it to the Library; and we'll see what your father says to such *loving.*"

She sprang at her precious epistles, but I held them above my head; and then she poured out further frantic entreaties that I would burn them—do anything rather than show them. And being really fully as much inclined to laugh as scold—for I esteemed it all girlish vanity—I at length relented in a measure, and asked,—

"If I consent to burn them, will you promise faithfully, neither to send nor receive a letter again, nor a book (for I perceive you have sent him books), nor locks of hair, nor rings, nor playthings?"

"We don't send playthings!" cried Catherine, her pride overcoming her shame.

"Nor anything at all, then, my lady," I said. "Unless you will, here I go."

"I promise, Ellen!" she cried, catching my dress. "Oh, put them in the fire, do, do!"

But when I proceeded to open a place with the poker, the sacrifice was too painful to be borne. She earnestly supplicated that I would spare her one or two.

"One or two, Ellen, to keep for Linton's sake!"

I unknotted the handkerchief, and commenced dropping them in from an angle, and the flame curled up the chimney.

"I will have one, you cruel wretch!" she screamed, darting her hand into the fire, and drawing forth some half-consumed fragments, at the expense of her fingers.

"Very well—and I will have some to exhibit to papa!" I answered, shaking back the rest into the bundle, and turning anew to the door.

She emptied her blackened pieces into the flames, and motioned me to finish the immolation. It was done; I stirred up the ashes, and interred them under a shovelfull of coals; and she mutely, and with a sense of intense injury, retired to her private apartment. I descended to tell my master that the young lady's qualm of sickness was almost gone, but I judged it best for her to lie down a while. She wouldn't dine; but she reappeared at tea, pale, and red about the eyes, and marvellously subdued in outward aspect. Next morning, I answered the letter by a slip of paper, inscribed, "Master Heathcliff is requested to send no more notes to Miss Linton, as she will not receive them." And, thenceforth, the little boy came with vacant pockets.

# Chapter 22

SUMMER drew to an end, and early autumn: it was past Michaelmas, but the harvest was late that year, and a few of our fields were still uncleared. Mr. Linton and his daughter would frequently walk out among the reapers; at the carrying of the last sheaves, they stayed till dusk, and the evening happening to be chill and damp, my master caught a bad cold that settled obstinately on his lungs, and confined him indoors throughout the whole of the winter, nearly without intermission.

Poor Cathy, frightened from her little romance, had been considerably sadder and duller since its abandonment; and her father insisted on her reading less, and taking more exercise. She had his companionship no longer; I esteemed it a duty to supply its lack, as much as possible, with mine: an inefficient substitute; for I could only spare two or three hours, from my numerous diurnal occupations, to follow her footsteps, and then my society was obviously less desirable than his.

On an afternoon in October, or the beginning of November—a fresh watery afternoon, when the turf and paths were rustling with moist, withered leaves, and the cold, blue sky was half hidden by clouds—dark grey streamers, rapidly mounting from the west, and boding abundant rain—I requested my young lady to forego her ramble, because I was certain of showers. She refused; and I unwillingly donned a cloak, and took my umbrella to accompany her on a stroll to the bottom of the park: a formal walk which she generally affected if low-spirited—and that she invariably was when Mr. Edgar had been worse than ordinary, a thing never known from his confession, but guessed both by her and me, from his increased silence and the melancholy of his countenance. She went sadly on: there was no running or bounding now, though the chill wind might well have tempted her to race. And often, from the side of my eye, I could detect her raising a hand, and brushing something off her cheek. I gazed round for a means of diverting her thoughts. On one side of the road rose a high, rough bank, where hazels and stunted oaks, with their roots half-exposed, held uncertain tenure: the soil was too loose for the latter; and strong winds had blown some nearly horizontal. In summer, Miss Catherine delighted to climb along these trunks, and sit in the branches, swinging twenty feet above the ground; and I, pleased with her agility and her light, childish heart, still considered it proper to scold every time I caught her at such an elevation, but so that she knew there was no real necessity for descending. From dinner to tea she would lie in her breeze-rocked cradle, doing nothing except singing old songs—my nursery lore—to herself, or watching the birds, joint tenants, feed and entice their young ones to fly: or nestling with closed lids, half thinking, half dreaming, happier than words can express.

"Look, miss!" I exclaimed, pointing to a nook under the roots of one twisted tree. "Winter is not here yet. There's a little flower up yonder, the last bud from the multitude of blue-bells that clouded those turf steps in July with a lilac mist. Will you clamber up, and pluck it to show to papa?"

Cathy stared a long time at the lonely blossom trembling in its earthy shelter, and replied, at length—

"No, I'll not touch it: but it looks melancholy, does it not, Ellen?"

"Yes," I observed, "about as starved and sackless as you: your cheeks are bloodless; let us take hold of hands and run. You're so low, I dare say I shall keep up with you."

"No," she repeated, and continued sauntering on, pausing, at intervals, to muse over a bit of moss, or a tuft of blanched grass, or a fungus spreading its bright orange among the heaps of brown foliage; and, ever and anon, her hand was lifted to her averted face.

"Catherine, why are you crying, love?" I asked, approaching and putting my arm over her shoulder. "You mustn't cry, because papa has a cold; be thankful it is nothing worse."

She now put no further restraint on her tears; her breath was stifled by sobs.

"Oh, it *will* be something worse," she said. "And what shall I do when papa and you leave me, and I am by myself? I can't forget your words, Ellen; they are always in my ear. How life will be changed, how dreary the world will be, when papa and you are dead."

"None can tell, whether you won't die before us," I replied. "It's wrong to anticipate evil. We'll hope there are years and years to come before any of us go: master is young, and I am strong, and hardly forty-five. My mother lived till eighty, a canty dame to the last. And suppose Mr. Linton were spared till he saw sixty, that would be more years than you have counted, miss. And would it not be foolish to mourn a calamity above twenty years beforehand?"

"But Aunt Isabella was younger than papa," she remarked, gazing up with timid hope to seek further consolation.

"Aunt Isabella had not you and me to nurse her," I replied. "She wasn't as happy as master: she hadn't as much to live for. All you need do, is to wait well on your father, and cheer him by letting him see you cheerful; and avoid him anxiety on any subject: mind that, Cathy! I'll not disguise but you might kill him, if you were wild and reckless, and cherished a foolish, fanciful affection for the son of a person who would be glad to have him in his grave; and allowed him to discover that you fretted over the separation he has judged it expedient to make."

"I fret about nothing on earth except papa's illness," answered my companion. "I care for nothing in comparison with papa. And I'll never—never—oh, never, while I have my senses, do an act or say a word to vex him. I love him better than myself, Ellen; and I know it by this: I pray every night that I may live after him; because I would rather be

96

miserable than that he should be: that proves I love him better than myself."

"Good words," I replied. "But deeds must prove it also; and after he is well, remember you don't forget resolutions formed in the hour of fear."

As we talked, we neared a door that opened on the road; and my young lady, lightening into sunshine again, climbed up and seated herself on the top of the wall, reaching over to gather some hips that bloomed scarlet on the summer branches of the wild rose trees, shadowing the highway side: the lower fruit had disappeared, but only birds could touch the upper, except from Cathy's present station. In stretching to pull them, her hat fell off; and as the door was locked, she proposed scrambling down to recover it. I bid her be cautious lest she got a fall, and she nimbly disappeared. But the return was no such easy matter: the stones were smooth and neatly cemented, and the rosebushes and blackberry stragglers could yield no assistance in re-ascending. I, like a fool, didn't recollect that, till I heard her laughing and exclaiming—

"Ellen! you'll have to fetch the key, or else I must run round to the porter's lodge. I can't scale the ramparts on this side!"

"Stay where you are," I answered, "I have my bundle of keys in my pocket: perhaps I may manage to open it; if not, I'll go."

Catherine amused herself with dancing to and fro before the door, while I tried all the large keys in succession. I had applied the last, and found that none would do; so, repeating my desire that she would remain there, I was about to hurry home as fast as I could, when an approaching sound arrested me. It was the trot of a horse; Cathy's dance stopped also.

"Who is that?" I whispered.

"Ellen, I wish you could open the door," whispered back my companion, anxiously.

"Ho, Miss Linton!" cried a deep voice (the rider's), "I'm glad to meet you. Don't be in haste to enter, for I have an explanation to ask and obtain."

"I shan't speak to you, Mr. Heathcliff," answered Catherine. "Papa says you are a wicked man, and you hate both him and me; and Ellen says the same."

"That is nothing to the purpose," said Heathcliff. (He it was.) "I don't hate my son, I suppose; and it is concerning him that I demand your attention. Yes; you have cause to blush. Two or three months since, were you not in the habit of writing to Linton? making love in play, eh? You deserved, both of you, flogging for that! You especially, the elder; and less sensitive, as it turns out. I've got your letters, and if you give me any pertness I'll send them to your father. I presume you grew weary of the amusement and dropped it, didn't you? Well, you dropped Linton with it into a Slough of Despond. He was in earnest: in love, really. As true as I live, he's dying for you; breaking his heart at your fickleness: not figuratively, but actually. Though Hareton has made him a standing jest for six weeks, and I have used more serious measures, and attempted to frighten him out of his idiocy, he gets worse daily; and he'll be under the sod before summer, unless you restore him!"

"How can you lie so glaringly to the poor child?" I called from the inside. "Pray ride on! How can you deliberately get up such paltry false-hoods? Miss Cathy, I'll knock the lock off with a stone: you won't believe that vile nonsense. You can feel in yourself, it is impossible that a person should die for love of a stranger."

"I was not aware there were eaves-droppers," muttered the detected villain. "Worthy Mrs. Dean, I like you, but I don't like your double-dealing," he added aloud. "How could *you* lie so glaringly, as to affirm I hated the 'poor child?' and invent bugbear stories to terrify her from my door-stones? Catherine Linton (the very name warms me), my bonny lass, I shall be from home all this week; go and see if I have not spoken truth: do, there's a darling! Just imagine your father in my place, and Linton in yours; then think how you would value your careless lover if he refused to stir a step to comfort you, when your father himself entreated him; and don't, from pure stupidity, fall into the same error. I swear, on my salvation, he's going to his grave, and none but you can save him!"

The lock gave way and I issued out.

"I swear Linton is dying," repeated Heathcliff, looking hard at me. "And grief and disappointment are hastening his death. Nelly, if you won't let her go, you can walk over yourself. But I shall not return till this time next week; and I think your master himself would scarcely object to her visiting her cousin!"

"Come in," said I, taking Cathy by the arm and half forcing her to re-enter; for she lingered, viewing with troubled eyes the features of the speaker, too stern to express his inward deceit.

He pushed his horse close, and, bending down, observed:

"Miss Catherine, I'll own to you that I have little patience with Linton; and Hareton and Joseph have less. I'll own that he's with a harsh set. He pines for kindness, as well as love; and a kind word from you would be his best medicine. Don't mind Mrs. Dean's cruel cautions; but be generous, and contrive to see him. He dreams of you day and night, and cannot be persuaded that you don't hate him, since you neither write nor call."

I closed the door, and rolled a stone to assist the loosened lock in hold-ing it; and spreading my umbrella, I drew my charge underneath: for the rain began to drive through the moaning branches of the trees, and warned us to avoid delay. Our hurry prevented any comment on the en-counter with Heathcliff, as we stretched towards home; but I divined in-stinctively that Catherine's heart was clouded now in double darkness. Her features were so sad, they did not seem hers: she evidently regarded what she had heard as every syllable true.

The master had retired to rest before we came in. Cathy stole to his room to inquire how he was; he had fallen asleep. She returned, and asked me to sit with her in the library. We took our tea together; and afterwards she lay down on the rug, and told me not to talk, for she was weary. I got a book, and pretended to read. As soon as she supposed me absorbed in my occupation, she recommenced her silent weeping; it appeared, at present, her favourite diversion. I suffered her to enjoy it a while; then I expostulated: deriding and ridiculing all Mr. Heathcliff's assertions about his son, as if I were certain she would coincide. Alas! I hadn't skill to counteract the effect his account had produced: it was just what he intended.

"You may be right, Ellen," she answered; "but I shall never feel at ease till I know. And I must tell Linton it is not my fault that I don't write, and convince him that I shall not change."

What use were anger and protestations against her silly credulity? We parted that night—hostile; but next day beheld me on the road to Wuthering Heights, by the side of my wilful young mistress's pony. I couldn't bear to witness her sorrow: to see her pale, dejected countenance, and heavy eyes; and I yielded, in the faint hope that Linton himself might prove, by his reception of us, how little of the tale was founded on fact.

## Chapter 23

THE rainy night had ushered in a misty morning—half-frost, half-drizzle— and temporary brooks crossed our path—gurgling from the uplands. My feet were thoroughly wetted; I was cross and low; exactly the humour suited for making the most of these disagreeable things. We entered the farmhouse by the kitchenway, to ascertain whether Mr. Heathcliff were really absent: but I put slight faith in his own affirmation.

Joseph seemed sitting in a sort of elysium alone, beside a roaring fire, a quart of ale on the table near him, bristling with large pieces of toasted oat-cake; and his black, short pipe in his mouth. Catherine ran to the hearth to warm herself. I asked if the master were in? My question remained so long unanswered, that I thought the old man had grown deaf, and repeated it louder.

"Na—ay!" he snarled, or rather screamed through his nose. "Na—ay! yah muh goa back whear yah coom frough."

"Joseph!" cried a peevish voice, simultaneously with me, from the inner room. "How often am I to call you? There are only a few red ashes now. Joseph! come this moment."

Vigorous puffs, and a resolute stare into the grate declared he had no ear for this appeal. The housekeeper and Hareton were invisible; one gone on an errand, and the other at his work, probably. We knew Linton's tones, and entered.

"Oh, I hope you'll die in a garret! starved to death," said the boy, mistaking our approach for that of his negligent attendant.

He stopped, on observing his error; his cousin flew to him.

"Is that you, Miss Linton?" he said, raising his head from the arm of the great chair, in which he reclined. "No—don't kiss me: it takes my breath. Dear me! Papa said you would call," continued he, after recovering a little from Catherine's embrace: while she stood by looking very contrite. "Will you shut the door, if you please? you left it open; and those—those *detestable* creatures won't bring coals to the fire. It's so cold!"

I stirred up the cinders, and fetched a scuttle full myself. The invalid complained of being covered with ashes; but he had a tiresome cough, and looked feverish and ill, so I did not rebuke his temper.

"Well, Linton," murmured Catherine, when his corrugated brow relaxed. "Are you glad to see me? Can I do you any good?"

"Why didn't you come before?" he asked. "You should have come, instead of writing. It tired me dreadfully, writing those long letters. I'd far rather have talked to you. Now, I can neither bear to talk, nor anything else. I wonder where Zillah is! Will you (looking at me) step into the kitchen and see?"

I had received no thanks for my other service; and being unwilling to run to and fro at his behest, I replied—

"Nobody is out there but Joseph."

"I want to drink," he exclaimed fretfully, turning away. "Zillah is constantly gadding off to Gimmerton since papa went: it's miserable! And I'm obliged to come down here—they resolved never to hear me upstairs."

"Is your father attentive to you, Master Heathcliff?" I asked, perceiving Catherine to be checked in her friendly advances.

"Attentive? He makes *them* a little more attentive at least," he cried. "The wretches! Do you know, Miss Linton, that brute Hareton laughs at me! I hate him! indeed, I hate them all: they are odious beings."

Cathy began searching for some water; she lighted on a pitcher in the dresser, filled a tumbler, and brought it. He bid her add a spoonful of wine from a bottle on the table; and having swallowed a small portion, appeared more tranquil, and said she was very kind.

"And are you glad to see me?" asked she, reiterating her former question, and pleased to detect the faint dawn of a smile.

"Yes, I am. It's something new to hear a voice like yours!" he replied. "But I have been vexed, because you wouldn't come. And papa swore it was owing to me: he called me a pitiful, shuffling, worthless thing; and said you despised me; and if he had been in my place, he would be more the master of the Grange than your father, by this time. But you don't despise me, do you Miss——"

100

"I wish you would say Catherine, or Cathy," interrupted my young lady. "Despise you? No! Next to papa and Ellen, I love you better than anybody living. I don't love Mr. Heathcliff, though; and I dare not come when he returns: will he stay away many days?"

"Not many," answered Linton; "but he goes on to the moors frequently, since the shooting season commenced; and you might spend an hour or two with me in his absense. Do say you will. I think I should not be peevish with you: you'd not provoke me, and you'd always be ready to help me, wouldn't you?"

"Yes," said Catherine, stroking his long soft hair; "if I could only get papa's consent, I'd spend half my time with you. Pretty Linton! I wish you were my brother."

"And then you would like me as well as your father?" observed he, more cheerfully. "But papa says you would love me better than him and all the world, if you were my wife; so I'd rather you were that."

"No, I should never love anybody better than papa," she returned gravely. "And people hate their wives sometimes; but not their sisters and brothers: and if you were the latter, you would live with us, and papa would be as fond of you as he is of me."

Linton denied that people ever hated their wives; but Cathy affirmed they did, and in her wisdom, instanced his own father's aversion to her aunt. I endeavoured to stop her thoughtless tongue. I couldn't succeed till everything she knew was out. Master Heathcliff, much irritated, asserted her relation was false.

"Papa told me; and papa not does tell falsehoods," she answered pertly.

"*My* papa scorns yours!" cried Linton. "He calls him a sneaking fool."

"Yours is a wicked man," retorted Catherine; "and you are very naughty to dare to repeat what he says. He must be wicked to have made Aunt Isabella leave him as she did."

"She didn't leave him," said the boy: "you shan't contradict me."

"She did," cried my young lady.

"Well, I'll tell *you* something!" said Linton. "Your mother hated your father: now then."

"Oh!" exclaimed Catherine, too enraged to continue.

"And she loved mine," added he.

"You little liar! I hate you now!" She panted, and her face grew red with passion.

"She did! she did!" sang Linton, sinking into the recess of his chair, and leaning back his head to enjoy the agitation of the other disputant, who stood behind.

"Hush, Master Heathcliff!" I said; "that's your father's tale, too, I suppose."

"It isn't: you hold your tongue!" he answered. "She did, she did, Catherine! she did, she did!"

Cathy, beside herself, gave the chair a violent push, and caused him to

101

fall against one arm. He was immediately seized by a suffocating cough that soon ended his triumph. It lasted so long that it frightened even me. As to his cousin, she wept with all her might: aghast at the mischief she had done: though she said nothing. I held him till the fit exhausted itself. Then he thrust me away, and leant his head down silently. Catherine quelled her lamentations also, took a seat opposite, and looked solemnly into the fire.

"How do you feel now, Master Heathcliff?" I inquired, after waiting ten minutes.

"I wish *she* felt as I do," he replied: "spiteful, cruel thing! Hareton never touches me: he never struck me in his life. And I was better to-day: and there——" his voice died on a whimper.

"*I* didn't strike you!" muttered Cathy, chewing her lip to prevent another burst of emotion.

He sighed and moaned like one under great suffering, and kept it up for a quarter of an hour; on purpose to distress his cousin apparently, for whenever he caught a stifled sob from her he put renewed pain and pathos into the inflections of his voice.

"I'm sorry I hurt you, Linton," she said at length, racked beyond endurance. "But *I* couldn't have been hurt by that little push, and I had no idea that you could, either: you're not much, are you, Linton? Don't let me go home thinking I've done you harm. Answer! speak to me."

"I can't speak to you," he murmured; "you've hurt me so, that I shall lie awake all night choking with this cough. If you had it you'd know what it was: but *you'll* be comfortably asleep while I'm in agony, and nobody near me. I wonder how you would like to pass those fearful nights!" And he began to wail aloud, for very pity of himself.

"Since you are in the habit of passing dreadful nights," I said, "it won't be miss who spoils your ease: you'd be the same had she never come. However, she shall not disturb you again; and perhaps you'll get quieter when we leave you."

"Must I go?" asked Catherine dolefully, bending over him. "Do you want me to go, Linton?"

"You can't alter what you've done," he replied pettishly, shrinking from her, "unless you alter it for the worse by teasing me into a fever."

"Well, then, I must go?" she repeated.

"Let me alone, at least," said he; "I can't bear your talking."

She lingered, and resisted my persuasions to depart a tiresome while; but as he neither looked up nor spoke, she finally made a movement to the door and I followed. We were recalled by a scream. Linton had slid from his seat on to the hearthstone, and lay writhing in the mere perverseness of an indulged plague of a child, determined to be as grievous and harassing as it can. I thoroughly gauged his disposition from his behaviour, and saw at once it would be folly to attempt humouring him. Not so my companion: she ran back in terror, knelt down, and cried, and

102

soothed and entreated, till he grew quiet from lack of breath: by no means from compunction at distressing her.

"I shall lift him on to the settle," I said, "and he may roll about as he pleases: we can't stop to watch him. I hope you are satisfied, Miss Cathy, that *you* are not the person to benefit him; and that his condition of health is not occasioned by attachment to you. Now, then, there he is! Come away: as soon as he knows there is nobody by to care for his nonsense, he'll be glad to lie still."

She placed a cushion under his head, and offered him some water; he rejected the latter, and tossed uneasily on the former, as if it were a stone or a block of wood. She tried to put it more comfortably.

"I can't do with that," he said; "it's not high enough."

Catherine brought another to lay above it.

"That's *too* high," murmured the provoking thing.

"How must I arrange it, then?" she asked despairingly.

He twined himself up to her, as she half knelt by the settle, and converted her shoulder into a support.

"No, that won't do," I said. "You'll be content with the cushion, Master Heathcliff. Miss has wasted so much time on you already: we cannot remain five minutes longer."

"Yes, yes, we can!" replied Cathy. "He's good and patient now. He's beginning to think I shall have far greater misery than he will to-night, if I believe he is the worse for my visit; and then I dare not come again. Tell the truth about it, Linton; for I mustn't come, if I have hurt you."

"You must come, to cure me," he answered. "You ought to come, because you have hurt me: you know you have extremely! I was not as ill when you entered as I am at present—was I?"

"But you've made yourself ill by crying and being in a passion."

"I didn't do it all," said his cousin. "However, we'll be friends now. And you want me: you would wish to see me sometimes, really?"

"I told you I did," he replied impatiently. "Sit on the settle and let me lean on your knee. That's as mamma used to do, whole afternoons together. Sit quite still and don't talk: but you may sing a song, if you can sing; or you may say a nice long interesting ballad—one of those you promised to teach me; or a story. I'd rather have a ballad, though: begin."

Catherine repeated the longest she could remember. The employment pleased both mightily. Linton would have another, and after that another, notwithstanding my strenuous objections; and so they went on till the clock struck twelve, and we heard Hareton in the court, returning for his dinner.

"And to-morrow, Catherine, will you be here to-morrow?" asked young Heathcliff, holding her frock as she rose reluctantly.

"No," I answered, "nor next day neither." She, however, gave a different response evidently, for his forehead cleared as she stooped and whispered in his ear.

"You won't go to-morrow, recollect, miss!" I commenced, when we were out of the house. "You are not dreaming of it, are you?"

She smiled.

"Oh, I'll take good care," I continued: "I'll have that lock mended, and you can escape by no way else."

"I can get over the wall," she said, laughing. "The Grange is not a prison, Ellen, and you are not my gaoler. And besides, I'm almost seventeen: I'm a woman. And I'm certain Linton would recover quickly if he had me to look after him. I'm older than he is, you know, and wiser: less childish, am I not? And he'll soon do as I direct him, with some slight coaxing. He's a pretty little darling when he's good. I'd make such a pet of him, if he were mine. We should never quarrel, should we, after we were used to each other? Don't you like him, Ellen?"

"Like him!" I exclaimed. "The worst-tempered bit of a sickly slip that ever struggled into its teens. Happily, as Mr. Heathcliff conjectured, he'll not win twenty. I doubt whether he'll see spring, indeed. And small loss to his family whenever he drops off. And lucky it is for us that his father took him: the kinder he was treated, the more tedious and selfish he'd be. I'm glad you have no chance of having him for a husband, Miss Catherine."

My companion waxed serious at hearing this speech. To speak of his death so regardlessly, wounded her feelings.

"He's younger than I," she answered, after a protracted pause of meditation, "and he ought to live the longest: he will—he must live as long as I do. He's as strong now as when he first came in to the north; I'm positive of that. It's only a cold that ails him, the same as papa has. You say papa will get better, and why shouldn't he?"

"Well, well," I cried, "after all, we needn't trouble ourselves; for listen, miss,—and mind, I'll keep my word,—if you attempt going to Wuthering Heights again, with or without me, I shall inform Mr. Linton, and, unless he allow it, the intimacy with your cousin must not be revived."

"It has been revived," muttered Cathy, sulkily.

"Must not be continued, then," I said.

"We'll see," was her reply, and she set off at a gallop, leaving me to toil in the rear.

We both reached home before our dinner-time; my master supposed we had been wandering through the park, and therefore he demanded no explanation of our absence. As soon as I entered, I hastened to change my soaked shoes and stockings; but sitting such a while at the Heights had done the mischief. On the succeeding morning I was laid up, and during three weeks I remained incapacitated for attending to my duties: a calamity never experienced prior to that period, and never, I am thankful to say, since.

My little mistress behaved like an angel, in coming to wait on me, and cheer my solitude: the confinement brought me exceedingly low. It is wearisome, to a stirring active body: but few have slighter reasons for complaint than I had. The moment Catherine left Mr. Linton's room, she appeared at my bed-side. Her day was divided between us; no amusement usurped a minute: she neglected her meals, her studies, and her play; and she was the fondest nurse that ever watched. She must have had a warm heart, when she loved her father so, to give so much to me. I said her days were divided between us; but the master retired early, and I generally needed nothing after six o'clock, thus the evening was her own. Poor thing! I never considered what she did with herself after tea. And though frequently, when she looked in to bid me good-night, I remarked a fresh colour in her cheeks and a pinkness over her slender fingers; instead of fancying the hue borrowed from a cold ride across the moors, I laid it to the charge of a hot fire in the library.

## Chapter 24

AT THE close of three weeks, I was able to quit my chamber, and move about the house. And on the first occasion of my sitting up in the evening, I asked Catherine to read to me, because my eyes were weak. We were in the library, the master having gone to bed: she consented, rather unwillingly, I fancied; and imagining my sort of books did not suit her, I bid her please herself in the choice of what she perused. She selected one of her own favourites, and got forward steadily about an hour; then came frequent questions.

"Ellen, are you not tired? Hadn't you better lie down now? You'll be sick, keeping up so long, Ellen."

"No, no, dear, I'm not tired," I returned, continually.

Perceiving me immovable, she essayed another method of showing her disrelish for her occupation. It changed to yawning and stretching, and—

"Ellen, I'm tired."

"Give over then and talk," I answered.

That was worse: she fretted and sighed, and looked at her watch till eight, and finally went to her room, completely overdone with sleep; judging by her peevish, heavy look, and the constant rubbing she inflicted on her eyes. The following night she seemed more impatient still; and on the third from recovering my company, she complained of a head-ache, and left me. I thought her conduct odd; and having remained alone a long while, I resolved on going and inquiring whether she were better, and asking her to come and lie on the sofa, instead of upstairs in the dark. No

Catherine could I discover upstairs, and none below. The servants affirmed they had not seen her. I listened at Mr. Edgar's door; all was silence. I returned to her apartment, extinguished my candle, and seated myself in the window.

The moon shone bright; a sprinkling of snow covered the ground, and I reflected that she might, possibly, have taken it into her head to walk about the garden, for refreshment. I did detect a figure creeping along the inner fence of the park; but it was not my young mistress: on its merging into the light, I recognised one of the grooms. He stood a considerable period, viewing the carriage-road through the grounds; then started off at a brisk pace, as if he had detected something, and reappeared presently, leading miss's pony; and there she was, just dismounted, and walking by its side. The man took his charge stealthily across the grass towards the stable. Cathy entered by the casement-window of the drawing-room, and glided noiselessly up to where I awaited her. She put the door gently too, slipped off her snowy shoes, untied her hat, and was proceeding, unconscious of my espionage, to lay aside her mantle, when I suddenly rose and revealed myself. The surprise petrified her an instant: she uttered an inarticulate exclamation, and stood fixed.

"My dear Miss Catherine," I began, too vividly impressed by ler recent kindness to break into a scold, "where have you been riding out at this hour? And why should you try to deceive me, by telling a tale? Where have you been? Speak."

"To the bottom of the park," she stammered. "I didn't tell a tale."

"And nowhere else?" I demanded.

"No," was the muttered reply.

"Oh, Catherine!" I cried, sorrowfully. "You know you have been doing wrong, or you wouldn't be driven to uttering an untruth to me. That does grieve me. I'd rather be three months ill, than hear you frame a deliberate lie."

She sprang forward, and bursting into tears, threw her arms round my neck.

"Well, Ellen, I'm so afraid of you being angry," she said. "Promise not to be angry, and you shall know the very truth: I hate to hide it."

We sat down in the window-seat; I assured her I would not scold, whatever her secret might be, and I guessed it, of course; so she commenced—

"I've been to Wuthering Heights, Ellen, and I've never missed going a day since you fell ill; except thrice before, and twice after you left your room. I gave Michael books and pictures to prepare Minny every evening, and to put her back in the stable: you mustn't scold *him* either, mind. I was at the Heights by half-past six, and generally stayed till half-past eight, and then galloped home. It was not to amuse myself that I went: I was often wretched all the time. Now and then I was happy: once in a week perhaps. At first, I expected there would be sad work persuading you to let me keep my word to Linton: for I had engaged to call again next day, when we quitted him; but, as you stayed up stairs on the morrow, I escaped that trouble. While Michael was refastening the lock of the park door in the afternoon, I got possession of the key, and told him how my cousin wished me to visit him, because he was sick, and couldn't come to the Grange; and how papa would object to my going: and then I negotiated with him about the pony. He is fond of reading, and he thinks of leaving soon to get married; so he offered, if I would lend him books out of the library, to do what I wished: but I preferred giving him my own, and that satisfied him better.

"On my second visit, Linton seemed in lively spirits; and Zillah (that is their housekeeper) made us a clean room and a good fire, and told us that, as Joseph was out at a prayer-meeting and Hareton Earnshaw was off with his dogs—robbing our woods of pheasants, as I heard afterwards—we might do what we liked. She brought me some warm wine and ginger-bread, and appeared exceedingly good-natured; and Linton sat in the arm-chair, and I in the little rocking-chair on the hearth-stone, and we laughed and talked so merrily, and found so much to say: we planned where we would go, and what we would do in summer. I needn't repeat that, because you would call it silly.

"One time, however, we were near quarrelling. He said the pleasantest manner of spending a hot July day was lying from morning till evening on a bank of heath in the middle of the moors, with the bees humming dreamily about among the bloom, and the larks singing high up over head, and the blue sky and bright sun shining steadily and cloudlessly. That was his most perfect idea of heaven's happiness: mine was rocking in a rustling green tree, with a west wind blowing, and bright white clouds flitting rapidly above; and not only larks, but throstles, and blackbirds, and linnets, and cuckoos pouring out music on every side, and the moors seen at a distance, broken into cool dusky dells; but close by great swells of long grass undulating in waves to the breeze; and woods and sounding water, and the whole world awake and wild with joy. He wanted all to lie in an ecstasy of peace; and I wanted all to sparkle and dance in a glorious jubilee. I said his heaven would be only half alive; and he said mine would be drunk: I said I should fall asleep in his; and he said he could not breathe in mine, and began to grow very snappish. At last, we agreed to try both, as soon as the right weather came; and then we kissed each other and were friends. .

"After sitting still an hour, I looked at the great room with its smooth uncarpeted floor, and thought how nice it would be to play in, if we removed the table; and I asked Linton to call Zillah in to help us, and we'd have a game at blind man's buff; she should try to catch us; you used to, you know, Ellen. He wouldn't: there was no pleasure in it, he said; but he consented to play at ball with me. We found two in a cupboard, among a heap of old toys, tops, and hoops, and battledores, and shuttle-cocks. One was marked C., and the other H.; and I wished to have the C., because that stood for Catherine, and the H. might be for Heathcliff, his name; but the bran came out of H., and Linton didn't like it. I beat him constantly: and he got cross again, and coughed, and returned to his chair. That night, though, he easily recovered his good humour: he was charmed with two or three pretty songs—*your* songs, Ellen; and when I was obliged to go, he begged and intreated me to come the following evening; and I promised. Minny and I went flying home as light as air; and I dreamt of Wuthering Heights and my sweet, darling cousin, till morning.

"On the morrow I was sad; partly because you were poorly, and partly that I wished my father knew, and approved of my excursions: but it was beautiful moonlight after tea; and, as I rode on, the gloom cleared. I shall have another happy evening I thought to myself; and what delights me more, my pretty Linton will. I trotted up their garden, and was turning round to the back, when that fellow Earnshaw met me, took my bridle, and bid me go in by the front entrance. He patted Minny's neck, and said she was a bonny beast and appeared as if he wanted me to speak to him. I only told him to leave my horse alone, or else it would kick him. He answered in his vulgar accent, 'It wouldn't do mitch hurt if it did!' and surveyed its legs with a smile. I was half inclined to make it try; however, he moved off to open the door, and as he raised the latch, he looked up to the inscription above, and said, with a stupid mixture of awkwardness and elation:

" 'Miss Catherine! I can read yon, now.'

" 'Wonderful,' I exclaimed. 'Pray let us hear you—you *are* grown clever!'

"He spelt, and drawled over by syllables, the name—'Hareton Earnshaw.'

" 'And the figures?' I cried, encouragingly, perceiving that he came to a dead halt.

" 'I cannot tell them yet,' he answered.

" 'Oh, you dunce!' I said, laughing heartily at his failure.

"The fool stared, with a grin hovering about his lips, and a scowl gathering over his eyes, as if uncertain whether he might not join in my mirth: whether it were not pleasant familiarity, or what it really was, contempt. I settled his doubts, by suddenly retrieving my gravity and desiring him to walk away, for I came to see Linton, not him. He reddened—I saw that by the moonlight—dropped his hand from the latch, and skulked off, a picture of mortified vanity. He imagined himself to be as accomplished as Linton, I suppose, because he could spell his own name; and was marvellously discomfited that I didn't think the same."

"Stop, Miss Catherine, dear!" I interrupted. "I shall not scold, but I don't like your conduct there. If you had remembered that Hareton was your cousin as much as Master Heathcliff, you would have felt how improper it was to behave in that way. At least, it was praiseworthy ambition for him to desire to be as accomplished as Linton; and probably he did not learn merely to show off: you had made him ashamed of his ignorance before, I have no doubt; and he wished to remedy it and please you. To sneer at his imperfect attempt was very bad breeding. Had *you* been brought up in his circumstances, would you be less rude? He was as quick and as intelligent a child as ever you were; and I'm hurt that he should be despised now, because that base Heathcliff has treated him so unjustly."

"Well, Ellen, you won't cry about it, will you?" she exclaimed, surprised at my earnestness. "But wait, and you shall hear if he conned his ABC to please me; and if it were worth while being civil to the brute. I entered; Linton was lying on the settle, and half got up to welcome me.

"'I'm ill to-night, Catherine, love,' he said; 'and you must have all the talk, and let me listen. Come, and sit by me. I was sure you wouldn't break your word, and I'll make you promise again, before you go.'

"I knew now that I mustn't tease him, as he was ill; and I spoke softly and put no questions, and avoided irritating him in any way. I had brought some of my nicest books for him; he asked me to read a little of one, and I was about to comply, when Earnshaw burst the door open: having gathered venom with reflection. He advanced direct to us, seized Linton by the arm, and swung him off the seat.

"'Get to thy own room'! he said, in a voice almost inarticulate with passion; and his face looked swelled and furious. 'Take her there if she comes to see thee: thou shalln't keep me out of this. Begone wi' ye both!'

"He swore at us, and left Linton no time to answer, nearly throwing him into the kitchen; and he clenched his fist as I followed, seemingly longing to knock me down. I was afraid for a moment, and I let one volume fall; he kicked it after me, and shut us out. I heard a malignant, crackly laugh by the fire, and turning, beheld that odious Joseph standing and rubbing his bony hands, and quivering.

"'I wer sure he'd sarve ye out! He's a grand lad! He's getten t'raight sperrit in him! *He* knaws—Ay, he knaws, as weel as I do, who sud be t'maister yonder—Ech, ech, ech! He made ye skift properly! Ech, ech, ech!'

"'Where must we go?' I asked of my cousin, disregarding the old wretch's mockery.

"Linton was white and trembling. He was not pretty then, Ellen: oh no! he looked frightful: for his thin face and large eyes were wrought into an expression of frantic, powerless fury. He grasped the handle of the door, and shook it: it was fastened inside.

"'If you don't let me in I'll kill you!—If you don't let me in, I'll kill you!' he rather shrieked than said. 'Devil! devil!—I'll kill you—I'll kill you!'

"Joseph uttered his croaking laugh again.

" 'Thear, that's t'father!' he cried. 'That's father! We've allas summat o' either side in us. Niver heed, Hareton, lad—dunnut be 'feard—he
cannot get at thee!'

"I took hold of Linton's hands, and tried to pull him away; but he
shrieked so shockingly that I dared not proceed. At last his cries were
choked by a dreadful fit of coughing; blood gushed from his mouth, and
he fell on the gorund. I ran into the yard, sick with terror; and called for
Zillah, as loud as I could. She soon heard me: she was milking the cows
in a shed behind the barn, and hurrying from her work, she inquired what
there was to do? I hadn't breath to explain; dragging her in, I looked
about for Linton. Earnshaw had come out to examine the mischief he had
caused, and he was then conveying the poor thing upstairs. Zillah and
I ascended after him; but he stopped me at the top of the steps, and said
I shouldn't go in: I must go home. I exclaimed that he had killed Linton,
and I *would* enter. Joseph locked the door, and declared I should do, 'no
sich stuff,' and asked me whether I were 'bahn to be as mad as him.' I
stood crying, till the housekeeper reappeared. She affirmed he would be
better in a bit, but he couldn't do with that shrieking and din; and she took
me, and nearly carried me into the house.

"Ellen, I was ready to tear my hair off my head! I sobbed and wept so
that my eyes were almost blind; and the ruffian you have such sympathy
with stood opposite: presuming every now and then to bid me 'wisht,' and
denying that it was his fault; and, finally, frightened by my assertions that
I would tell papa, and that he should be put in prison and hanged, he
commenced blubbering himself, and hurried out to hide his cowardly
agitation. Still, I was not rid of him: when at length they compelled me
to depart, and I had got some hundred yards off the premises, he suddenly
issued from the shadow of the roadside, and checked Minny and took
hold of me.

" 'Miss Catherine, I'm ill grieved,' he began, 'but it's rayther too bad——'

"I gave him a cut with my whip, thinking perhaps he would murder me.
He let go, thundering one of his horrid curses, and I galloped home more
than half out of my senses.

"I didn't bid you good night that evening, and I didn't go to Wuthering
Heights the next: I wished to go exceedingly; but I was strangely excited,
and dreaded to hear that Linton was dead, sometimes; and sometimes
shuddered at the thought of encountering Hareton. On the third day I
took courage: at least, I couldn't bear longer suspense, and stole off once
more. I went at five o'clock, and walked; fancying I might manage to
creep into the house, and up to Linton's room, unobserved. However, the
dogs gave notice of my approach. Zillah received me, and saying 'the lad
was mending nicely,' showed me into a small, tidy, carpeted apartment,
where, to my inexpressible joy, I beheld Linton laid on a little sofa, reading one of my books. But he would neither speak to me nor look at me,
through a whole hour, Ellen; he has such an unhappy temper. And what

110

quite confounded me, when he did open his mouth, it was to utter the falsehood that I had occasioned the uproar, and Hareton was not to blame! Unable to reply, except passionately, I got up and walked from the room. He sent after me a faint 'Catherine!' He did not reckon on being answered so: but I wouldn't turn back; and the morrow was the second day on which I stayed at home, nearly determined to visit him no more. But it was so miserable going to bed and getting up, and never hearing anything about him, that my resolution melted into air before it was properly formed. It *had* appeared wrong to take the journey once; now it seemed wrong to refrain. Michael came to ask if he must saddle Minny; I said 'Yes,' and considered myself doing a duty as she bore me over the hills. I was forced to pass the front window to get to the court: it was no use trying to conceal my presence.

"'Young master is in the house,' said Zillah, as she saw me making for the parlour. I went in; Earnshaw was there also, but he quitted the room directly. Linton sat in the great arm-chair half asleep; walking up to the fire, I began in a serious tone, partly meaning it to be true—

"'As you don't like me, Linton, and as you think I come on purpose to hurt you, and pretend that I do so every time, this is our last meeting: let us say good-bye; and tell Mr. Heathcliff that you have no wish to see me, and that he mustn't invent any more falsehoods on the subject.'

"'Sit down and take your hat off, Catherine,' he answered. 'You are so much happier than I am, you ought to be better. Papa talks enough of my defects, and shows enough scorn of me, to make it natural I should doubt myself. I doubt whether I am not altogether as worthless as he calls me, frequently; and then I feel so cross and bitter, I hate everybody! I *am* worthless, and bad in temper, and bad in spirit, almost always; and, if you choose, you *may* say good-bye: you'll get rid of an annoyance. Only, Catherine, do me this justice: believe that if I might be as sweet, and as kind, and as good as you are, I would be; as willingly, and more so, than as happy and as healthy. And believe that your kindness has made me love you deeper than if I deserved your love: and though I couldn't, and cannot help showing my nature to you, I regret it and repent it; and shall regret and repent it till I die!'

"I felt he spoke the truth; and I felt I must forgive him, and, though he should quarrel the next moment, I must forgive him again. We were reconciled; but we cried, both of us, the whole time I stayed: not entirely for sorrow; yet I *was* sorry Linton had that distorted nature. He'll never let his friends be at ease, and he'll never be at ease himself! I have always gone to his little parlour, since that night; because his father returned the day after.

"About three times, I think, we have been merry and hopeful, as we were the first evening; the rest of my visits were dreary and troubled: now with his selfishness and spite, and now with his sufferings: but I've learned to endure the former with nearly as little resentment as the latter. Mr.

Heathcliff purposely avoids me: I have hardly seen him at all. Last Sunday, indeed, coming earlier than usual, I heard him abusing poor Linton, cruelly, for his conduct of the night before. I can't tell how he knew of it, unless he listened. Linton had certainly behaved provokingly: however, it was the business of nobody but me, and I interrupted Mr. Heathcliff's lecture by entering and telling him so. He burst into a laugh, and went away, saying he was glad I took that view of the matter. Since then, I've told Linton he must whisper his bitter things. Now, Ellen, you have heard all. I can't be prevented from going to Wuthering Heights, expect by inflicting misery on two people; whereas, if you'll only not tell papa, my going need disturb the tranquillity of none. You'll not tell, will you? It will be very heartless, if you do."

"I'll make up my mind on that point by to-morrow, Miss Catherine," I replied. 'It requires some study; and so I'll leave you to your rest, and go think it over."

I thought it over aloud, in my master's presence; walking straight from her room to his, and relating the whole story: with the exception of her conversations with her cousin, and any mention of Hareton. Mr. Linton was alarmed and distressed, more than he would acknowledge to me. In the morning, Catherine learnt my betrayal of her confidence, and she learnt also that her secret visits were to end. In vain she wept and writhed against the interdict, and implored her father to have pity on Linton: all she got to comfort her was a promise that he would write and give him leave to come to the Grange when he pleased; but explaining that he must no longer expect to see Catherine at Wuthering Heights. Perhaps, had he been aware of his nephew's disposition and state of health, he would have seen fit to withhold even that slight consolation.

## Chapter 25

"These things happened last winter, sir," said Mrs. Dean; "hardly more than a year ago. Last winter, I did not think, at another twelve months' end, I should be amusing a stranger to the family with relating them! Yet, who knows how long you'll be a stranger? You're too young to rest always contented, living by yourself; and I some way fancy no one could see Catherine Linton and not love her. You smile; but why do you look so lively and interested, when I talk about her? and why have you asked me to hang her picture over your fireplace? and why——"

"Stop, my good friend!" I cried. "It may be very possible that _I_ should love her; but would she love me? I doubt it too much to venture my tranquillity by running into temptation: and then my home is not here. I'm of the busy world, and to its arms I must return. Go on. Was Catherine obedient to her father's commands?"

"She was," continued the housekeeper. "Her affection for him was still the chief sentiment in her heart; and he spoke without anger: he spoke in the deep tenderness of one about to leave his treasure and perils and foes, where his remembered words would be the only aid that he could bequeath to guide her. He said to me, a few days afterwards:

"'I wish my nephew would write, Ellen, or call. Tell me, sincerely, what you think of him: is he changed for the better, or is there a prospect of improvement, as he grows a man?'

"'He's very delicate, sir,' I replied; 'and scarcely likely to reach manhood: but this I can say, he does not resemble his father; and if Miss Catherine had the misfortune to marry him, he would not be beyond her control: unless she were extremely and foolishly indulgent. However, master, you'll have plenty of time to get acquainted with him, and see whether he would suit her: it wants four years and more to his being of age.'

Edgar sighed; and, walking to the window, looked out towards Gimmerton Kirk. It was a misty afternoon, but the February sun shone dimly, and we could just distinguish the two fir-trees in the yard, and the sparely-scattered grave-stones.

"I've prayed often," he half-soliloquised, "for the approach of what is coming; and now I begin to shrink, and fear it. I thought the memory of the hour I came down that glen a bridegroom would be less sweet than the anticipation that I was soon, in a few months, or, possibly, weeks, to be carried up, and laid in its lonely hollow! Ellen, I've been very happy with my little Cathy: through winter nights and summer days she was a living hope at my side. But I've been as happy musing by myself among those stones, under that old church: lying, through the long June evenings, on the green mound of her mother's grave, and wishing—yearning for the time when I might lie beneath it. What can I do for Cathy? How must I quit her? I'd not care one moment for Linton being Heathcliff's son; nor for his taking her from me, if he could console her for my loss. I'd not care that Heathcliff gained his ends, and triumphed in robbing me of my last blessing! But should Linton be unworthy—only a feeble tool to his father—I cannot abandon her to him! And, hard though it be to crush her buoyant spirit, I must persevere in making her sad while I live, and leaving her solitary when I die. Darling! I'd rather resign her to God, and lay her in the earth before me."

"Resign her to God as it is, sir," I answered, "and if we should lose you—which may He forbid—under His providence, I'll stand her friend and counsellor to the last. Miss Catherine is a good girl: I don't fear that she will go wilfully wrong; and people who do their duty are always finally rewarded."

Spring advanced; yet my master gathered no real strength, though he resumed his walks in the grounds with his daughter. To her inexperienced notions, this itself was a sign of convalescence; and then his cheek was often flushed, and his eyes were bright: she felt sure of his recovering. On her seventeenth birthday, he did not visit the churchyard: it was raining, and I observed—

"You'll surely not go out to-night, sir?"

He answered—

"No, I'll defer it this year a little longer."

He wrote again to Linton, expressing his great desire to see him; and, had the invalid been presentable, I've no doubt his father would have permitted him to come. As it was, being instructed, he returned an answer, intimating that Mr. Heathcliff objected to his calling at the Grange; but his uncle's kind remembrance delighted him, and he hoped to meet him, sometimes, in his rambles, and personally to petition that his cousin and he might not remain so long utterly divided.

That part of his letter was simple, and probably his own. Heathcliff knew he could plead eloquently for Catherine's company, then.

"I do not ask," he said, "that she may visit here; but, am I never to see her, because my father forbids me to go to her home, and you forbid her to come to mine? Do, now and then, ride with her towards the Heights; and let us exchange a few words, in your presence! We have done nothing to deserve this separation; and you are not angry with me: you have no reason to dislike me, you allow, yourself. Dear uncle! send me a kind note to-morrow, and leave to join you anywhere you please, except at Thrushcross Grange. I believe an interview would convince you that my father's character in not mine: he affirms I am more your nephew than his son; and though I have faults which render me unworthy of Catherine, she has excused them, and for her sake, you should also. You inquire after my health—it is better; but while I remain cut off from all hope, and doomed to solitude, or the society of those who never did and never will like me, how can I be cheerful and well?"

Edgar, though he felt for the boy, could not consent to grant his request; because he could not accompany Catherine. He said, in summer, perhaps, they might meet: meantime, he wished him to continue writing at intervals, and engaged to give him what advice and comfort he was able by letter; being well aware of his hard position in his family. Linton complied; and had he been unrestrained, would probably have spoiled all by filling his epistles with complaints and lamentations: but his father kept a sharp watch over him; and, of course, insisted on every line that my master sent being shown; so, instead of penning his peculiar personal sufferings and distresses, the themes constantly uppermost in his thoughts, he harped on the cruel obligation of being held asunder from his friend and love; and gently intimated that Mr. Linton must allow an interview soon, or he should fear he was purposely deceiving him with empty promises.

Cathy was a powerful ally at home; and, between them they at length persuaded my master to acquiesce in their having a ride or a walk together about once a week, under my guardianship, on the moors nearest the Grange: for June found him still declining. Though he had set aside a yearly portion of his income for my young lady's fortune, he had a natural desire that she might retain—or at least return in a short time to—the house of her ancestors; and he considered her only prospect of doing that was by a union with his heir; he had no idea that the latter was failing almost as fast as himself; nor had any one, I believe: no doctor visited the Heights, and no one saw Master Heathcliff to make a report of his condition among us. I, for my part, began to fancy my forebodings were false, and that he must be actually rallying, when he mentioned riding and walking on the moors, and seemed so earnest in pursuing his object. I could not picture a father treating a dying child as tyrannically and wickedly as I afterwards learned Heathcliff had treated him, to compel this apparent eagerness: his efforts redoubling the more imminently his avaricious and unfeeling plans were threatened with defeat by death.

## Chapter 26

SUMMER was already past its prime, when Edgar reluctantly yielded his assent to their entreaties, and Catherine and I set out on our first ride to join her cousin. It was a close, sultry day: devoid of sunshine, but with a sky too dappled and hazy to threaten rain; and our place of meeting had been fixed at the guide-stone, by the cross-roads. On arriving there, however, a little herd-boy, despatched as a messenger, told us that—

"Maister Linton wer just o' this side th' Heights: and he'd be mitch obleeged to us to gang on a bit further."

"Then Master Linton has forgot the first injunction of his uncle," I observed: "he bid us keep on the Grange land, and here we are off at once."

"Well, we'll turn our horses' heads round, when we reach him," answered my companion, "our excursion shall lie towards home."

But when we reached him, and that was scarcely a quarter of a mile from his own door, we found he had no horse; and we were forced to dismount, and leave ours to graze. He lay on the heath, awaiting our approach, and did not rise till we came within a few yards. Then he walked so feebly, and looked so pale, that I immediately exclaimed—

"Why, Master Heathcliff, you are not fit for enjoying a ramble, this morning. How ill you do look!"

Catherine surveyed him with grief and astonishment: she changed the ejaculation of joy on her lips, to one of alarm; and the congratulation on their long-postponed meeting, to an anxious inquiry, whether he were worse than usual?

"No—better—better!" he panted, trembling, and retaining her hand as if he needed its support, while his large blue eyes wandered timidly over her; the hollowness round them transforming to haggard wildness the languid expression they once possessed.

"But you have been worse," persisted his cousin; "worse than when I saw you last; you are thinner, and—"

"I'm tired," he interrupted, hurriedly. "It is too hot for walking, let us rest here. And, in the morning, I often feel sick—papa says I grow so fast."

Badly satisfied, Cathy sat down, and he reclined beside her.

"This is something like your paradise," said she making an effort at cheerfulness. "You recollect the two days we agreed to spend in the place and way each thought pleasantest? This is nearly yours, only there are clouds; but then they are so soft and mellow: it is nicer than sunshine. Next week, if you can, we'll ride down to the Grange Park, and try mine."

Linton did not appear to remember what she talked of; and he had evidently great difficulty in sustaining any kind of conversation. His lack of interest in the subjects she started, and his equal incapacity to contribute to her entertainment, were so obvious that she could not conceal her disappointment. An indefinite alteration had come over his whole person and manner. The pettishness that might be caressed into fondness, had yielded to a listless apathy; there was less of the peevish temper of a child which frets and teases on purpose to be soothed, and more of the self-absorbed moroseness of a confirmed invalid, repelling consolation, and ready to regard the good-humoured mirth of others, as an insult. Catherine perceived, as well as I did, that he held it rather a punishment, than a gratification, to endure our company; and she made no scruple of proposing, presently, to depart. That proposal, unexpectedly, roused Linton from his lethargy, and threw him into a strange state of agitation. He glanced fearfully towards the Heights, begging she would remain another half-hour, at least.

"But, I think," said Cathy, "you'd be more comfortable at home than sitting here; and I cannot amuse you to-day, I see, by my tales, and songs, and chatter: you have grown wiser than I, in these six months; you have little taste for my diversions now: or else, if I could amuse you, I'd willingly stay."

"Stay to rest yourself," he replied. "And Catherine, don't think, or say that I'm *very* unwell: it is the heavy weather and heat that make me dull; and I walked about, before you came, a great deal for me. Tell uncle, I'm in tolerable health, will you?"

"I'll tell him that *you* say so, Linton. I couldn't affirm that you are," observed my young lady, wondering at his pertinacious assertion of what was evidently an untruth.

"And be here again next Thursday," continued he, shunning her puzzled gaze. "And give him my thanks for permitting you to come—my best thanks, Catherine. And—and if you *did* meet my father, and he asked you about me, don't lead him to suppose that I've been extremely silent and stupid: don't look sad and downcast, as you *are* doing—he'll be angry."

"I care nothing for his anger," exclaimed Cathy, imagining she would be its object.

"But I do," said her cousin, shuddering. "*Don't* provoke him against me, Catherine, for he is very hard."

"Is he severe to you, Master Heathcliff?" I inquired. "Has he grown weary of indulgence, and passed from passive to active hatred?"

Linton looked at me, but did not answer; and, after keeping her seat by his side another ten minutes, during which his head fell drowsily on his breast, and he uttered nothing except suppressed moans of exhaustion or pain, Cathy began to seek solace in looking for bilberries, and sharing the produce of her researches with me: she did not offer them to him, for she saw further notice would only weary and annoy.

"Is it half an hour now, Ellen?" she whispered in my ear, at last. "I can't tell why we should stay. He's asleep, and papa will be wanting us back."

"Well, we must not leave him asleep," I answered; "wait till he wakes, and be patient. You were mighty eager to set off, but your longing to see poor Linton has soon evaporated!"

"Why did *he* wish to see me?" returned Catherine. "In his crossest humours, formerly, I liked him better than I do in his present curious mood. It's just as if it were a task he was compelled to perform—this interview—for fear his father should scold him. But I'm hardly going to come to give Mr. Heathcliff pleasure; whatever reason he may have for ordering Linton to undergo this penance. And, though I'm glad he's better in health, I'm sorry he's so much less pleasant, and so much less affectionate to me."

"You think *he* is better in health, then?" I said.

"Yes," she answered; "because he always made such a great deal of his sufferings, you know. He is not tolerably well, as he told me to tell papa; but he's better, very likely."

"There you differ with me, Miss Cathy," I remarked; "I should conjecture him to be far worse."

Linton here started from his slumber in bewildered terror, and asked if any one had called his name.

"No," said Catherine; "unless in dreams. I cannot conceive how you manage to doze out of doors, in the morning."

"I thought I heard my father," he gasped, glancing up to the frowning nab above us. "You are sure nobody spoke?"

"Quite sure," replied his cousin. "Only Ellen and I were disputing concerning your health. Are you truly stronger, Linton, than when we separated in winter? If you be, I'm certain one thing is not stronger—your regard for me: speak,—are you?"

The tears gushed from Linton's eyes as he answered, "Yes, yes, I am!" And, still under the spell of the imaginary voice, his gaze wandered up and down to detect its owner. Cathy rose. "For to-day we must part," she said. "And I won't conceal that I have been sadly disappointed with our meeting; though I'll mention it to nobody but you: not that I stand in awe of Mr. Heathcliff."

"Hush," murmured Linton; "for God's sake, hush! He's coming." And he clung to Catherine's arm, striving to detain her; but at that announcement she hastily disengaged herself, and whistled to Minny, who obeyed her like a dog.

"I'll be here next Thursday," she cried, springing to the saddle. "Good-bye. Quick, Ellen!"

And so we left him, scarcely conscious of our departure, so absorbed was he in anticipating his father's approach.

Before we reached home, Catherine's displeasure softened into a perplexed sensation of pity and regret, largely blended with vague, uneasy doubts about Linton's actual circumstances, physical and social: in which I partook, though I counselled her not to say much; for a second journey would make us better judges. My master requested an account of our ongoings. His nephew's offering of thanks was duly delivered, Miss Cathy gently touching on the rest: I also threw a little light on his inquiries, for I hardly knew what to hide, and what to reveal.

# Chapter 27

SEVEN days glided away, every one marking its course by the henceforth rapid alteration of Edgar Linton's state. The havoc that months had previously wrought was now emulated by the inroads of hours. Catherine, we would fain have deluded yet; but her own quick spirit refused to delude her: it divined in secret, and brooded on the dreadful probability, gradually ripening into certainty. She had not the heart to mention her ride, when Thursday came round; I mentioned it for her, and obtained permission to order her out of doors: for the library, where her father stopped a short time daily—the brief period he could bear to sit up—and his chamber, had become her whole world. She grudged each moment that did not find her bending over his pillow, or seated by his side. Her countenance grew wan with watching and sorrow, and my master gladly dismissed her to what he flattered himself would be a happy change of scene and society;

drawing comfort from the hope that she would not now be left entirely alone after his death.

He had a fixed idea, I guessed by several observations he let fall, that, as his nephew resembled him in person, he would resemble him in mind; for Linton's letters bore few or no indications of his defective character. And I, through pardonable weakness, refrained from correcting the error; asking myself what good there would be in disturbing his last moments with information that he had neither power nor opportunity to turn to account.

We deferred our excursion till the afternoon; a golden afternoon of August: every breath from the hills so full of life, that it seemed whoever respired it, though dying, might revive. Catherine's face was just like the landscape—shadows and sunshine flitting over it in rapid succession; but the shadows rested longer, and the sunshine was more transient; and her poor little heart reproached itself for even that passing forgetfulness of its cares.

We discerned Linton watching at the same spot he had selected before. My young mistress alighted, and told me that, as she was resolved to stay a very little while, I had better hold the pony and remain on horseback; but I dissented: I wouldn't risk losing sight of the charge committed to me a minute; so we climbed the slope of heath together. Master Heathcliff received us with greater animation on this occasion: not the animation of high spirits though, nor yet of joy; it looked more like fear.

"It is late!" he said, speaking short and with difficulty. "Is not your father very ill? I thought you wouldn't come."

"*Why* won't you be candid?" cried Catherine, swallowing her greeting. "Why cannot you say at once you don't want me? It is strange, Linton, that for the second time you have brought me here on purpose, apparently, to distress us both, and for no reason besides!"

Linton shivered, and glanced at her, half supplicating, half ashamed; but his cousin's patience was not sufficient to endure this enigmatical behaviour.

"My father *is* very ill," she said; "and why am I called from his bedside? Why didn't you send to absolve me from my promise, when you wished I wouldn't keep it? Come! I desire an explanation: playing and trifling are completely banished out of my mind; and I can't dance attendance on your affections now!"

"My affections!" he murmured; "what are they? For Heaven's sake, Catherine, don't look so angry! Despise me as much as you please; I am a worthless, cowardly wretch: I can't be scorned enough; but I'm too mean for your anger. Hate my father, and spare me for contempt."

"Nonsense!" cried Catherine, in a passion. "Foolish, silly boy! And there! he trembles, as if I were really going to touch him! You needn't bespeak contempt, Linton: anybody will have it spontaneously at your service. Get off! I shall return home: it is folly dragging you from the

119

hearthstone, and pretending—what do we pretend? Let go my frock! If I pitied you for crying and looking so very frightened, you should spurn such pity. Ellen, tell him how disgraceful this conduct is. Rise, and don't degrade yourself into an abject reptile—*don't*!"

With streaming face and an expression of agony, Linton had thrown his nerveless frame along the ground: he seemed convulsed with exquisite terror.

"Oh!" he sobbed, "I cannot bear it! Catherine, Catherine, I'm a traitor, too, and I dare not tell you! But leave me, and I shall be killed! *Dear* Catherine, my life is in your hands: and you have said you loved me, and if you did, it wouldn't harm you. You'll not go, then? kind, sweet, good Catherine! And perhaps you *will* consent—and he'll let me die with you!"

My young lady, on witnessing his intense anguish, stooped to raise him. The old feeling of indulgent tenderness overcame her vexation, and she grew thoroughly moved and alarmed.

"Consent to what?" she asked. "To stay! Tell me the meaning of this strange talk, and I will. You contradict your own words, and distract me! Be calm and frank, and confess at once all that weighs on your heart. You wouldn't injure me, Linton, would you? You wouldn't let any enemy hurt me, if you could prevent it? I'll believe you are a coward for yourself, but not a cowardly betrayer of your best friend."

"But my father threatened me," gasped the boy, clasping his attenuated fingers, "and I dread him—I dread him! I *dare* not tell!"

"Oh, well!" said Catherine, with scornful compassion, "keep your secret: *I'm* no coward. Save yourself: I'm not afraid!"

Her magnanimity provoked his tears: he wept wildly, kissing her supporting hands, and yet could not summon courage to speak out. I was cogitating what the mystery might be, and determined Catherine should never suffer, to benefit him, or anyone else, by my good will; when hearing a rustle among the ling, I looked up and saw Mr. Heathcliff almost close upon us, descending the Heights. He didn't cast a glance towards my companions, though they were sufficiently near for Linton's sobs to be audible; but hailing me in the most hearty tone he assumed to none besides, and the sincerity of which I couldn't avoid doubting, he said—

"It is something to see you so near to my house, Nelly. How are you at the Grange? Let us hear. The rumour goes," he added in a lower tone, "that Edgar Linton is on his deathbed: perhaps they exaggarate his illness?"

"No; my master is dying," I replied: "it is true enough. A sad thing it will be for us all, but a blessing for him!"

"How long will he last, do you think?" he asked.

"I don't know," I said.

"Because," he continued, looking at the two young people, who were fixed under his eye—Linton appeared as if he could not venture to stir or raise his head, and Catherine could not move, on his account—"because

120

that lad yonder seems determined to beat me; and I'd thank his uncle to be quick, and go before him. Hallo! has the whelp been playing that game long? I *did* give him some lessons about snivelling. Is he pretty lively with Miss Linton generally?"

"Lively? no—he has shown the greatest distress," I answered. "To see him, I should say, that instead of rambling with his sweetheart on the hills, he ought to be in bed, under the hands of a doctor."

"He shall be, in a day or two," muttered Heathcliff. "But first—get up, Linton! Get up!" he shouted. "Don't grovel on the ground there: up, this moment!"

Linton had sunk prostrate again in another paroxysm of helpless fear, caused by his father's glance towards him, I suppose; there was nothing else to produce such humiliation. He made several efforts to obey, but his little strength was annihilated for the time, and he fell back again with a moan. Mr. Heathcliff advanced, and lifted him to lean against a ridge of turf.

"Now," said he, with curbed ferocity, "I'm getting angry; and if you don't command that paltry spirit of yours—*Damn* you! get up directly!"

"I will, father," he panted. "Only, let me alone, or I shall faint. I've done as you wished, I'm sure. Catherine will tell you that I—that I—have been cheerful. Ah! keep by me, Catherine; give me your hand."

"Take mine," said his father; "stand on your feet. There now—she'll lend you her arm: that's right, look at *her.* You would imagine I was the devil himself, Miss Linton, to excite such horror. Be so kind as to walk home with him, will you? He shudders if I touch him."

"Linton, dear!" whispered Catherine, "I can't go to Wuthering Heights: papa has forbidden me. He'll not harm you: why are you so afraid?"

"I can never re-enter that house," he answered. "I'm *not* to re-enter it without you!"

"Stop!" cried his father. "We'll respect Catherine's filial scruples. Nelly, take him in, and I'll follow your advice concerning the doctor, without delay."

"You'll do well," replied I. "But I must remain with my mistress: to mind your son is not my business."

"You are very stiff," said Heathcliff, "I know that: but you'll force me to pinch the baby and make it scream before it moves your charity. Come, then, my hero. Are you willing to return, escorted by me?"

He approached once more, and made as if he would seize the fragile being; but, shrinking back, Linton clung to his cousin, and implored her to accompany him, with a frantic importunity that admitted no denial. However I disapproved, I couldn't hinder her: indeed, how could she have refused him herself? What was filling him with dread we had no means of discerning; but there he was, powerless under its gripe, and any addition seemed capable of shocking him into idiocy. We reached the threshold; Catharine walked in, and I stood waiting till she had conducted the invalid to a chair, expecting her out immediately; when Mr. Heathcliff, pushing me forward, exclaimed—

"My house is not stricken with the plague, Nelly; and I have a mind to be hospitable to-day: sit down, and allow me to shut the door."

He shut and locked it also. I started.

"You shall have tea before you go home," he added. "I am by myself. Hareton is gone with some cattle to the Lees, and Zillah and Joseph are off on a journey of pleasure; and, though I'm used to being alone, I'd rather have some interesting company, if I can get it. Miss Linton, take your seat by *him*. I give you what I have: the present is hardly worth accepting; but I have nothing else to offer. It is Linton, I mean. How she does stare! It's odd what a savage feeling I have to anything that seems afraid of me! Had I been born where laws are less strict and tastes less dainty, I should treat myself to a slow vivisection of those two, as an evening's amusement."

He drew in his breath, struck the table, and swore to himself, "By hell! I hate them."

"I'm not afraid of you!" exclaimed Catherine, who could not hear the latter part of his speech. She stepped close up; her black eyes flashing with passion and resolution. "Give me that key: I will have it!" she said. "I wouldn't eat or drink here, if I were starving."

Heathcliff had the key in his hand that remained on the table. He looked up, seized with a sort of surprise at her boldness; or, possibly, reminded by her voice and glance, of the person from whom she inherited it. She snatched at the instrument, and half-succeeded in getting it out of his loosened fingers: but her action recalled him to the present; he recovered it speedily.

"Now, Catherine Linton," he said, "stand off, or I shall knock you down; and that will make Mrs. Dean mad."

Regardless of this warning, she captured his closed hand and its contents again. "We *will* go!" she repeated, exerting her utmost efforts to cause the iron muscles to relax; and finding that her nails made no impression, she applied her teeth pretty sharply. Heathcliff glanced at me a glance that kept me from interfering a moment. Catherine was too intent on his fingers to notice his face. He opened them suddenly, and resigned the object of dispute; but, ere she had well secured it, he seized her with the liberated hand, and, pulling her on his knee, administered with the other a shower of terrific slaps on both sides of the head, each sufficient to have fulfilled his threat, had she been able to fall.

At this diabolical violence I rushed on him furiously. "You villain!" I began to cry, "you villain!" A touch on the chest silenced me: I am stout, and soon put out of breath; and, what with that and the rage, I staggered dizzily back, and felt ready to suffocate, or to burst a blood-vessel. The scene was over in two minutes; Catherine, released, put her two hands to her temples, and looked just as if she were not sure whether

122

her ears were off or on. She trembled like a reed, poor thing, and leant against the table perfectly bewildered.

"I know how to chastise children, you see," said the scoundrel, grimly, as he stooped to repossess himself of the key, which had dropped to the floor. "Go to Linton, now, as I told you; and cry at your ease! I shall be your father, to-morrow—all the father you'll have in a few days—and you shall have plenty of that. You can bear plenty; you're no weakling: you shall have a daily taste, if I catch such a devil of a temper in your eyes again!"

Cathy ran to me instead of Linton, and knelt down and put her burning cheek on my lap, weeping aloud. Her cousin had shrunk into a corner of the settle, as quiet as a mouse, congratulating himself, I dare say, that the correction had lighted on another than him. Mr. Heathcliff, perceiving us all confounded, rose, and expeditiously made the tea himself. The cups and saucers were laid ready. He poured it out, and handed me a cup.

"Wash away your spleen," he said. "And help your own naughty pet and mine. It is not poisoned, though I prepared it. I'm going out to seek your horses."

Our first thought, on his departure, was to force an exit somewhere. We tried the kitchen door, but that was fastened outside: we looked at the windows—they were too narrow for even Cathy's little figure.

"Master Linton," I cried, seeing we were regularly imprisoned; "you know what your diabolical father is after, and you shall tell us, or I'll box your ears, as he has done your cousin's."

"Yes, Linton. you must tell," said Catherine. "It was for your sake I came; and it will be wickedly ungrateful if you refuse."

"Give me some tea, I'm thirsty, and then I'll tell you," he answered. "Mrs. Dean, go away. I don't like you standing over me. Now, Catherine, you are letting your tears fall into my cup. I won't drink that. Give me another."

Catherine pushed another to him, and wiped her face. I felt disgusted at the little wretch's composure, since he was no longer in terror for himself. The anguish he had exhibited on the moor subsided as soon as ever he entered Wuthering Heights; so I guessed he had been menaced with an awful visitation of wrath if he failed in decoying us there; and, that accomplished, he had no further immediate fears.

"Papa wants us to be married," he continued, after sipping some of the liquid. "And he knows your papa wouldn't let us marry now; and he's afraid of my dying, if we wait; so we are to be married in the morning, and you are to stay here all night; and, if you do as he wishes, you shall return home next day, and take me with you."

"Take you with her, pitiful changeling?" I exclaimed. "*You* marry? Why the man is mad! or he thinks us fools, every one. And do you imagine that beautiful young lady, that healthy, hearty girl, will tie herself to a little perishing monkey like you? Are you cherishing the notion that *anybody*, let alone Miss Catherine Linton, would have you for a husband? You want whipping for bringing us in here at all, with your dastardly puling tricks; and—don't look so silly, now! I've a very good mind to shake you severely, for your contemptible treachery, and your imbecile conceit."

I did give him a slight shaking; but it brought on the cough, and he took to his ordinary resource of moaning and weeping, and Catherine rebuked me.

"Stay all night? No," she said, looking slowly round. "Ellen, I'll burn that door down, but I'll get out."

And she would have commenced the execution of her threat directly, but Linton was up in alarm for his dear self again. He clasped her in his two feeble arms sobbing—

"Won't you have me, and save me? not let me come to the Grange? Oh! darling Catherine! you mustn't go and leave, after all. You *must* obey my father—you *must!*"

"I must obey my own," she replied, "and relieve him from this cruel suspense. The whole night! What would he think? he'll be distressed already. I'll either break or burn a way out of the house. Be quiet! You're in no danger; but if you hinder me—Linton, I love papa better than you!"

The mortal terror he felt for Mr. Heathcliff's anger restored to the boy his coward's eloquence. Catherine was near distraught: still, she persisted that she must go home, and tried entreaty in her turn, persuading him to subdue his selfish agony. While they were thus occupied, our jailer re-entered.

"Your beasts have trotted off," he said, "and—now Linton! snivelling again? What has she been doing to you? Come, come—have done, and get to bed. In a month or two, my lad, you'll be able to pay her back for her present tyrannies with a vigorous hand. You're pining for pure love, are you not? nothing else in the world: and she shall have you! There to bed! Zillah won't be here to-night; you must undress yourself. Hush! hold your noise! Once in your own room, I'll not come near you: you needn't fear. By chance, you've managed tolerably. I'll look to the rest."

He spoke these words, holding the door open for his son to pass; and the latter achieved his exit exactly as a spaniel might, which suspected the person who attended on it of designing a spiteful squeeze. The lock was resecured. Heathcliff approached the fire, where my mistress and I stood silent. Catherine looked up, and instinctively raised her hand to her cheek: his neighbourhood revived a painful sensation. Anybody else would have been incapable of regarding the childish act with sternness, but he scowled on her, and muttered—

"Oh! you are not afraid of me? Your courage is well disguised: you *seem* damnably afraid!"

"I *am* afraid now," she replied, "because, if I stay, papa will be miserable; and how can I endure making him miserable—when he—when he—Mr. Heathcliff, *let* me go home! I promise to marry Linton: papa would like me to: and I love him. Why should you wish to force me to do what I'll willingly do of myself?"

"Let him dare to force you!" I cried. "There's law in the land, thank God! there is; though we be in an out-of-the-way-place. I'd inform if he were my own son: and it's felony without benefit of clergy!"

"Silence!" said the ruffian. "To the devil with your clamour! I don't want *you* to speak. Miss Linton, I shall enjoy myself remarkably in thinking your father will be miserable: I shall not sleep for satisfaction. You could have hit on no surer way of fixing your residence under my roof for the next twenty-four hours, than informing me that such an event would follow. As to your promise to marry Linton, I'll take care you shall keep it; for you shall not quit this place till it is fulfilled."

"Send Ellen, then, to let papa know I'm safe!" exclaimed Catherine, weeping bitterly. "Or marry me now. Poor papa! Ellen, he'll think we're lost, What shall we do?"

"Not he! He'll think you are tired of waiting on him, and run off for a little amusement," answered Heathcliff. "You cannot deny that you entered my house of your own accord, in contempt of his injunctions to the contrary. And it is quite natural that you should desire amusement at your age; and that you would weary of nursing a sick man, and that man *only* your father. Catherine, his happiest days were over when your days began. He cursed you, I dare say, for coming into the world (I did, at least); and it would just do if he cursed you as *he* went out of it. I'd join him. I don't love you! How should I? Weep away. As far as I can see, it will be your chief diversion hereafter; unless Linton makes amends for other losses: and your provident parent appears to fancy he may. His letters of advice and consolation entertained me vastly. In his last he recommended my jewel to be careful of his; and kind to her when he got her. Careful and kind—that's paternal. But Linton requires his whole stock of care and kindness for himself. Linton can play the little tyrant well. He'll undertake to torture any number of cats, if their teeth be drawn and their claws pared. You'll be able to tell his uncle fine tales of his *kindness*, when you get home again, I assure you."

"You're right there!" I said; "explain your son's character. Show his resemblance to yourself; and then, I hope, Miss Cathy will think twice before she takes the cockatrice!"

"I don't much mind speaking of his amiable qualities now," he answered; "because she must either accept him or remain a prisoner, and you along with her, till your master dies. I can detain you both, quite concealed, here. If you doubt, encourage her to retract her word, and you'll have an opportunity of judging!"

"I'll not retract my word," said Catherine. "I'll marry him within this hour, if I may go to Thrushcross Grange afterwards. Mr. Heathcliff, you're a cruel man, but you're not a fiend; and you won't, from *mere* malice, destroy irrevocably all my happiness. If papa thought I had left him on purpose, and if he died before I returned, could I bear to live? I've given over crying: but I'm going to kneel here, at your knee; and I'll not get up, and I'll not take my eyes from your face till you look back at me! No, don't turn away! *do* look! You'll see nothing to provoke you. I don't hate you. I'm not angry that you struck me. Have you never loved *anybody* in all your life, uncle? *never?* Ah! you must look once. I'm so wretched, you can't help being sorry and pitying me."

"Keep your eft's fingers off; and move, or I'll kick you!" cried Heathcliff, brutally repulsing her. "I'd rather be hugged by a snake. How the devil can you dream of fawning on me? I *detest* you!"

He shrugged his shoulders: shook himself, indeed, as if his flesh crept with aversion; and thrust back his chair; while I got up, and opened my mouth, to commence a downright torrent of abuse. But I was rendered dumb in the middle of the first sentence, by a threat that I should be shown into a room by myself the very next syllable I uttered. It was growing dark—we heard the sound of voices at the garden gate. Our host hurried out instantly: *he* had his wits about him; *we* had not. There was a talk of two or three minutes, and he returned alone.

"I thought it had been your cousin Hareton," I observed to Catherine. "I wish he would arrive! Who knows but he might take our part?"

"It was three servants sent to seek you from the Grange," said Heathcliff, overhearing me. "You should have opened a lattice and called out: but I could swear that chit is glad you didn't. She's glad to be obliged to say, I'm certain."

At learning the chance we had missed, we both gave vent to our grief without control; and he allowed us to wail on till nine o'clock. Then he bid us go upstairs, through the kitchen, to Zillah's chamber; and I whispered my companion to obey: perhaps we might contrive to get through the window there, or into a garret, and out by its skylight. The window, however, was narrow, like those below, and the garret trap was safe from our attempts; for we were fastened in as before. We neither of us lay down: Catherine took her station by the lattice, and watched anxiously for morning; a deep sigh bringing the only answer I could obtain to my frequent entreaties that she would try to rest. I seated myself in a chair, and rocked to and fro, passing harsh judgment on my many derelictions of duty; from which, it struck me then, all the misfortunes of my employers sprang. It was not the case, in reality, I am aware; but it was, in my imagination, that dismal night; and I thought Heathcliff himself less guilty than I.

At seven o'clock he came, and inquired if Miss Linton had risen. She ran to the door immediately, and answered, "Yes." "Here, then," he said, opening it, and pulling her out. I rose to follow, but he turned the lock again. I demanded my release.

"Be patient," he replied! "I'll send up your breakfast in a while."

I thumped on the panels, and rattled the latch angrily; and Catherine asked why I was still shut up? He answered, I must try to endure it another hour, and they went away. I endured it two or three hours; at length, I heard a footstep; not Heathcliff's.

"I've brought you something to eat," said a voice; "oppen t' door!"

Complying eagerly, I beheld Hareton, laden with food enough to last me all day.

"Tak it," he added, thrusting the tray into my hand.

"Stay one minute," I began.

"Nay," cried he, and retired, regardless of any prayers I could pour forth to detain him.

And there I remained enclosed the whole day, and the whole of the next night; and another, and another. Five nights and four days I remained, altogether, seeing nobody but Hareton, once every morning; and he was a model of a jailer: surly, and dumb, and deaf to every attempt at moving his sense of justice or compassion.

## *Chapter 28*

ON THE fifth morning, or rather afternoon, a different step approached—lighter and shorter; and, this time, the person entered the room. It was Zillah; donned in her scarlet shawl, with a black silk bonnet on her head, and a willow basket swung on her arm.

"Eh, dear! Mrs. Dean!" she exclaimed. "Well! there is a talk about you at Gimmerton. I never thought but you were sunk in the Black-horse marsh, and missy with you, till master told me you'd been found, and he'd lodged you here! What! and you must have got on an island, sure? And how long were you in the hole? Did master save you, Mrs. Dean? But you're not so thin—you've not been so poorly, have you?"

"Your master is a true scoundrel!" I replied. "But he shall answer for it. He needn't have raised that tale: it shall all be laid bare!"

"What do you mean?" asked Zillah. "It's not his tale: they tell that in the village—about your being lost in the marsh: and I calls to Eearnshaw, when I come in—'Eh, they's queer things, Mr. Hareton, happened since I went off. It's sad pity of that likely young lass, and cant Nelly Dean.' He stared. I thought he had not heard aught, so I told him the rumour. The master listened, and he just smiled to himself, and said, 'If they have been in the marsh, they are out now, Zillah. Nelly Dean is lodged, at this minute, in your room. You can tell her to flit, when you go up; here is the key. The bog-water got into her head, and she would have run home quite flighty; but I fixed her till she came round to her senses. You can bid her go to the Grange at once, if she is able, and carry a message from me, that her young lady will follow in time to attend the squire's funeral.'"

"Mr. Edgar is not dead?" I gasped. "Oh! Zillah, Zillah!"

"No, no; sit you down, my good mistress," she replied, "you're right sickly yet. He's not dead; Doctor Kenneth thinks he may last another day. I met him on the road and asked."

Instead of sitting down, I snatched my outdoor things, and hastened below, for the way was free. On entering the house, I looked about for someone to give information of Catherine. The place was filled with sunshine, and the door stood wide open; but nobody seemed at hand. As I hesitated whether to go off at once, or return and seek my mistress, a slight cough drew my attention to the hearth. Linton lay on the settle, sole tenant, sucking a stick of sugar-candy, and pursuing my movements with apathetic eyes. "Where is Miss Catherine?" I demanded, sternly, supposing I could frighten him into giving intelligence, by catching him thus, alone. He sucked on like an innocent.

"Is she gone?" I said.

"No," he replied; "she's upstairs: she's not to go; we won't let her."

"You won't let her, little idiot!" I exclaimed. "Direct me to her room immediately, or I'll make you sing out sharply."

"Papa would make you sing out, if you attempted to get there," he answered. "He says I'm not to be soft with Catherine: she's my wife, and it's shameful that she should wish to leave me. He says, she hates me and wants me to die, that she may have my money; but she shan't have it; and she shan't go home! She never shall—she may cry, and be sick as much as she pleases!"

I considered it best to depart without seeing Mr. Heathcliff, and bring a rescue for my young lady from the Grange. On reaching it, the astonishment of my fellow-servants to see me, and their joy also, was intense; and when they heard that their little mistress was safe, two or three were about to hurry up and shout the news at Mr. Edgar's door: but I bespoke the announcement of it, myself. How changed I found him, even in those few days! He lay an image of sadness and resignation waiting his death. Very young he looked; though his actual age was thirty-nine, one would have called him ten years younger, at least. He thought of Catherine; for he murmured her name. I touched his hand, and spoke.

"Catherine is coming, dear master!" I whispered; "she is alive and well; and will be here, I hope, to-night."

I trembled at the first effects of this intelligence: he half rose up, looked eagerly round the apartment, and then sank back in a swoon. As soon as he recovered, I related our compulsory visit, and detention at the

128

Heights. I said Heathcliff forced me to go in: which was not quite true. I uttered as little as possible against Linton; nor did I describe all his father's brutal conduct—my intentions being to add no bitterness, if I could help it, to his already overflowing cup.

He divined that one of his enemy's purposes was to secure the personal property, as well as the estate, to his son: or rather himself; yet why he did not wait till his decease was a puzzle to my master, because ignorant how nearly he and his nephew would quit the world together. However, he felt that his will had better be altered: instead of leaving Catherine's fortune at her own disposal, he determined to put it in the hands of trustees for her use during life, and for her children, if she had any, after her. By that means, it could not fall to Mr. Heathcliff should Linton die.

Having received his orders. I despatched a man to fetch the attorney, and four more, provided with serviceable weapons, to demand my young lady of her jailer. Both parties were delayed very late. The single servant returned first. He said Mr. Green, the lawyer, was out when he arrived at his house, and he had to wait two hours for his re-entrance; and then Mr. Green told him he had a little business in the village that must be done; but he would be at Thrushcross Grange before morning. The four men came back unaccompanied also. They brought word that Catherine was ill: too ill to quit her room; and Heathcliff would not suffer them to see her. I scolded the stupid fellows well for listening to that tale, which I would not carry to my master; resolving to take a whole bevy up to the Heights, at daylight, and storm it literally, unless the prisoner were quietly surrendered to us. Her father *shall* see her, I vowed, and vowed again, if that devil be killed on his own doorstones in trying to prevent it!

Happily, I was spared the journey and the trouble. I had gone downstairs at three o'clock to fetch a jug of water; and was passing through the hall with it in my hand, when a sharp knock at the front door made me jump. "Oh! it is Green," I said, recollecting myself—"only Green," and I went on, intending to send somebody else to open it; but the knock was repeated: not loud, and still importunately. I put the jug on the bannister and hastened to admit him myself. The harvest moon shone clear outside. It was not the attorney. My own sweet little mistress sprang on my neck, sobbing:

"Ellen! Ellen! Is papa alive?"

"Yes," I cried: "yes, my angel, he is. God be thanked, you are safe with us again!"

She wanted to run, breathless as she was, upstairs to Mr. Linton's room; but I compelled her to sit down on a chair, and made her drink, and washed her pale face, chafing it into a faint colour with my apron. Then I said I must go first, and tell of her arrival; imploring her to say, she should be happy with young Heathcliff. She stared, but soon comprehending why I counselled her to utter the falsehood, she assured me she would not complain.

I couldn't abide to be present at their meeting. I stood outside the chamber-door a quarter of an hour, and hardly ventured near the bed, then. All was composed, however: Catherine's despair was as silent as her father's joy. She supported him calmly, in appearance; and he fixed on her features his raised eyes, that seemed dilating with ecstasy.

He died blissfully, Mr. Lockwood: he died so. Kissing her cheek, he murmured,—

"I am going to her; and you darling child shall come to us!" and never stirred or spoke again; but continued that rapt, radiant gaze, till his pulse imperceptibly stopped and his soul departed. None could have noticed the exact minute of his death, it was so entirely without a struggle.

Whether Catherine had spent her tears, or whether the grief were too weighty to let them flow, she sat there dry-eyed till the sun rose: she sat till noon, and would still have remained brooding over that deathbed, but I insisted on her coming away and taking some repose. It was well I succeeded in removing her; for at dinner-time appeared the lawyer, having called at Wuthering Heights to get his instructions how to behave. He had sold himself to Mr. Heathcliff: that was the cause of his delay in obeying my master's summons. Fortunately, no thought of worldly affairs crossed the latter's mind, to disturb him, after his daughter's arrival.

Mr. Green took upon himself to order everything and everybody about the place. He gave all the servants, but me, notice to quit. He would have carried his delegated authority to the point of insisting that Edgar Linton should not be buried beside his wife, but in the chapel, with his family. There was the will, however, to hinder that, and my loud protestations against any infringement of its directions. The funeral was hurried over; Catherine, Mrs. Linton Heatchcliff now, was suffered to stay at the Grange till her father's corpse had quitted it.

She told me that her anguish had at last spurred Linton to incur the risk of liberating her. She heard the men I sent disputing at the door, and she gathered the sense of Heathcliff's answer. It drove her desperate. Linton, who had been conveyed up to the little parlour soon after I left, was terrified into fetching the key before his father re-ascended. He had the cunning to unlock and re-lock the door, without shutting it; and when he should have gone to bed, he begged to sleep with Hareton, and his petition was granted for once. Catherine stole out before the break of day. She dare not try the doors, lest the dogs should raise an alarm; she visited the empty chambers and examined their windows; and, luckily, lighting on her mother's she got easily out of its lattice, and on to the ground by means of the fir-tree close by. Her accomplice suffered for his share in the escape, notwithstanding his timid contrivances.

130

# Chapter 29

THE evening after the funeral, my young lady and I were seated in the library; now musing mournfully—one of us despairingly—on our loss, now venturing conjectures as to the gloomy future.

We had just agreed the best destiny which could await Catherine, would be a permission to continue resident at the Grange; at least during Linton's life: he being allowed to join her there, and I to remain as housekeeper. That seemed rather too favourable an arrangement to be hoped for; and yet I did hope, and began to cheer up under the prospect of retaining my home and my employment, and, above all, my beloved young mistress; when a servant—one of the discarded ones, not yet departed—rushed hastily in, and said, "that devil Heathcliff" was coming through the court: should he fasten the door in his face?

If we had been mad enough to order that proceeding, we had not time. He made no ceremony of knocking or announcing his name: he was master, and availed himself of the master's privilege to walk straight in, without saying a word. The sound of our informant's voice directed him to the library; he entered, and motioning him out, shut the door.

It was the same room into which he had been ushered, as a guest, eighteen years before: the same moon shone through the window; and the same autumn landscape lay outside. We had not yet lighted a candle, but all the apartment was visible, even to the portraits on the wall: the splendid head of Mrs. Linton, and the graceful one of her husband. Heathcliff advanced to the hearth. Time had little altered his person either. There was the same man: his dark face rather sallower and more composed, his frame a stone or two heavier, perhaps, and no other difference. Catherine had risen, with an impulse to dash out, when she saw him.

"Stop!" he said, arresting her by the arm. "No more runnings away! Where would you go? I'm come to fetch you home; and I hope you'll be a dutiful daughter, and not encourage my son to further disobedience. I was embarrassed how to punish him when I discovered his part in the business: he's such a cobweb, a pinch would annihilate him; but you'll see by his look that he has received his due! I brought him down one evening, the day before yesterday, and just set him in a chair, and never touched him afterwards. I sent Hareton out, and we had the room to ourselves. In two hours, I called Joseph to carry him up again; and since then my presence is as potent on his nerves as a ghost: and I fancy he sees me often, though I am not near. Hareton says he wakes and shrieks in the night by the hour together, and calls you to protect him from me; and, whether you like your precious mate or not, you must come: he's your concern now; I yield all my interest in him to you."

"Why not let Catherine continue here?" I pleaded, "and send Master

Linton to her. As you hate them both, you'd not miss them: they *can* only be a daily plague to your unnatural heart."

"I'm seeking a tenant for the Grange," he answered; "and I want my children about me, to be sure. Besides, that lass owes me her services for her bread. I'm not going to nurture her in luxury and idleness after Linton is gone. Make haste and get ready, now; and don't oblige me to compel you."

"I shall," said Catherine. "Linton is all I have to love in the world, and though you have done what you could to make him hateful to me, and me to him, you *cannot* make us hate each other. And I defy you to hurt him when I am by, and I defy you to frighten me!"

"You are a boastful champion," replied Heathcliff; "but I don't like you well enough to hurt him: you shall get the full benefit of the torment, as long as it lasts. It is not I who will make him hateful to you—it is his own sweet spirit. He's as bitter as gall at your desertion and its consequences: don't expect thanks for this noble devotion. I heard him draw a pleasant picture to Zillah of what he would do if he were as strong as I: the inclination is there, and his very weakness will sharpen his wits to find a substitute for strength."

"I know he has a bad nature," said Catherine: "he's your son. But I'm glad I've a better, to forgive it; and I know he loves me, and for that reason I love him. Mr. Heathcliff, *you* have *nobody* to love you; and, however miserable you make us, we shall still have the revenge of thinking that your cruelty arises from your greater misery. You *are* miserable, are you not? Lonely, like the devil, and envious like him? *Nobody* loves you—*nobody* will cry for you when you die! I wouldn't be you!"

Catherine spoke with a kind of dreary triumph: she seemed to have made up her mind to enter into the spirit of her future family, and draw pleasure from the griefs of her enemies.

"You shall be sorry to be yourself presently," said her father-in-law, "if you stand there another minute. Begone, witch, and get your things!"

She scornfully withdrew. In her absence, I began to beg for Zillah's place at the Heights, offering to resign mine to her; but he would suffer it on no account. He bid me be silent; and then, for the first, time, allowed himself a glance round the room and a look at the pictures. Having studied Mrs. Linton's, he said—

"I shall have that home. Not because I need it, but——" He turned abruptly to the fire, and continued, with what, for lack of a better word, I must call a smile "I'll tell you what I did yesterday! I got the sexton, who was digging Linton's grave, to remove the earth off her coffin-lid, and I opened it. I thought, once, I would have stayed there: when I saw her face again—it is hers yet!—he had hard work to stir me; but he said it would change if the air blew on it, and so I struck one side of the coffin loose, and covered it up: not Linton's side, damn him! I wish he'd been soldered in lead. And I bribed the sexton to pull it away when I'm laid there, and slide mine out too; I'll have it made so: and then by the time Linton gets to us he'll not know which is which!"

"You were very wicked, Mr. Heathcliff!" I exclaimed.

He resumed his meditation on the picture, took it down and leant it against the sofa to contemplate it to better advantage; and while so occupied Catherine entered, announcing that she was ready, when her pony should be saddled.

"Send that over to-morrow," said Heathcliff to me; then turning to her, he added, "You may do without your pony: it is a fine evening, and you'll need no ponies at Wuthering Heights; for what journeys you take, your own feet will serve you. Come along."

"Good-bye, Ellen!" whispered my dear little mistress. As she kissed me, her lips felt like ice. "Come and see me, Ellen; don't forget."

"Take care you do no such thing, Mrs. Dean!" said her new father. "When I wish to speak to you I'll come here. I want none of your prying at my house!"

He signed her to precede him; and casting back a look that cut my heart, she obeyed. I watched them, from the window, walk down the garden. Heathcliff fixed Catherine's arm under his: though she disputed the act at first evidently; and with rapid strides he hurried her into the alley, whose trees concealed them.

## *Chapter 30*

I HAVE paid a visit to the Heights, but I have not seen her since she left: Joseph held the door in his hand when I called to ask after her, and wouldn't let me pass. He said Mrs. Linton was "thrang," and the master was not in. Zillah has told me something of the way they go on, otherwise I should hardly know who was dead and who living. She thinks Catherine haughty, and does not like her, I can guess by her talk. My young lady asked some aid of her when she first came; but Mr. Heathcliff told her to follow her own business, and let his daughter-in-law look after herself; and Zillah willingly acquiesced, being a narrow-minded selfish woman. Catherine evinced a child's annoyance at this neglect; repaid it with contempt, and thus enlisted my informant among her enemies, as securely as if she had done her some great wrong. I had a long talk with Zillah about six weeks ago, a little before you came, one day when we fore-gathered on the moor; and this is what she told me.

"The first thing Mrs. Linton did," she said, "on her arrival at the Heights, was to run upstairs, without even wishing good evening to me and Joseph; she shut herself into Linton's room and remained till morning. Then, while the master and Earnshaw were at breakfast, she entered the house, and asked all in a quiver if the doctor might be sent for? her cousin was very ill.

"'We know that!' answered Heathcliff; 'but his life is not worth a farthing, and I won't spend a farthing on him.'

"'But I cannot tell how to do,' she said; 'and if nobody will help me, he'll die!'

"'Walk out of the room,' cried the master, 'and let me never hear a word more about him! None here care what becomes of him; if you do, act the nurse; if you do not, lock him up and leave him.'

"Then she began to bother me, and I said I'd had enough plague with the tiresome thing; we each had our tasks, and her's was to wait on Linton. Mr. Heathcliff bid me leave that labour to her.

"How they managed together, I can't tell. I fancy he fretted a great deal, and moaned hisseln night and day; and she had precious little rest: one could guess by her white face and heavy eyes. She sometimes came into the kitchen all wildered like, and looked as if she would fain beg assistance; but I was not going to disobey the master: I never dare disobey him, Mrs. Dean; and, though I thought it wrong that Kenneth should not be sent for, it was no concern of mine either to advise or complain, and I always refused to meddle. Once or twice, after we had gone to bed, I happened to open my door again and seen her sitting crying on the stairs' top; and then I've shut myself in quick, for fear of being moved to interfere. I did pity her then; I'm sure, still I didn't wish to lose my place, you know.

"At last, one night she came boldly into my chamber, and frightened me out of my wits, by saying,—

"'Tell Mr. Heathcliff that his son is dying—I'm sure he is, this time. Get up instantly, and tell him.'

"Having uttered this speech, she vanished again. I lay a quarter of an hour listening and trembling. Nothing stirred—the house was quiet.

"She's mistaken, I said to myself. He's got over it. I needn't disturb them; and I began to doze. But my sleep was marred a second time by a sharp ringing of the bell—the only bell we have, put up on purpose for Linton; and the master called to me to see what was the matter, and inform them that he wouldn't have that noise repeated.

"I delivered Catherine's message. He cursed to himself, and in a few minutes came out with a lighted candle, and proceeded to their room. I followed. Mrs. Heathcliff was seated by the bedside, with her hands folded on her knees. Her father-in-law went up, held the light to Linton's face, looked at him, and touched him; afterwards he turned to her.

"'Now—Catherine,' he said, 'how do you feel?'

"She was dumb.

"'How do you feel, Catherine?' he repeated.

"'He's safe, and I'm free,' she answered: 'I should feel well—but,' she continued, with a bitterness she couldn't conceal, 'you have left me so long to struggle against death alone, that I feel and see only death! I feel like death!'

"And she looked like it, too! I gave her a little wine. Hareton and Joseph, who had been wakened by the ringing and the sound of feet, and heard our talk from outside, now entered. Joseph was fain, I believe, of the lad's removal; Hareton seemed a thought bothered: though he was more taken up with staring at Catherine than thinking of Linton. But the master bid him get off to bed again: we didn't want his help. He afterwards made Joseph remove the body to his chamber, and told me to return to mine, and Mr. Heathcliff remained by herself.

"In the morning, he sent me to tell her she must come down to breakfast: she had undressed, and appeared going to sleep, and said she was ill; at which I hardly wondered. I informed Mr. Heathcliff, and he replied:

"'Well, let her be till after the funeral; and go up now and then to get her what is needful; and, as soon as she seems better, tell me.'"

Cathy stayed upstairs a fortnight, according to Zillah; who visited her twice a day, and would have been rather more friendly, but her attempts at increasing kindness were proudly and promptly repelled.

Heathcliff went up once, to show her Linton's will. He had bequeathed the whole of his, and what had been her, moveable property to his father: the poor creature was threatened, or coaxed, into that act during her week's absence, when his uncle died. The lands, being a minor, he could not meddle with. However, Mr. Heathcliff has claimed them and kept them and kept them in his wife's right and his also: I suppose legally; at any rate, Catherine, destitute of cash and friends, cannot disturb his possession.

"Nobody," said Zillah, "ever approached her door, except that once, but I; and nobody asked anything about her. The first occasion of her coming down into the house was on a Sunday afternoon. She had cried out, when I carried up her dinner, that she couldn't bear any longer being in the cold; and I told her the master was going to Thrushcross Grange, and Earnshaw and I need'nt hinder her from descending; so, as soon as she heard Heathcliff's horse trot off, she made her appearance, donned in black, and her yellow curls combed back behind her ears as plain as a Quaker: she couldn't comb them out.

"Joseph and I generally go to chapel on Sundays:" the kirk, you know, has no minister now, explained Mrs. Dean; and they call the Methodist's or Baptist's place (I can't say which it is), at Gimmerton, a chapel. "Joseph had gone," she continued, "but I thought proper to bide at home. Young folks are always the better for an elder's over-looking; and Hareton, with all his bashfulness, isn't a model of nice behaviour. I let him know that his cousin would very likely sit with us, and she had been always used to see the Sabbath respected; so he had as good leave his guns and bits of indoor work alone, while she stayed. He coloured up at the news, and cast his eyes over his hands and clothes. The train-oil and gunpowder were shoved out of sight in a minute. I saw he meant to give her his company; and I guessed, by his way, he wanted to be presentable; so, laughing, as I durst not laugh when the master is by, I offered to help him, if he would, and joked at his confusion. He grew sullen, and began to swear.

"Now, Mrs. Dean," Zillah went on, seeing me not pleased by her manner, "you happen to think your young lady too fine for Mr. Hareton; and happen you're right: but I own I should love well to bring her pride a peg lower. And what will all her learning and daintiness do for her, now? She's as poor as you or I: poorer, I'll be bound: you're saving, and I'm doing my little all that road."

Hareton allowed Zillah to give him her aid; and she flattered him into a good-humour; so, when Catherine came, half forgetting her former insults, he tried to make himself agreeable, by the housekeeper's account.

"Missis walked in," she said, "as chill as an icicle, and as high as a princess. I got up and offered her my seat in the arm-chair. No, she turned up her nose at my civility. Earnshaw rose, too, and bid her come to the settle, and sit close by the fire: he was sure she was starved.

"'I've been starved a month and more,' she answered, resting on the word as scornful as she could.

"And she got a chair for herself, and placed it at a distance from both of us. Having sat till she was warm, she began to look round, and discovered a number of books in the dresser; she was instantly upon her feet again, stretching to reach them: but they were too high up. Her cousin, after watching her endeavours a while, at last summoned courage to help her; she held her frock, and he filled it with the first that came to hand.

"That was a great advance for the lad. She didn't thank him; still, he felt gratified that she had accepted his assistance, and ventured to stand behind as she examined them, and even to stoop and point out what struck his fancy in certain old pictures which they contained; nor was he daunted by the saucy style in which she jerked the page from his finger: he contented himself with going a bit further back, and looking at her instead of the book. She continued reading, or seeking for something to read. His attention became, by degrees, quite centred in the study of her thick, silky curls: her face he couldn't see, and she couldn't see him. And, perhaps, not quite awake to what he did, but attracted like a child to a candle, at last he proceeded from staring to touching; he put out his hand and stroked one curl, as gently as if it were a bird. He might have stuck a knife into her neck, she started round in such a taking.

"'Get away, this moment! How dare you touch me? Why are you stopping there?' she cried, in a tone of disgust. 'I can't endure you! I'll go upstairs again, if you come near me.'

"Mr. Hareton recoiled, looking as foolish as he could do: he sat down in the settle very quiet, and she continued turning over her volumes another half hour; finally, Earnshaw crossed over, and whispered to me.

"'Will you ask her to read to us, Zillah? I'm stalled of doing naught; and I do like—I could like to hear her! Dunnot say I wanted it, but ask of yoursel'n.'

"'Mr. Hareton wishes you would read to us, ma'am,' I said, immediately. 'He'd take it very kind—he'd be much obliged.'

"She frowned; and looking up, answered—

"'Mr. Hareton, and the whole set of you, will be good enough to understand that I reject any pretence at kindness you have the hypocrisy to offer! I despise you, and will have nothing to say to any of you! When I would have given my life for one kind word, even to see one of your faces, you all kept off. But I won't complain to you! I'm driven down here by the cold; not either to amuse you or enjoy your society.'

"'What could I ha' done?' began Earnshaw. 'How wa I to blame?'

"'Oh! you are an exception,' answered Mrs. Heathcliff. 'I never missed such a concern as you.'

"'But I offered more than once, and asked,' he said, kindling up at her pertness, 'I asked Mr. Heathcliff to let me wake for you——'

"'Be silent! I'll go out of doors, or anywhere, rather than have your disagreeable voice in my ear!' said my lady.

Hareton muttered she might go to hell, for him! and unslinging his gun, restrained himself from his Sunday occupations no longer. He talked now, freely enough; and she presently saw fit to retreat to her solitude: but the frost had set in, and, in spite of her pride, she was forced to condescend to our company, more and more. However, I took care there should be no further scorning at my good-nature: ever since, I've been as stiff as herself; and she has no lover or liker among us: and she does not deserve one; for, let them say the least word to her, and she'll curl back without respect of any one! She'll snap at the master himself, and as good as dares him to thrash her; and the more hurt she gets, the more venomous she grows."

At first, on hearing this account from Zillah, I determined to leave my situation, take a cottage, and get Catherine to come and live with me: but Mr. Heathcliff would as soon permit that as he would set up Hareton in an independent house; and I can see no remedy, at present, unless she could marry again: and that scheme does not come within my province to arrange.

Thus ended Mrs. Dean's story. Notwithstanding the doctor's prophecy, I am rapidly recovering strength; and though it be only the second week in January, I propose getting out on horseback in a day or two, and riding over to Wuthering Heights, to inform my landlord that I shall spend the next six months in London; and, if he likes, he may look out for another tenant to take my place after October. I would not pass another winter here for much.

## Chapter 31

YESTERDAY was bright, calm, and frosty. I went to the Heights as I proposed: my housekeeper entreated me to bear a little note from her to her young lady, and I did not refuse, for the worthy woman was not conscious of anything odd in her request. The front door stood open, but the jealous gate was fastened, as at my last visit; I knocked, and invoked Earnshaw from among the garden beds; he unchained it, and I entered. The fellow is as handsome a rustic as need be seen. I took particular notice of him this time; but then he does his best, apparently, to make the least of his advantages.

I asked if Mr. Heathcliff were at home? He answered, No; but he would be in at dinner-time. It was eleven o'clock, and I announced my intention of going in and waiting for him, at which he immediately flung down his tools and accompanied me, in the office of watchdog, not as a substitute for the host.

We entered together; Catherine was there, making herself useful in preparing some vegetables for the approaching meal; she looked more sulky and less spirited than when I had seen her first. She hardly raised her eyes to notice me, and continued her employment with the same disregard to common forms of politeness as before; neve returning my bow and good-morning by the slightest acknowledgment.

"She does not seem so amiable," I thought, "as Mrs. Dean would persuade me to believe. She's a beauty, it is true, but not an angel."

Earnshaw surlily bid her remove her things to the kitchen. "Remove them yourself," she said pushing them from her as soon as she had done; and retiring to a stool by the window, where she began to carve figures of birds and beasts out of the turnip parings in her lap. I approached her, pretending to desire a view of the garden; and, as I fancied, adroitly dropped Mrs. Dean's note on to her knee, unnoticed by Hareton—but she asked aloud, "What is that?" And chucked it off.

"A letter from your old acquaintance, the housekeeper at the Grange," I answered; annoyed at her exposing my kind deed, and fearful lest it should be imagined a missive of my own. She would gladly have gathered it up at this information, but Hareton beat her; he seized and put it in his waistcoat, saying Mr. Heathcliff should look at it first. Threat, Catherine silently turned her face from us, and, very stealthily, drew out her pocket-handkerchief and applied it to her eyes; and her cousin, after struggling a while to keep down his softer feelings, pulled out the letter and flung it on the floor beside her, as ungraciously as he could. Catherine caught and perused it eagerly; then she put a few qestions to me concerning the inmates, rational and irrational, of her former home; and gazing towards the hills, murmured in soliloquy:

"I should like to be riding Minny down there! I should like to be climb-

138

ing up there! Oh! I'm tired—I'm *stalled*, Hareton!" And she leant her pretty head back against the sill, with half a yawn and half a sigh, and lapsed into an aspect of abstracted sadness: neither caring nor knowing whether we remarked her.

"Mrs. Heathcliff," I said, after sitting some time mute, "you are not aware that I am an acquaintance of yours? so intimate that I think it strange you won't come and speak to me. My housekeeper never wearies of talking about and praising you; and she'll be greatly disappointed if I return with no news of or from you, except that you received her letter and said nothing!"

She appeared to wonder at this speech and asked.—

"Does Ellen like you?"

"Yes, very well," I replied hesitatingly.

"You must tell her," she continued, "that I would answer her letter, but I have no materials for writing: not even a book from which I might tear a leaf."

"No books!" I exclaimed. "How do you contrive to live here without them? if I may take the liberty to inquire. Though provided with a large library, I'm frequently very dull at the Grange; take my books away, and I should be desperate!"

"I was always reading, when I had them," said Catherine; "and Mr. Heathcliff never reads; so he took it into his head to destroy my books. I have not had a glimpse of one for weeks. Only once, I searched through Joseph's store of theology, to his great irritation; and once, Hareton, I came upon a secret stock in your room—some Latin and Greek, and some tales and poetry: all old friends. I brought the last here—and you gathered them, as a magpie gathers silver spoons, for the mere love of stealing! They are of no use to you; or else you concealed them in the bad spirit that as you cannot enjoy them nobody else shall. Perhaps *your* envy counselled Mr. Heathcliff to rob me of my treasures? But I've most of them written on my brain and printed in my heart, and you cannot deprive me of those?"

Earnshaw blushed crimson when his cousin made this revelation of his private literary accumulations, and stammered an indignant denial of her accusations.

"Mr. Hareton is desirous of increasing his amount of knowledge," I said, coming to his rescue. "He is not *envious* but *emulous* of your attainments. He'll be a clever scholar in a few years."

"And he wants me to sink into a dunce, meantime," answered Catherine. "Yes, I hear him trying to spell and read to himself, and pretty blunders he makes! I wish you would repeat Chevy Chase as you did yesterday: it was extremely funny. I heard you; and I heard you turning over the dictionary to seek out the hard words, and then cursing because you could not read their explanations!"

The young man evidently thought it too bad that he should be laughed at for his ignorance, and then laughed at for trying to remove it. I had a similar notion; and, remembering Mrs. Dean's anecdote of his first attempt at enlightening the darkness in which he had been reared, I observed:

"But, Mrs. Heathcliff, we have each had a commencement, and each stumbled and tottered on the threshold; had our teachers scorned us instead of aiding, we should stumble and totter yet."

"Oh!" she replied, "I don't wish to limit his acquirements: still, he has no right to appropriate what is mine, and make it ridiculous to me with his vile mistakes and mispronunciations! Those books, both prose and verse, are consecrated to me by other associations; and I hate to have them debased and profaned in his mouth! Besides, of all, he has selected my favourite pieces that I love the most to repeat, as if out of deliberate malice."

Hareton's chest heaved in silence a minute: he laboured under a severe sense of mortification and wrath, which it was no easy task to suppress. I rose, and, from a gentlemanly idea of relieving his embarrassment, took up my station in the doorway, surveying the external prospect as I stood. He followed my example, and left the room; but presently reappeared, bearing half a dozen volumes in his hands, which he threw into Catherine's lap, exclaiming,—

"Take them! I never want to hear, or read, or think of them again!"

"I won't have them now," she answered. "I shall connect them with you, and hate them."

She opened one that had obviousy been turned over often, and read a portion in the drawling tone of beginner; then laughed, and threw it from her. "And listen," she continued, provokingly, commencing a verse of an old ballad in the same fashion.

But his self-love would endure no further torment: I heard, and not altogether disapprovingly, a manual check given to her saucy tongue. The little wretch had done her utmost to hurt her cousin's sensitive though uncultivated feelings, and a physical argument was the only mode he had of balancing the account, and repaying its effects on the inflictor. He afterwards gathered the books and hurled them on the fire. I read in his countenance what anguish it was to offer that sacrifice to spleen. I fancied that as they consumed, he recalled the pleasure they had already imparted, and the triumph and ever-increasing pleasure he had anticipated from them, and I fancied I guessed the incitement to his secret studies also. He had been content with daily labour and rough animal enjoyments, till Catherine crossed his path. Shame at her scorn, and hope of her approval, were his first prompters to higher pursuits; and, instead of guarding him from one and winning him to the other, his endeavours to raise himself had produced just the contrary result.

"Yes; that's all the good that such a brute as you can get from them!" cried Catherine, sucking her damaged lip, and watching the conflagration with indignant eyes.

"You'd *better* hold your tongue, now," he answered fiercely.

And his agitation precluded further speech; he advanced hastily to the entrance, where I made way for him to pass. But ere he had crossed the door-stones, Mr. Heathcliff, coming up the causeway, encountered him, and laying hold of his shoulder asked:

"What's to do now, my lad?"

"Naught, naught," he said, and broke away to enjoy his grief and anger in solitude.

Heathcliff gazed after him, and sighed.

"It will be odd if I thwart myself," he muttered, unconscious that I was behind him. "But when I look for his father in his face, I find *her* every day more! How the devil is he so like? I can hardly bear to see him."

He bent his eyes to the ground, and walked moodily in. There was a restless, anxious expression in his countenance I had never remarked there before; and he looked sparer in person. His daughter-in-law, on perceiving him through the window, immediately escaped to the kitchen, so that I remained alone.

"I'm glad to see you out of doors again, Mr. Lockwood," he said, in reply to my greeting; "from selfish motives partly: I don't think I could readily supply your loss in this desolation. I've wondered more than once what brought you here."

"An idle whim, I fear, sir," was my answer; "or else an idle whim is going to spirit me away. I shall set out for London next week; and I must give you warning that I feel no disposition to retain Thrushcross Grange beyond the twelve months I agreed to rent it. I believe I shall not live there any more."

"Oh, indeed; you're tired of being banished from the world, are you?" he said. "But if you're coming to plead off paying for a place you won't occupy, your journey is useless: I never relent in exacting my due from any one."

"I'm coming to plead off nothing about it," I exclaimed, considerably irritated. "Should you wish it, I'll settle with you now," and I drew my note-book from my pocket.

"No, no," he replied coolly; "you'll leave sufficient behind to cover your debts, if you fail to return: I'm not in such a hurry. Sit down and take your dinner with us; a guest that is safe from repeating his visit can generally be made welcome. Catherine, bring the things in: where are you?"

Catherine reappeared, bearing a tray of knives and forks.

"You may get your dinner with Joseph," muttered Heathcliff aside, "and remain in the kitchen till he is gone."

She obeyed his directions very punctually: perhaps she had no temptation to transgress. Living among clowns and misanthropists, she probably cannot appreciate a better class of people when she meets them.

With Mr. Heathcliff, grim and saturnine, on the one hand, and Hareton, absolutely dumb, on the other, I made a somewhat cheerless meal, and bade adieu early. I would have departed by the back way, to get a last glimpse of Catherine and annoy old Joseph; but Hareton received orders to lead up my horse, and my host himself escorted me to the door, so I could not fulfil my wish.

"How dreary life gets over in that house!" I reflected, while riding down the road. "What a realization of something more romantic than a fairy tale it would have been for Mrs. Linton Heathcliff, had she and I struck up an attachment, as her good nurse desired, and migrated together into the stirring atmosphere of the town!"

## Chapter 32

1802. This September I was invited to devastate the moors of a friend in the north, and on my journey to his abode, I unexpectedly came within fifteen miles of Gimmerton. The ostler at a roadside public-house was holding a pail of water to refresh my horses, when a cart of very green oats, newly reaped, passed by, and he remarked—

"Yon's frough Gimmerton, nah! They're allas three wick' after other folk wi' ther hervest."

"Gimmerton?" I repeated—my residence in that locality had already grown dim and dreamy. "Ah! I know. How far is it from this?"

"Happen fourteen mile' o'er th' hills; and a rough road," he answered.

A sudden impulse seized me to visit Thrushcross Grange. It was scarcely noon, and I conceived that I might as well pass the night under my own roof as in an inn. Besides, I could spare a day easily to arrange matters with my landlord, and thus save myself the trouble of invading the neighbourhood again. Having rested a while, I directed my servant to inquire the way to the village; and, with great fatigue to our beasts, we managed the distance in some three hours.

I left him there, and proceeded down the valley alone. The grey church looked greyer, and the lonely churchyard lonelier. I distinguished a moor sheep cropping the short turf on the graves. It was sweet, warm weather—too warm for travelling; but the heat did not hinder me from enjoying the delightful scenery above and below: had I seen it nearer August, I'm sure it would have tempted me to waste a month among its solitudes. In winter nothing more dreary, in summer nothing more divine, than those glens shut in by hills, and those bluff, bold swells of heath.

I reached the Grange before sunset, and knocked for admittance; but the family had retreated into the back premises, I judged, by one thin, blue wreath curling from the kitchen chimney, and they did not hear. I rode into the court. Under the porch, a girl of nine or ten sat knitting, and an old woman reclined on the horse-steps, smoking a meditative pipe.

"Is Mrs. Dean within?" I demanded of the dame.

"Mistress Dean? Nay!" she answered, "shoo doesn't bide here: shoo's up at th' Heights."

"Are you the housekeeper, then?" I continued.

"Eea, aw keep th' hause," she replied.

"Well, I'm Mr. Lockwood, the master. Are there any rooms to lodge me in, I wonder? I wish to stay all night."

"T' maister!" she cried in astonishment. "Whet, whoiver knew yah wur coming? Yah sud ha' send word. They's nowt norther dry nor mensful abaht t' place: nowt there isn't!"

She threw down her pipe and bustled in, the girl followed, and I entered too; soon perceiving that her report was true, and, moreover, that I had almost upset her wits by my unwelcome apparition, I bade her be composed. I would go out for a walk; and, meantime, she must try to prepare a corner of a sitting-room for me to sup in, and a bedroom to sleep in. No sweeping or dusting, only good fire and dry sheets were necessary. She seemed willing to do her best; though she thrust the hearth-brush into the grates in mistake for the poker, and mal-appropriated several other articles of her craft: but I retired, confiding in her energy for a resting-place against my return. Wuthering Heights was the goal of my proposed excursion. An after-thought brought me back, when I had quitted the court.

"All well at the Heights?" I inquired of the woman.

"Eea, f'r owt ee knaw!" she answered, skurrying away with a pan of hot cinders.

I would have asked why Mrs. Dean had deserted the Grange, but it was impossible to delay her at such a crisis, so I turned away and made my exit, rambling leisurely along, with the glow of a sinking sun behind, and the mild glory of a rising moon in front—one fading, and the other brightening—as I quitted the park, and climbed the stony by-road branching off to Mr. Heathcliff's dwelling. Before I arrived in sight of it, all that remained of day was a beamless amber light along the west: but I could see every pebble of the path, and every blade of grass, by that splendid moon. I had neither to climb the gate nor to knock—it yielded to my hand. That is an improvement, I thought. And I noticed another, by the aid of my nostrils; a fragrance of stocks and wallflowers wafted on the air from amongst the homely fruit trees.

Both doors and lattices were open; and yet, as is usually the case in a coal district, a fine, red fire illumined the chimney: the comfort which the eye derives from it renders the extra heat endurable. But the house of Wuthering Heights is so large, that the inmates have plenty of space for withdrawing out of its influence; and accordingly, what inmates there were had stationed themselves not far from one of the windows. I could both see them and hear them talk before I entered, and looked and listened in consequence; being moved thereto by a mingled sense of curiosity and envy, that grew as I lingered.

"Con-*trary*!" said a voice as sweet as a silver bell—"That for the third time, you dunce! I'm not going to tell you again. Recollect, or I'll pull your hair!"

"Contrary, then," answered another, in deep but softened tones. "And now, kiss me, for minding so well."

"No, read it over first correctly, without a single mistake."

The male speaker began to read: he was a young man, respectably dressed and seated at a table, having a book before him. His handsome features glowed with pleasure, and his eyes kept impatiently wandering from the page to a small white hand over his shoulder, which recalled him by a smart slap on the cheek, whenever its owner detected such signs of inattention. Its owner stood behind; her light, shining ringlets blending, at intervals, with his brown locks, as she bent to superintend his studies; and her face—it was lucky he could not see her face, or he would never have been so steady. I could; and I bit my lip in spite, at having thrown away the chance I might have had of doing something besides staring at its smiting beauty.

The task was done, not free from further blunders; but the pupil claimed a reward, and received at least five kisses: which, however, he generously returned. Then they came to the door, and from their conversation I judged they were about to issue out and have a walk on the moors. I supposed I should be condemned in Hareton Earnshaw's heart, if not by his mouth, to the lowest pit in the infernal regions, if I showed my unfortunate person in his neighbourhood then; and feeling very mean and malignant, I skulked round to seek refuge in the kitchen. There was unobstructed admittance on that side also; and at the door sat my old friend Nelly Dean, sewing and singing a song. I advanced; and recognising me directly, she jumped to her feet, crying—

"Why, bless you, Mr. Lockwood! How could you think of returning in this way? All's shut up at Thrushcross Grange. You should have given us notice!"

"I've arranged to be accomodated there, for as long as I shall stay," I answered. "I depart again to-morrow. And how are you transplanted here, Mrs. Dean? tell me that."

"Zillah left, and Mr. Heathcliff wished me to come, soon after you went to London, and stay till you returned. But, step in, pray! Have you walked from Gimmerton this evening?"

"From the Grange," I replied; "and while they make me lodging room there, I want to finish my business with your master; because I don't think of having another opportunity in a hurry."

"What business, sir?" said Nelly, conducting me into the house. "He's gone out at present, and won't return soon."

144

"About the rent," I answered.

"Oh! then it is with Mrs. Heathcliff you must settle," she observed; "or rather with me. She has not learnt to manage her affairs yet, and I act for her: there's nobody else."

I looked surprised.

"Ah! you have not heard of Heathcliff's death, I see," she continued.

"Heathcliff dead!" I exclaimed, astonished. "How long ago?"

"Three months since: but sit down, and let me take your hat, and I'll tell you all about it."

She furnished me with the sequel of Heathcliff's history. Had he a "queer" end, as she expressed it.

I was summoned to Wuthering Height's, within a fortnight of your leaving us, she said; and I obeyed joyfully, for Catherine's sake. My first interview with her grieved and shocked me: she had altered so much since our separation. Mr. Heathcliff did not explain his reasons for taking a new mind about my coming here; he only told me he wanted me, and he was tired of seeing Catherine: I must make the little parlour my sitting-room, and keep her with me. It was enough if he were obliged to see her once or twice a day. She seemed pleased at this arrangement; and, by, degrees, I smuggled over a great number of books, and other articles, that had formed her amusement at the Grange; and flattered myself we should get on in tolerable comfort. The delusion did not last long. Catherine, contented at first, in a brief space grew irritable and restless. For one thing, she was forbidden to move out of the garden, and it fretted her sadly to be confined to its narrow bounds as spring drew on; for another, in following the house, I was forced to quit her frequently, and she complained of loneliness: she preferred quarrelling with Joseph in the kitchen to sitting at peace in her solitude. I did not mind their skirmishes; but Hareton was often obliged to seek the kitchen also, when the master wanted to have the house to himself; and though in the beginning she either left it at his approach, or quietly joined in my occupations, and shunned remarking or addressing him—and though he was always as sullen and silent as possible —after a while, she changed her behaviour, and became incapable of letting him alone: talking at him; commenting on his stupidity and idleness; expressing her wonder how he could endure the life he lived—how he could sit a whole evening staring into the fire, and dozing.

"I know why Hareton never speaks, when I am in the kitchen," she exclaimed, on one occasion. "He is afraid I shall laugh at him. Ellen, what do you think? He began to teach himself to read once; and, because I laughed, he burned his books, and dropped it: was he not a fool?"

"Were not you naughty?" I said; "answer me that."

"Perhaps I was," she went on; "but I did not expect him to be so silly. Hareton, if I gave you a book, would you take it now? I'll try!"

She placed one she had been perusing on his hand; he flung it off, and muttered, if she did not give over, he would break her neck.

"Well, I shall put it here," she said, "in a table drawer; and I'm going to bed."

Then she whispered to me to watch whether he touched it, and departed. But he would not come near it; and so I informed her in the morning, to her great disappointment. I saw she was sorry for his persevering sulkiness and indolence: her conscience reproved her for frightening him off improving himself: she had done it effectually. But her ingenuity was at work to remedy the injury: while I ironed, or pursued other such stationary employments as I could not well do in the parlour, she would bring some pleasant volume and read it aloud to me. When Hareton was there, she generally paused in an interesting part, and left the book lying about: that she did repeatedly; but he was as obstinate as a mule, and, instead of snatching at her bait, in wet weather he took to smoking with Joseph.

Mr. Heathcliff, who grew more and more disinclined to society, had almost banished Earnshaw from his apartment. Owing to an accident at the commencement of March, he became for some days a fixture in the kitchen. His gun burst while out on the hills by himself; a splinter cut his arm, and he lost a good deal of blood before he could reach home. The consequence was that, perforce, he was condemned to the fireside and tranquillity, till he made it up again. It suited Catherine to have him there: at any rate, it made her hate her room upstairs more than ever: and she would compel me to find out business below, that she might accompany me.

On Easter Monday, Joseph went to Gimmerton fair with some cattle; and, in the afternoon, I was busy getting up linen in the kitchen. Earnshaw sat, morose as usual, at the chimney corner, and my little mistress was beguiling an idle hour with drawing pictures on the window panes; varying her amusement by smothered bursts of songs, and whispered ejaculations, and quick glances of annoyance and impatience in the direction of her cousin, who steadfastly smoked, and looked into the grate. At a notice that I could do with her no longer intercepting my light, she removed to the hearthstone. I bestowed little attention on her proceedings, but, presently, I heard her begin:

"I've found out, Hareton, that I want—that I'm glad—that I should like you to be my cousin now, if you had not grown so cross to me, and so rough."

Hareton returned no answer.

"Hareton, Hareton, Hareton! do you hear?" she continued.

"Get off wi' ye!" he growled, with uncompromising gruffness.

"Let me take that pipe," she said, cautiously advancing her hand and abstracting it from his mouth.

Before he could attempt to recover it, it was broken, and behind the fire. He swore at her and seized another.

"Stop," she cried, "you must listen to me first; and I can't speak while those clouds are floating in my face."

"Will you go to the devil!" he exclaimed, ferociously, "and let me be!"

"No," she persisted, "I won't: I can't tell what to do to make you talk to me; and you are determined not to understand. When I call you stupid, I don't mean anything: I don't mean that I despise you. Come, you shall take notice of me, Hareton: you are my cousin, and you shall own me."

"I shall have naught to do wi' you and your mucky pride, and your damned mocking tricks!" he answered. "I'll go to hell, body and soul, before I look sideways after you again. Side out o' t' gate, now; this minute!"

Catherine frowned, and retreated to the window-seat chewing her lip, and endeavouring, by humming an eccentric tune, to conceal a growing tendency to sob.

"You should be friends with your cousin, Mr. Hareton," I interrupted, "since she repents of her sauciness. It would do you a great deal of good: it would make you another man, to have her for a companion."

"A companion!" he cried; "when she hates me, and does not think me fit to wipe her shoon! Nay, if it made me a king, I'd not be scorned for seeking her good-will any more."

"It is not I who hate you, it is you who hate me!" wept Cathy, no longer disguising her trouble. "You hate me as much as Mr. Heathcliff does, and more."

"You're a damned liar," began Earnshaw: "why have I made him angry, by taking your part, then, a hundred times? and that when you sneered at and despised me, and—Go on plaguing me, and I'll step in yonder, and say you worried me out of the kitchen!"

"I didn't know you took my part," she answered, drying her eyes; "and I was miserable and bitter at everybody; but now I thank you, and beg you to forgive me: what can I do besides?"

She returned to the hearth, and frankly extended her hand. He blackened and scowled like a thunder-cloud, and kept his fists resolutely clenched, and his gaze fixed on the ground. Catherine, by instinct, must have divined it was obdurate perversity, and not dislike, that prompted this dogged conduct; for, after remaining an instant undecided, she stooped and impressed on his cheek a gentle kiss. The little rogue thought I had not seen her, and, drawing back, she took her former station by the window, quite demurely.

Whether the kiss convinced Hareton, I cannot tell: he was very careful, for some minutes, that his face should not be seen, and when he did raise it, he was sadly puzzled where to turn his eyes.

Catherine employed herself in wrapping a handsome book neatly in white paper, and having tied it with a bit of ribbon, and addressed it to "Mr. Hareton Earnshaw," she desired me to be her ambassadress, and convey the present to its destined recipient.

"And tell him, if he'll take it I'll come and teach him to read it right," she said; "and, if he refuse it, I'll go upstairs, and never tease him again."

I carried it, and repeated the message; anxiously watched by my employer. Hareton would not open his fingers, so I laid it on his knee. He did not strike it off, either. I returned to my work. Catherine leaned her hand and arms on the table, till she heard the slight rustle of the covering being removed; then she stole away, and quietly seated herself beside her cousin. He trembled, and his face glowed: all his rudeness and all his surly harshness had deserted him: he could not summon courage, at first, to utter a syllable in reply to her questioning look, and her murmured petition.

"Say you forgive me, Hareton, do. You can make me so happy by speaking that little word."

He muttered something inaudible.

"And you'll be my friend?" added Catherine, interrogatively.

"Nay, you'll be ashamed of me every day of your life," he answered; "and the more ashamed, the more you know of me; and I cannot bide it."

"So you won't be my friend?" she said, smiling as sweet as honey, and creeping close up.

I overheard no further distinguishable talk, but, on looking round again, I perceived two such radiant countenances bent over the page of the accepted book, that I did not doubt the treaty had been ratified on both sides; and the enemies were, thenceforth, sworn allies.

The intimacy thus commenced, grew rapidly; though it encountered temporary interruptions. Earnshaw was not to be civilized with a wish, and my young lady was no philosopher, and no paragon of patience; but both their minds tending to the same point—one loving and desiring to esteem, and the other loving and desiring to be esteemed—they contrived in the end to reach it.

You see, Mr. Lockwood, it was easy enough to win Mrs. Heathcliff's heart. But now, I'm glad you did not try. The crown of all my wishes will be the union of those two. I shall envy no one on their wedding-day: there won't be a happier woman than myself in England!

## Chapter 33

ON THE morrow of that Monday, Earnshaw was still unable to follow his ordinary employments, and therefore remaining about the house, I speedily found it would be impracticable to retain my charge beside me, as heretofore. She got downstairs before me, and out into the garden, where she had seen her cousin performing some easy work; and when I went to bid them come to breakfast, I saw she had persuaded him to clear a large space of ground from currant and gooseberry bushes, and they were busy planning together an importation of plants from the Grange.

I was terrified at the devastation which had been accomplished in a brief half-hour; the black-currant trees were the apple of Joseph's eye, and she had just fixed her choice of a flower bed in the midst of them.

"There! That will be all shown to the master," I exclaimed, "the minute it is discovered. And what excuse have you to offer for taking such liberties with the garden? We shall have a fine explosion on the head of it: see if we don't! Mr. Hareton, I wonder you should have no more wit, than to go and make that mess at her bidding!"

"I'd forgotten they were Joseph's," answered Earnshaw, rather puzzled; "but I'll tell him I did it."

We always ate our meals with Mr. Heathcliff. I held the mistress's post in making tea and carving; so I was indispensable at table. Catherine usually sat by me, but to-day she stole nearer to Hareton; and I presently saw she would have no more discretion in her friendship than she had in her hostility.

"Now, mind you don't talk with and notice your cousin too much," were my whispered instructions as we entered the room. "It will certainly annoy Mr. Heathcliff, and he'll be mad at you both."

"I'm not going to," she answered.

The minute after, she had sidled to him, and was sticking primroses in his plate of porridge.

He dared not speak to her there: he dared hardly look; and yet she went on teasing, till he was twice on the point of being provoked to laugh. I frowned, and then she glanced towards the master: whose mind was occupied on other subjects than his company, as his countenance evinced; and she grew serious for an instant, scrutinizing him with deep gravity. Afterwards she turned, and recommenced her nonsense; at last, Hareton uttered a smothered laugh. Mr. Heathcliff started; his eye rapidly surveyed our faces. Catherine met it with her accustomed look of nervousness and yet defiance, which he abhorred.

"It is well you are out of my reach," he exclaimed. "What fiend possesses you to stare back at me, continually, with those infernal eyes? Down with them! and don't remind me of your existence again. I thought I had cured you of laughing."

"It was me," muttered Hareton.

"What do you say?" demanded the master.

Hareton looked at his plate, and did not repeat the confession. Mr. Heathcliff looked at him a bit, and then silently resumed his breakfast and his interrupted musing. We had nearly finished, and the two young people prudently shifted wider asunder, so I anticipated no further disturbance during that sitting: when Joseph appeared at the door, revealing by his quivering lip and furious eyes, that the outrage committed on his precious shrubs was detected. He must have seen Cathy and her cousin about the spot before he examined it, for his jaws worked like those of a cow chewing its cud, and rendered his speech difficult to understand. "It's yon flaysome, graceless quean, that's witched our lad, wi' her bold een and her forrard ways—till—Nay! it fair brusts my heart! He's forgotten all I've done for him, and made on him, and goan and riven up a whole row o' t' grandest currant trees, i' t' garden!" and here he lamented outright; unmanned by a sense of his bitter injuries, and Earnshaw's ingratitude and dangerous condition.

"Is the fool drunk?" asked Mr. Heathcliff. "Hareton, is it you he's finding fault with?"

"I've pulled up two or three bushes," replied the young man; "but I'm going to set 'em again."

"And why have you pulled them up?" said the master.

Catherine wisely put in her tongue.

"We wanted to plant some flowers there," she cried. "I'm the only person to blame, for I wished him to do it."

"And who the devil gave *you* leave to touch a stick about the place?" demanded her father-in-law, much surprised. "And who ordered *you* to obey her!" he added, turning to Hareton.

The latter was speechless; his cousin replied—

"You shouldn't grudge a few yards of earth for me to ornament, when you have taken all my land!"

"Your land, insolent slut! You never had any," said Heathcliff.

"And my money," she continued; returning his angry glare, and meantime biting a piece of crust, the remnant of her breakfast.

"Silence!" he exclaimed. "Get done, and begone!"

"And Hareton's land and his money," pursued the reckless thing. "Hareton and I are friends now; and I shall tell him all about you!"

The master seemed confounded a moment: he grew pale, and rose up, eyeing her all the while, with an expression of mortal hate.

"If you strike me, Hareton will strike you," she said; "so you may as well sit down."

"If Hareton does not turn you out of the room, I'll strike him to hell," thundered Heathcliff. "Damnable witch! dare you pretend to rouse him against me? Off with her! Do you hear? Fling her into the kitchen! I'll kill her, Ellen Dean, if you let her come into my sight again!"

Hareton tried, under his breath, to persuade her to go.

"Drag her away!" he cried, savagely. "Are you staying to talk?" And he approached to execute his own command.

"He'll not obey you, wicked man, any more," said Catherine; "and he'll soon detest you as much as I do."

"Wisht! wisht!" muttered the young man, reproachfully. "I will not hear you speak so to him. Have done."

"But you won't let him strike me?" she cried.

"Come, then," he whispered, earnestly.

It was too late: Heathcliff had caught hold of her.

"Now, *you* go!" he said to Earnshaw. "Accursed witch! this time she has provoked me when I could not bear it; and I'll make her repent it for ever!"

He had his hand in her hair; Hareton attempted to release her locks, entreating him not to hurt her that once. Heathcliff's black eyes flashed; he seemed ready to tear Catherine to pieces, and I was just worked up to risk coming to the rescue, when of a sudden his fingers relaxed; he shifted his grasp from her head to her arm, and gazed intently in her face. Then he drew his hand over his eyes, stood a moment to collect himself apparently, and turning anew to Catherine, said, with assumed calmness—"You must learn to avoid putting me in a passion, or I shall really murder you some time! Go with Mrs. Dean, and keep with her; and confine your insolence to her ears. As to Hareton Earnshaw, if I see him listen to you, I'll send him seeking his bread where he can get it! Your love will make him an outcast and a beggar. Nelly, take her; and leave me, all of you! Leave me!"

I led my young lady out: she was too glad of her escape to resist; the other followed, and Mr. Heathcliff had the room to himself till dinner. I had counselled Catherine to dine upstairs; but, as soon as he perceived her vacant seat, he sent me to call her. He spoke to none of us, ate very little, and went out directly afterwards, intimating that he should not return before evening.

I came in to sit with them, after I had done my work; and I felt so soothed and comforted to watch them, that I did not notice how time got on. You know, they both appeared in a measure my children: I had long been proud of one; and now, I was sure, the other would be a source of equal satisfaction. His honest, warm, and intelligent nature shook off rapidly the clouds of ignorance and degradation in which it had been bred; and Catherine's sincere commendations acted as a spur to his industry.

While I admired and they laboured, dusk drew on, and with it returned the master. He came upon us quite unexpectedly, entering by the front way, and had a full view of the whole three, ere we could raise our heads to glance at him. Well, I reflected, there was never a pleasanter, or more harmless sight; and it will be a burning shame to scold them. The red firelight glowed on their two bonny heads, and revealed their faces animated with the eager interest of children; for, though he was twenty-three and she eighteen, each had so much of novelty to feel and learn, that neither experienced nor evinced the sentiments of sober disenchanted maturity.

They lifted their eyes together, to encounter Mr. Heathcliff: perhaps you have never remarked that their eyes are precisely similar, and they are

151

those of Catherine Earnshaw. The present Catherine has no other likeness to her, except a breadth of forehead, and a certain arch of the nostril that makes her appear rather haughty, whether she will or not. With Hareton the resemblance is carried farther: it is singular at all times, *then* it was particularly striking; because his senses were alert, and his mental faculties wakened to unwonted activity. I suppose this resemblance disarmed Mr. Heathcliff: he walked to the hearth in evident agitation; but it quickly subsided as he looked at the young man: or, should I say, altered its character; for it was there yet. He took the book from his hand, and glanced at the open page, then returned it without any observation; merely signing Catherine away: her companion lingered very little behind her, and I was about to depart also, but he bid me sit still.

"It is a poor conclusion, is it not?" he observed, having brooded a while on the scene he had just witnessed: "and absurd termination to my violent exertions? I get levers and mattocks to demolish the two houses, and train myself to be capable of working like Hercules, and when everything is ready and in my power, I find the will to lift a slate off either roof has vanished! My old enemies have not beaten me; now would be the precise time to revenge myself on their representatives: I could do it; and none could hinder me. But where is the use? I don't care for striking: I can't take the trouble to raise my hand! That sounds as if I had been labouring the whole time only to exhibit a fine trait of magnanimity. It is far from being the case: I have lost the faculty of enjoying their destruction, and I am too idle to destroy for nothing.

"Nelly, there is a strange change approaching: I'm in its shadow at present. I take so little interest in my daily life, that I hardly remember to eat and drink. Those two who have left the room are the only objects which retain a distinct material appearance to me; and that appearance causes me pain, amounting to agony. About *her* I won't speak: and I don't desire to think; but I earnestly wish she were invisible: her presence invokes only maddening sensations. *He* moves me differently: and yet if I could do it without seeming insane, I'd never see him again! You'll perhaps think me rather inclined to become so," he added, making an effort to smile, "if I try to describe the thousand forms of past associations and ideas he awakens or embodies. But you'll not talk of what I tell you; and my mind is so eternally secluded in itself, it is tempting at last to turn it out to another.

"Five minutes ago, Hareton seemed a personification of my youth, not a human being: I felt to him in such a variety of ways, that it would have been impossible to have accosted him rationally. In the first place, his startling likeness to Catherine connected him fearfully with her. That, however, which you may suppose the most potent to arrest my imagination, is actually the least: for what is not connected with her to me? and what does not recall her? The entire world is a dreadful collection of memoranda that she did exist, and that I have lost her! Well, Hareton's aspect was the ghost of my immortal love; of my wild endeavours to hold my right; my degradation, my pride, my happiness, and my anguish—

"But what do you mean by a *change*, Mr. Heathcliff?" I said, alarmed at his manner: though he was neither in danger of losing his senses, nor dying, according to my judgment: he was quite strong and healthy; and, as to his reason, from childhood he had a delight in dwelling on dark things, and entertaining odd fancies. He might have had a monomania on the subject of his departed idol; but on every other point his wits were as sound as mine.

"I shall not know that till it comes," he said, "I'm only half conscious of it now."

"You have no feeling of illness, have you?" I asked.

"No, Nelly, I have not," he answered.

"Then you are not afraid of death?" I pursued.

"Afraid? No!" he replied. "I have neither a fear nor a presentiment, nor a hope of death. Why should I? With my hard constitution and temperate mode of living, and unperilous occupations, I ought to, and probably *shall*, remain above ground till there is scarcely a black hair on my head. And yet I cannot continue in this condition! I have to remind myself to breathe—almost to remind my heart to beat! And it is like bending back a stiff spring: it is by compulsion that I do the slightest act not prompted by one thought; and by compulsion that I notice anything dead or alive, which is not associated with one universal idea. I have a single wish, and my whole being and faculties are yearning to attain it. They have yearned towards it so long, and so unwaveringly, that I'm convinced it *will* be reached—and *soon*—because it has devoured my existence: I am swallowed up in the anticipation of its fulfilment. My confessions have not relieved me; but they may account for some otherwise unaccountable phases of humour which I show. O God! It is a long fight, I wish it were over!"

He began to pace the room, muttering terrible things to himself, till I was inclined to believe, as he said Joseph did, that conscience had turned his heart to an earthly hell. I wondered greatly how it would end.

## Chapter 34

FOR SOME days after that evening, Mr. Heathcliff shunned meeting us at meals; yet he would not consent formally to exclude Hareton and Cathy. He had an aversion to yielding so completely to his feelings, choosing rather to absent himself; and eating once in twenty-four hours seemed sufficient sustenance for him.

One night, after the family were in bed, I heard him go downstairs, and out at the front door. I did not hear him re-enter, and in the morning I found he was still away. We were in April then: the weather was sweet and warm, the grass as green as showers and sun could make it, and the two dwarf apple-trees near the southern wall in full bloom. After breakfast, Catherine insisted on my bringing a chair and sitting with my work under the fir-trees at the end of the house. I was comfortably revelling in the spring fragrance around, and the beautiful soft blue overhead, when my young lady, who had run down near the gate to procure some primrose roots for a border, returned only half laden, and informed us that Mr. Heathcliff was coming in. "And he spoke to me," she added, with a perplexed countenance.

"What did he say?" asked Hareton

"He told me to begone as fast as I could," she answered. "But he looked so different from his usual look that I stopped a moment to stare at him."

"How?" he inquired.

"Why, almost bright and cheerful. No, *almost* nothing—*very much* excited, and wild, and glad!" she replied.

"Night-walking amuses him, then," I remarked, affecting a careless manner: in reality as surprised as she was, and anxious to ascertain the truth of her statement; for to see the master looking glad would not be an everyday spectacle. I framed an excuse to go in. Heathcliff stood at the open door; he was pale, and he trembled: yet, certainly, he had a strange joyful glitter in his eyes, that altered the aspect of his whole face.

"Will you have some breakfast?" I said. "You must be hungry, rambling about all night!" I wanted to discover where he had been, but I did not like to ask directly.

"No, I'm not hungry," he answered, averting his head, and speaking rather contemptuously, as if he guessed I was trying to divine the occasion of his good humour.

I felt perplexed: I didn't know whether it were not a proper opportunity to offer a bit of admonition.

"I don't think it right to wander out of doors," I observed, "instead of being in bed: it is not wise, at any rate, this moist season. I dare say you'll catch a bad cold, or a fever: you have something the matter with you now!"

"Nothing but what I can bear," he replied; "and with the greatest pleasure, provided you'll leave me alone: get in, and don't annoy me."

I obeyed: and, in passing, I noticed he breathed as fast as a cat.

That noon he sat down to dinner with us, and received a heaped-up plate from my hands, as if he intended to make amends for previous fasting.

"I've neither cold nor fever, Nelly," he remarked, in allusion to my morning's speech; "and I'm ready to do justice to the food you give me."

He took his knife and fork, and was going to commence eating, when the inclination appeared to become suddenly extinct. He laid them on the table, looked eagerly towards the window, then rose and went out. We saw him walking to and fro in the garden while we concluded our meal.

I set his plate to keep warm on the fender; and after an hour or two he re-entered, when the room was clear, in no degree calmer: the same unnatural—it was unnatural—appearance of joy under his black brows; the same bloodless hue, and his teeth visible, now and then, in a kind of smile; his frame shivering, not as one shivers with chill or weakness, but as a tight-stretched cord vibrates—a strong thrilling, rather than trembling.

I will ask what is the matter, I thought; or who should? And I exclaimed—

"Have you heard any good news, Mr. Heathcliff? You look uncommonly animated."

"Where should good news come from to me?" he said. "I'm animated with hunger; and, seemingly, I must not eat."

"Your dinner is here," I returned; "why won't you get it?"

"I don't want it now," he muttered, hastily: "I'll wait till supper. And, Nelly, once for all, let me beg you to warn Hareton and the other away from me. I wish to be troubled by nobody: I wish to have this place to myself."

"Is there some new reason for this banishment?" I inquired. "Tell me why you are so queer, Mr. Heathcliff? Where were you last night? I'm not putting the question through idle curiosity, but——"

"You are putting the question through very idle curiosity," he interrupted, with a laugh. "Yet I'll answer it. Last night I was on the threshold of hell. To-day, I am within sight of my heaven."

He did not quit the house again that afternoon, and no one intruded on his solitude; till, at eight, I deemed it proper, though unsummoned, to carry a candle and his supper to him. He was leaning against the ledge of an open lattice, but not looking out: his face was turned to the interior gloom. I commenced shutting the casements, one after another, till I came to his.

"Must I close this?" I asked, in order to rouse him; for he would not stir.

The light flashed on his features as I spoke. Oh, Mr. Lockwood, I cannot express what a terrible start I got by the momentary view! Those deep black eyes! That smile, and ghastly paleness! It appeared to me, not Mr. Heathcliff, but a goblin; and, in my terror, I let the candle bend towards the wall, and it left me in darkness.

"Yes, close it," he replied, in his familiar voice. "There, that is pure awkwardness! Why did you hold the candle horizontally? Be quick, and bring another."

I hurried out in a foolish state of dread, and said to Joseph—

"The master wishes you to take him a light and re-kindle the fire." For I dare not go in myself again just then.

Joseph rattled some fire into the shovel, and went: but he brought it back immediately, with the supper-tray in his other hand, explaining that Mr. Heathcliff was going to bed, and he wanted nothing to eat till morning. We heard him mount the stairs directly; he did not proceed to his ordinary chamber, but turned into that with the panelled bed: its window, as I mentioned before, is wide enough for anybody to get through; and it struck me that he plotted another midnight excursion, of which he had rather we had no suspicion.

At dawn I rose, and went into the garden, as soon as I could see, to ascertain if there were any footmarks under his window. There were none. "He has staid at home," I thought, "and he'll be all right to-day." I prepared breakfast for the household, as was my usual custom, but told Hareton and Catherine to get theirs ere the master came down, for he lay late. They preferred taking it out of doors, under the trees, and I set a little table to accommodate them.

On my re-entrance, I found Mr. Heathcliff below. He and Joseph were conversing about some farming business; he gave clear, minute directions concerning the matter discussed, but he spoke rapidly, and turned his head continually aside, and had the same excited expression, even more exaggerated. When Joseph quitted the room he took his seat in the place he generally chose, and I put a basin of coffee before him. He drew it nearer, and then rested his arms on the table, and looked at the opposite wall, as I supposed, surveying one particular portion, up and down, with glittering, restless eyes, and with such eager interest that he stopped breathing during half a minute together.

"Come now," I exclaimed, pushing some bread against his hand, "eat and drink that, while it is hot: it has been waiting near an hour."

He didn't notice me, and yet he smiled. I'd rather have seen him gnash his teeth than smile so.

"Mr. Heathcliff! master!" I cried, "don't, for God's sake, stare as if you saw an unearthly vision."

"Don't, for God's sake, shout so loud," he replied. "Turn round, and tell me, are we by ourselves?"

"Of course," was my answer; "of course we are."

Still, I involuntarily obeyed him, as if I was not quite sure. With a sweep of his hand he cleared a vacant space in front among the breakfast things, and leant forward to gaze more at his ease.

Now, I perceived he was not looking at the wall; for when I regarded him alone, it seemed exactly that he gazed at something within two yards' distance. And whatever it was, it communicated, apparently, both pleasure and pain in exquisite extremes: at least the anguished, yet raptured, expression of his countenance suggested that idea. The fancied object was not fixed, either; his eyes pursued it with unwearied diligence, and, even in speaking to me, were never weaned away. I vainly reminded him of his protracted abstinence from food: if he stirred to touch anything in compliance with my entreaties, if he stretched his hand out to get a piece of bread, his fingers clenched before they reached it, and remained on the table, forgetful of their aim.

I sat, a model of patience, trying to attract his absorbed attention from its engrossing speculation; till he grew irritable, and got up, asking why I would not allow him to have his own time in taking his meals? and saying that on the next occasion, I needn't wait: I might set the things down and go. Having uttered these words he left the house, slowly sauntered down the garden path, and disappeared through the gate.

The hours crept anxiously by: another evening came. I did not retire to rest till late, and when I did, I could not sleep. He returned after midnight, and, instead of going to bed, shut himself into the room beneath. I listened, and tossed about, and, finally, dressed and descended. It was too irksome to lie there, harassing my brain with a hundred idle misgivings.

I distinguished Mr. Heathcliff's step, restlessly measuring the floor, and he frequently broke the silence by a deep inspiration, resembling a groan. He muttered detached words also; the only one I could catch was the name of Catherine, coupled with some wild term of endearment or suffering; and spoken as one would speak to a person present: low and earnest, and wrung from the depth of his soul. I had not courage to walk straight into the apartment; but I desired to divert him from his reverie, and therefore fell foul of the kitchen fire, stirred it, and began to scrape the cinders. It drew him forth sooner than I expected. He opened the door immediately, and said:

"Nelly, come here—is it morning? Come in with your light."

"It is striking four," I answered. "You want a candle to take upstairs: you might have lit one at this fire."

"No, I don't wish to go upstairs," he said. "Come in, and kindle *me* a fire, and do anything there is to do about the room."

"I must blow the coals red first, before I can carry any," I replied, getting a chair and the bellows.

He roamed to and fro, meantime, in a state approaching distraction; his heavy sighs succeeding each other so thick as to leave no space for common breathing between.

"I'm too happy; and yet I'm not happy enough. My soul's bliss kills my body, but does not satisfy itself."

"Happy, master?" I cried. "Strange happiness! If you would hear me without being angry, I might offer you some advice that would make you happier."

"What is that?" he asked. "Give it."

"You are aware, Mr. Heathcliff," I said, "that from the time you were thirteen years old, you have lived a selfish, unchristian life; and probably hardly had a Bible in your hands during all that period. You must have

157

forgotten the contents of the book, and you may not have space to search it now. Could it be hurtful to send for some one—some minister of any denomination, it does not matter which—to explain it, and show you how very far you have erred from its precepts; and how unfit you will be for its heaven, unless a change takes place before you die?"

"I'm rather obliged than angry, Nelly," he said, "for you remind me of the manner in which I desire to be buried. It is to be carried to the church-yard in the evening. You and Hareton may, if you please, accompany me: and mind, particularly, to notice that the sexton obeys my directions concerning the two coffins! No minister need come; nor need anything be said over me."

As soon as he heard the other members of the family stirring he retired to his den, and I breathed freer. Through the whole night, and far into the morning, we heard him groaning and murmuring to himself. Hareton was anxious to enter; but I requested admittance and tried to open the door, I found it locked; and Heathcliff bid us be damned. He was better, and would be left alone.

The following evening was very wet: indeed it poured down till day-dawn; and, as I took my morning walk round the house, I observed the master's window swinging open, and the rain driving straight in. He cannot be in bed, I thought: those showers would drench him through. He must either be up or out. But I'll make no more ado, I'll go boldly and look!

Having succeeded in obtaining entrance with another key, I ran to un-close the panels, for the chamber was vacant; quickly pushing them aside, I peeped in. Mr. Heathcliff was there—laid on his back. His eyes met mine keen and fierce, I started; and then he seemed to smile. I could not think him dead: but his face and throat were washed with rain; the bed-clothes dripped, and he was perfectly still. The lattice, flapping to and fro, had grazed one hand that rested on the sill; no blood trickled from the broken skin, and when I put my fingers to it, I could doubt no more: he was dead and stark!

I felt stunned by the awful event; and my memory unavoidably recurred to former times with a sort of oppressive sadness. But poor Hareton, the most wronged, was the only one who really suffered much. He sat by the corpse all night, weeping in bitter earnest. He pressed its hand, and kissed the sarcastic, savage face that every one else shrank from contemplating; and bemoaned him with that strong grief which springs naturally from a generous heart, though it be tough as tempered steel.

Mr. Kenneth was perplexed to pronounce of what disorder the master died. I concealed the fact of his having swallowed nothing for four days, fearing it might lead to trouble, and then, I am persuaded, he did not abstain on purpose: it was the consequence of his strange illness, not the cause.

We buried him, to the scandal of the whole neighbourhood, as he wish-ed. Earnshaw and I, the sexton, and six men to carry the coffin, comprehended the whole attendance. The six men departed when they had let it down into the grave: we stayed to see it covered. Hareton, with a streaming face, dug green sods, and laid them over the brown mould himself: at present it is as smooth and verdant as its companion mounds—and I hope its tenant sleeps as soundly. But the country folks, if you ask them, would swear on the Bible that he *walks:* there are those who speak to having met him near the church, and on the moor, and even within this house. Idle tales, you'll say, and so say I.

Yet, still, I don't like being out in the dark now; and I don't like being left by myself in this grim house: I cannot help it; I shall be glad when they leave it, and shift to the Grange.

"They are going to the Grange, then," I said.

"Yes," answered Mrs. Dean, "as soon as they are married, and that will be on New Year's day."

"And who will live here then?"

"Why, Joseph will take care of the house, and, perhaps, a lad to keep him company. They will live in the kitchen, and the rest will be shut up."

"For the use of such ghosts as choose to inhabit it," I observed.

"No, Mr. Lockwood," said Nelly, shaking her head. "I believe the dead are at peace: but it is not right to speak of them with levity."

At that moment the garden gate swung to; the ramblers were returning.

"*They* are afraid of nothing," I grumbled, watching their approach through the window. "Together, they would brave Satan and all his legions."

As they stepped on to the door-stones, and halted to take a last look at the moon—or, more correctly, at each other by her light—I felt irresistibly impelled to escape them again; and, pressing a remembrance into the hand of Mrs. Dean, and disregarding her expostulations at my rudeness, I vanished through the kitchen as they opened the house-door.

My walk home was lengthened by a diversion in the direction of the kirk. When beneath its walls I sought, and soon discovered, the three head-stones on the slope next the moor: the middle one grey, and half buried in heath; Edgar Linton's only harmonized by the turf and moss creeping up its foot; Heathcliff's still bare.

I lingered round them, under that benign sky: watched the moths fluttering among the heath and hare-bells, listened to the soft wind breathing through the grass, and wondered how any one could ever imagine unquiet slumbers for the sleepers in that quiet earth.

*Printed in Germany*